GIVING ME BUTTERFLIES

LENNY'S BARTENDERS BOOK #1

KATY MICHELE

To Max

*Thank you for pushing me to pursue my dream
and being there for me along the way.*

NOTE TO READER

Giving Me Butterflies is book #1 of the Lenny's Bartenders series, a contemporary romance series of three interconnected standalones.

Giving Me Butterflies contains topics that may be triggering to some readers. These topics include explicit sexual content, school shootings, panic attacks from trauma, grief, death of a sibling (off-page).

If any of these topics are triggering to you,
please do what you need to protect your peace. 🤍

PLAYLIST

"IS SHE GIVING ME BUTTERFLIES?"

Life @ 11 by A Day to Remember
Bad Day by Charlotte Sands
Break Your Little Heart by All Time Low
Thnks Fr Th Mmrs by Fall Out Boy
Rerun by Honey Revenge
All Downhill From Here by New Found Glory
Hate Me (Sometimes) by Stand Atlantic
Hard Times by Paramore
She's Out of Her Mind by Blink-182
Beautifully Tragic by Escape the Fate
The Only Exception by Paramore
Alone in a Room by Asking Alexandria
Coffee at Midnight by Stand Atlantic
2 Be Loved (Am I Ready) by Lizzo
Golden by Harry Styles
Still Into You by Paramore

PROLOGUE

DREW

IT WAS A NORMAL DAY.

Until it wasn't.

Everyone always told me that I'd be trapped in my class-room—with endless papers to grade, students to see, meet-ings to attend, parents to call, and colleagues to meet with.

But, it wasn't until we put as many desks and chairs against the door that I truly felt trapped.

CHAPTER 1
DREW

I WAKE up to my alarm playing—the sound that haunts my nightmares. The sound that means it was time to put my needs and well-being aside, for the next eight hours, and instead focus on the needs and well-being of twenty-four eleven- and twelve-year-olds.

With my eyes barely open, I reach over to where my phone is sitting on my bedside table and hit stop.

It's six in the morning, which means I have one hour to get ready and be out the door.

Not to mention, the sun isn't even up yet.

The December darkness is taking over southeastern Wisconsin, making it hard to want to go anywhere besides my bed. I wake up to darkness, drive home from work in darkness, and it feels like the only sunshine I've been getting is through the windows of my classroom.

One of the perks of being a teacher is having Winter Break over the holidays. It is always much-needed as we reach the point of the year where my students and I are no longer finding our footing or distracted by the excitement of a new school year. We are now at the point where a break is exactly what we all need. And we are so close.

I just have to get through today. It's important, as a teacher, to find the perks amidst the many downfalls of the profession. I'm only in my second year, yet the drive I had when I first started my full-time position is slowly fading. The students are wonderful, but exhausting, while the job itself is far more than just *teaching*.

I'm learning more and more that the fun parts of the job are what paint the picture for those on the outside, and they are few and far between.

I roll over to face my bedside table, my bed feeling more comfortable now than it did when I had seven hours of sleep ahead of me.

My eyelids feel heavy as I take my phone off the charger. Maybe some mindless scrolling on social media will trick my eyes into thinking they actually want to be open.

I unlock my phone, tap to open up Instagram, and am greeted by the familiar highlight reel of people I haven't talked to since high school or college. People I used to consider classmates and friends, now living lives worthy of posting.

As I scroll, I see the influx of new engagements, marriages, anniversaries, and babies, along with people participating in their favorite winter and holiday activities.

Can't relate.

My last Instagram post was from my college graduation, a year and a half ago, and I haven't added anything to my story since the end of summer that same year. Clicking on my profile, I look at that most recent photo, and I can still remember the cool wind taking turns with the warmth of the sun which couldn't decide if it wanted to be out or not on graduation day. May in Milwaukee makes for a lot of overcast days, but overcast days make for good pictures. I was lucky to get a few snapped of me, thanks to someone's parent.

The picture I decided to post, to announce my graduation,

shows a bright-eyed, newly-graduated teacher with the names of her students, from her student teaching assignment, on her decorated cap. My robe was black, which contrasted against my olive skin that was still pale from the winter months and too much time inside a school building. I have a light, sky-blue cord around my neck to represent my graduation from the School of Education, and my smile takes up most of my face.

The day I graduated college was the same day I got offered a sixth-grade teaching position for the following fall. It's safe to say that the day was a highlight, but there haven't been too many more to follow.

I'm not even really sure why I keep the app; it's just a reminder of where you are compared to others, and it's hard to remember that I'm where I want to be, even if I'm *years* away from an engagement ring or gender reveal post to prove it.

I somehow manage to find the motivation to pull myself out of bed, missing the warmth the second I'm out of my sheets. My barefoot steps make my floor creak as I walk out of my bedroom and across my living room.

My one-bedroom apartment reflects me perfectly: bookshelves filled with books I've read and books I plan to read—the plan-to-read section being far larger than the books-read section. My counter space is clear and uncluttered because I have enough clutter constantly spiraling in my mind, and I definitely don't need the space surrounding me to reflect the same.

My thermostat is set to sixty-five degrees at all times, even when I may slightly regret it on mornings like these, and I've acquired enough furniture and décor over the past six years of living alone to fill the space nicely.

It is the perfect size for me with one bathroom, a cute little kitchen, a cozy living space, and a perfect spot by the window for my desk and bookshelves. My apartment complex is right off the highway, a few towns over from where I teach, so the place is also great for my commute.

When I'm not at work, I spend a lot of time here, almost always alone, which I enjoy. Aside from when the loneliness decides to creep in which inevitably leads to a nightly visit from a familiar face.

When I get to my bathroom, I grab my toothbrush and toothpaste as I mindlessly click through Instagram stories of beaches, bars, and fancy cocktails with equally fancy dinners.

Once again, can't relate.

The stories come to an end, abruptly taking me back to my news feed—the brightness of my phone being the only light in the whole apartment.

I go to set my phone down next to the sink but completely miss, causing my phone to drop on the floor instead. The series of loud smacks and thumps echoes to an almost deafening volume. I flinch at each thump, not at the noise but more at how each thud is a reminder that not everyone in this complex gets up at 6 AM.

I spit my toothpaste out into the sink before letting out a sigh.

So this is how the day is going to go.

I'm absolutely sure I'll be hearing about this from my downstairs neighbor.

I pick up my phone and try not to wake the whole apartment complex this time as I set it down and then turn to the opposite wall to warm up the shower.

While I wait for the water to reach a temperature fit for my liking, I slide out of my oversized Fall Out Boy t-shirt and underwear and look into the mirror. Still surrounded by darkness and the gentle splashing of the water behind me, I look at my reflection before me.

How did I get here?

If you had asked me, six years ago, where I thought I'd be at twenty-four, and *here* was definitely not it. I would never have guessed that I'd be teaching at a school, in a small suburb of Milwaukee, a mile from Lake Michigan, close to where I went to college, but not too close to my hometown. Being in my second year of teaching sixth grade, I finally feel like I not only have a sense of control, but I'm in a place I want to stay and continue to grow. I'm not fumbling over my lessons, I learned from my mistakes my first year, I'm making good enough money for my solo lifestyle, and I've let go of everything that was holding me back to get to where I wanted to be.

Everything besides the high school boyfriend.

I slip my hand underneath the water to check the temperature. Still lukewarm, so I close the glass shower door, continuing to wait for it to warm up.

I've lived in apartment complexes for my whole adult life, this one being the one I plan on staying at for the foreseeable future. I moved into my first apartment at eighteen and lived there until I moved here about six months ago.

I'm used to the water taking a while to warm up, the subtle sound of footsteps around and above me, the daily decisions between the stairs or elevator, even the idea that there's almost always someone who can hear what you're doing in your own home.

I don't mind any of it.

I actually like the feeling of living alone, yet not alone, because you can feel the life existing around you, yet completely separate from you.

It makes living alone feel less lonely.

It makes my empty apartment feel less empty.

That's what makes apartment living perfect for me. It's the same way teaching is the profession for me because there are very few moments where the classroom is quiet, let alone silent.

I reach back into the shower to feel the water, and it's finally at an enjoyable temperature.

I step into the shower, feeling the hot water trickle over my cold body, my skin pebbling at the conflicting sensations. I turn to have my back face the source and close my eyes as I lean back to get my hair wet.

The warm water pours over me, warming my skin just enough. The droplets trickling down my neck, my chest, down my stomach, and then down my legs, pooling at my feet, just slightly.

Then, before I can realize it's happening, the loneliness I know all too well begins to trickle in too.

Being the only one in this shower, knowing I'll be by myself over the next ten days of Winter Break with no work or hormonal sixth graders to distract me, should make me feel excited. Excited for the endless books I can read, movies I can watch, bathroom breaks I can take. But instead, it reopens a hole in my stomach that I've tried to patch over so many times.

A hole that makes me feel lonely. Empty.

Empty enough to text *him*.

———

I met Reed Michaels my junior year of high school, so we know each other inside and out. When he comes over, the small talk is comfortable. Familiar. Just like the sex.

A hole that makes me feel lonely. Empty Sometimes, when I invite him over, I ask him about work. Sometimes I'll tell him about my day, but the conversations never go far.

Not like they did when we were seventeen and in love.

I feel my skin acclimate to the warm water, and I reach for my shampoo, as my mind revisits the latest memory I have of Reed and me

We were lying in my bed, wrapped in the covers, my head on his chest, feeling his heartbeat align with mine. The air was starting to cool, as if warning us that winter was on its way. The moonlight was shining through my open window on that November night, and the TV was playing in the background, just loud enough to fill the silence. I felt the cool air slip in, making my bare body melt into Reed's even more.

"Do you like being a teacher?" he asked, seemingly out of nowhere. Our pillow talk was close to nonexistent these days, so this question must have been weighing heavily on his mind.

I was taken aback but answered, "Yeah, I really do."

The first few months of my second year teaching sixth grade came to my mind, along with so many memories playing over in my brain, all leaving me with feelings of love and admiration for my students and our short time so far together. "I love the time I spend with the kids. The job can get hard at times, but I really do love it."

As my words lingered in the air around us, I felt his body tighten in the slightest measure—I thought maybe it was a reaction to the cool air at first.

I paused, wanting to explain how excited I was to be in my second year of teaching and how much I was looking forward to the year ahead, but I stopped myself as an awkward tension began to invade the atmosphere.

The realization that I walked away from him, from us—from what we used to be—to get to where I am today covered my mouth and wouldn't let me speak another word.

I wasn't sure if he was going to say something or if he had the same realization I just had. I thought maybe I should reroute the conversation, but my mind went blank.

A few moments passed with neither one of us saying a word. The hold he had around my waist loosened, and I thought maybe he fell asleep.

I was about to close my eyes, thinking he didn't want the conversation to continue. It was then he responded to my sentiment, and it wasn't what I wanted to hear from someone I've known for so many years. Someone who grew up with me and stuck with me even after all I put him through.

It was the answer of a stranger.

An answer that reminded me that our relationship was for one purpose and one purpose only.

"Why would you spend all that money to be an overpaid babysitter? And don't call them 'your kids,' that's weird."

The words struck me deep in the stomach where butterflies used to flutter. Any teacher will tell you that teaching is so much more than that.

On the surface, I brushed off the comment but still tried to stand my ground. I couldn't hide the betrayal I felt. "My job is a little more than babysitting, Reed." *He scoffed at my attempt to push back at him.*

Was that truly all he thought of me and my career?

I didn't even try to explain how I call them "my kids" because they are. I know all teachers understand. We call them our kids because they become more than a class list. I spend more time with my students than anyone else, and they do truly become part of my heart.

"I hope it was worth it," *he responds before letting go of me, in more ways than one, to roll over and go to sleep. I rolled over the other way creating more space between us.*

My mind squeezed out all the energy it had trying to forget about the tone of his voice when he said those words. Thinking about the doubts about myself I buried so deep. Feeling the loneliness I know all too well, even in Reed's presence.

Did I make a mistake becoming a teacher and letting go of what we planned so many years ago?

Reed didn't say anything more that night, and I couldn't find any more words to say to him.

He was gone before I woke up. This was a usual occurrence, but it stung more this time.

It hurt more than any other time before.

I decided that I should end this mess we were in before it got any more complicated than it already was. I should've ended it a long time ago, knowing that all we do is hurt each other in the end.

All I did was hurt him in high school, but he's the one hurting me now.

I reached over the spot where he lay just a few hours ago and grabbed my phone, the lingering scent of rain and burning wood—smoky yet calming—staining my sheets.

I deleted his number

I told myself I wouldn't reach out again.

A clean break.

Again.

I haven't seen him since that night because I'm holding my ground.

Also, because he hasn't reached out either.

And that hurts, a little more than I thought it would.

CHAPTER 2
DREW

REED MICHAELS WAS one of the few people who has been to my apartment since I moved here in June. He was also one of the few to have seen where I lived before here—a cheap, old, one-bedroom outside of the University of Milwaukee's campus.

I moved out of my parents' houses at eighteen, so I definitely had limited choices as to what I could afford back then, and I definitely don't miss the smell of stale beer that was stuck in the carpets.

Reed was also one of the two things from my hometown that trickled over into my life after high school. My best friend, Lacey, is the second of those two things, and, without her, there would have been no Reed.

Everyone in our hometown couldn't believe that the boy that wore flannel and work boots fell for the girl in skinny jeans, band tees, and box-dyed black hair.

Reed and I officially met about halfway through our junior year of high school even though we both lived in our small town our whole lives. We went to different elementary schools and middle schools, but all the schools funneled into our district's one high school.

The first two years, we had some classes together, but I never would have considered him to be someone I *knew*. We didn't truly meet until one morning when I was waiting for Lacey before school.

I was leaning against her locker, picking at the black nail polish on my fingernails when Reed showed up.

"Hey," I heard from behind me. I didn't turn to face the voice because I initially assumed it wasn't directed at me. Then, I heard it again.

"Hello?"

I turned and was struck by a sight I had never seen up close before. Reed's hair was damp from the snow falling hard that Tuesday morning in February, and the smell of gasoline and oil lingered on his clothes from helping his dad open up their family's auto repair shop. I felt his foggy blue eyes hook into me at that very moment, and I couldn't look away.

And I'm still, to this day, trying to unhook myself from the feeling I get in my stomach when those eyes are on me.

"Hey," I muttered, barely getting the word off my tongue.

"I'm Reed. You're Drew, right? Lacey's friend?" He ran one hand through his hair, moving the pieces that were falling over his eyes and revealed a crooked smile, his lips wavering to one side of his face. His other hand was holding his backpack that was slung over his shoulder.

"Uh yeah, that's me." My words made his smile deepen, exposing a single dimple on this left cheek.

I was expecting him to respond by politely asking me to move out of his way or something, but he didn't. He actually didn't say anything else that day. He just looked at me, and I couldn't tear away from his gaze.

His stare was enticing.

I watched his eyes move from my eyes to my lips then back up to my eyes, and the look on his face told me that he had already known the answer to his question before asking.

It told me he already knew who I was, but it told me he wanted to know me better.

It told me I was going to mean something to him. That he was going to mean something to me.

He swung his backpack off his shoulder and opened the locker next to the one I was waiting by. He put what he needed into his backpack, and closed his locker before heading down the hallway. I watched as he walked away, thinking that maybe I was wrong about the way he was looking at me.

Maybe our interaction was just a one-and-done. But then he looked over his shoulder, catching me staring, and my cheeks warmed at the smirk he sent me before he turned back around and continued on his way.

The days following, there was a flicker in my stomach every time I turned the corner to the hallway where his locker was.

A friendship between him and I budded during those moments I waited for Lacey in the morning or between classes at her locker. Those few minutes alone each morning allowed us to get to know each other more and more. Then, before I knew it, a relationship blossomed beyond that space, and we were as inseparable as two high schoolers could be.

We spent every moment we could together, falling further and further into the mutual infatuation that inevitably turned into my first experience with love.

I learned the little I knew about love from my parents, and for as long as I could remember, I longed for what it felt like to not have to work, hope, or long for love. For as long as I could remember, there was a hole in my stomach that left me feeling so lonely, so empty, so unlovable.

But, every time I was with Reed, I felt that hole fill, and I never wanted to let go of that feeling.

I never thought I would have to.

My mom and dad separated when my brother and I were

in the early years of elementary school—I was ten, and my brother was eight.

My parents were never married, making everything that followed their breakup much more messy. Between the custody battles and child support, my brother and I were pawns in their twisted game.

Since then, or maybe even before then, there were always inconsistencies between their love and care for us. The love we received was laced with control and the strain for power over each other, and my idea of what it felt like to receive love became so convoluted to the point that I don't think I knew what it felt to have love reciprocated.

Growing up, my parents each held me responsible for so many things, but they also held me responsible for reading their minds as to how *they* thought I should manage everything.

They always found something wrong with what I did, even when I was breaking my back to do everything they wanted. They wanted me to excel in school, but reminded me that I should be spending my free time working to earn my own money. I was expected to help out with my brother and around the house, but they also became worried that I didn't have any friends or a social life.

My brother suffered the same, causing him to find anywhere else to be rather than home as we got older. We drifted, never really having a relationship aside from shared experiences and DNA. With him avoiding their houses as much as possible, I was the only one left for my parents to put in the middle of their arguments and disagreements, both constantly using me as a figurative punching bag to complain about the other.

So, I always did everything I could, telling myself if I did everything they wanted, they would show me the uncondi- tional love I longed for.

It wasn't until I almost exploded under all the pressure,

my mom blaming *me* for my brother's unwillingness to spend any time at home was the straw that broke the camel's back. Reed and I were supposed to go out to dinner for our six month anniversary, and our last hooray of the summer before our senior year of high school, but we didn't even make it out of the car.

We had just parked in front of the restaurant, and he noticed I had been quiet the whole ride.

"Is everything okay, D?"

I answered with a nod because I didn't want to ruin the night.

"Are you sure?" He turned to face me, but I knew I wouldn't be able to hold anything in if I looked at him. "If you're okay, why can't you look at me?" Reed asked, as if he could read my mind.

I couldn't even form words because I felt the tears well up in my eyes, threatening to fall at any second.

He reached over to grab my hand that was sitting on my lap, and there was no more holding it in. The feeling of his touch sent me into full-blown sobs.

He grabbed my arm and pulled me onto his lap in the driver's seat. My legs on each side of his, he wrapped one arm tightly around my waist and put one hand on the back of my head as he pulled my head into his chest, giving me the space to cry.

I had confided in him how I felt about the position my parents put me in and how I never felt like I was doing enough to make them both happy, but that night, he didn't say a word. Maybe not knowing what to say, or knowing anything he said wouldn't make me feel better.

The comfort I felt just being in his arms gave me the space to let out the cries I had been carrying for so many years.

I sobbed into his chest until my eyes were raw, and he just held me until the cries faded, and my tears began to run out.

He stroked my back as I calmed down. "You're going to kill yourself if you keep this up. You're killing yourself trying to do everything they want," he said into my hair.

"I know," I whispered.

"You don't have to keep this up," he whispered back.

"I know," I whispered again.

"Then why do you let them make you so upset?"

"I'm just never good enough for them. I do what they tell me to and more, yet, I'm always in the wrong. I just can't do anything right." My voice was shaky from the residual tears, but I felt the sadness in my chest burn into anger, like a paper turning black from a flame. "I'm so sick of feeling this way. So sick of thinking I need them because I don't. I'm better off without them in my life." I turn my head, still against Reed's chest, and look out the window.

The sky was still lit by the slanting rays of the slowly setting sun, giving a warm orange tinge to the sky. The night looked warm and inviting, but Reed holding me tightly in the car felt safe and familiar.

In that moment, I realized that I was never going to meet my parents' unattainable expectations, and they would never see me as enough. But, I also realized that I didn't need them.

I didn't need them because I had Reed.

Once again, as if he could read my mind, Reed's palms warmed my cheeks as he brought my face to look at him. "You have me, Drew. And, that's all you need." His blue eyes had a gray tint that contradicted the warm sky, but in that moment, there was no place I would have rather been.

It began to make sense in my head.

His support, his comfort, his words.

This must be what love is supposed to feel like.

Reed helped me feel like I was enough.

Until who I was stopped being enough for him, too.

CHAPTER 3
DREW

I OPEN my eyes as I rinse the shampoo out of my hair and grab my conditioner. As I run the product through my hair, I tune out my thoughts of Reed, and my parents, and my past, and I begin to do what I do best: distract myself with work.

I go over my mental to-do list for when I get to school this morning.

1. Make copies of a graphic organizer for reading.
2. Edit the slides for this morning's lesson.
3. Write today's learning targets on the board.
4. Email students' families our weekly newsletter.

There's probably more I *should* do, but it's also the day before break. I can save some stuff for when we come back in January.

I put my conditioner down and grab my body wash, squeezing it into my hand. The crisp, citrusy smell wakes me up a little bit more as it mixes with the steam rising from the warm water.

As I lather myself with the lemony, sugary scent, I go over the schedule for the day, knowing I had to move some things around for the school's holiday assembly in the afternoon.

The thought then transforms into the holiday that is just around the corner, and I'm struck with the sudden realization that it's almost Christmas, and I have no plans. I feel the excitement I had for the day mold into a pit in my stomach.

Maybe I should call my mom to see what she's doing for Christmas Eve this year.

Or, I could call my dad.

The holidays are less than a week away, and I'm not sure if I want to spend them alone like I did last year.

But I'm not sure reaching out to my parents will be much better, even though I've made my peace, and we make it work.

I came to my own understanding that my relationship with both of my parents is what it is—never letting myself fall back into the place I was in as a child where I sacrificed my love for myself for theirs.

I realized it only hurt me, wanting more from each of them—more than what they are willing to give.

I would say that my relationship with my parents is closer to the relationship you have with distant aunts and uncles. You see each other every once in a while—usually for holidays or special occasions—and the conversations never run very deep. It's casual and polite, but I keep them at arms-length. There's love there, but more so out of obligation. It's not the kind of love you would want or expect to receive from a mom or dad.

Unlike my brother who turned eighteen and never looked back. He lives in Evanston now, and goes to school at Northwestern. He got there completely on his own—no thanks to mom or dad. Calvin and I keep in touch more now that we are adults, but we still have some room for our sibling-relationship to grow.

Last year was the first year I didn't go to my mom's for Christmas Eve or see my dad for New Years. I was way too busy trying to stay on top of my grading and planning while I was still finding my balance as a first-year teacher.

Or at least that's what I told them.

In reality, I didn't want to deal with their questions, thoughts, and opinions on my life choices, which I knew they would be both all too willing to share.

I could call Cal.

He's on break from school, and it might be a nice olive branch to extend. Reaching out could be the first step towards being in each other's lives again without the driving force of our parents separating us anymore.

I could also call Lacey.

My best friend.

But I haven't been a good best friend lately—ignoring her invites to have dinner with her and her boyfriend, Tyler.

They've been dating since our sophomore year of college and just closed on a house in August. They decided to come back to Lacey's—and my—hometown to "settle down and start their lives together."

At least, that's what Lacey said when I called to congratulate her. It was the first time we had talked all summer and the last time we've actually talked rather than texted.

Lacey's always been there for me, through the ups and downs of my relationship with my parents and Reed, and she has always supported me and my decisions.

We're the kind of friends who don't have to talk every day, but she's reached out less and less these past few months. I know she would be there if I ever needed, the same way I would be for her.

I really should call them both.

With my mental energy beginning to run low from the

plethora of things popping into my head this morning, I tell myself that there will be no more thinking about my parents, Reed, Cal, or Lacey… for now anyway.

I need to save this energy for my students.

I'll call Lacey this weekend to make plans for lunch while I'm off.

I'll text Cal later today to see if I can find a time to visit him since we're both on break.

I'll call my mom after school today, and I'll call my dad right after to see if I can stop by and see them both sometime next week.

And I will *not call Reed.*

I grab my towel and quickly dry off to start getting ready.

Walking back and forth between the bedroom and my bathroom, I realize I'm probably making too much noise for my downstairs neighbor's preference. But I can't help it. I may be stomping around, or closing drawers too loudly, or dropping too many things along the way, but he'll just have to deal because I'm now officially running late.

Too late to be concerned with the amount of noise I'm making.

Hopefully, he understands.

Although hopeful thinking about my neighbor hasn't gotten me too far these past six months.

I jump into some black jeans—one of my few pairs without holes—and throw a black turtleneck over my head, so I can finish putting on my mascara and twisting my damp hair into a claw clip. My hair falls a few inches below where a bra strap would be, so clipping it back keeps it out of the way.

Not too long ago, I dyed my dark brown hair red, making the green in my hazel eyes more apparent behind my dark lashes. I pull a few stands out of the clip to frame my face before swiping some bronzer on my cheeks to give my skin a little more color.

I can always skip the blush because my cheeks have a tendency to give my feelings away, meaning I naturally wear a few different blush shades a day without the need to apply them. The natural flush sits just behind the freckles on the high points of my cheeks and nose that lighten during this time of year.

Aside from the badge I wear around the neck, you could argue that I blend in with my students exceptionally well. I only stand just about five feet tall, never gaining any extra inches from my shoes of choice. My body hasn't changed much from my own middle school years, aside from growing to fit my jeans much nicer, but not enough to fill a bra.

Dressed and almost ready, I thank my past self for the purchase of a coffee maker with the pre-set brew time that saves me essential minutes in the morning. I like to make it to school by 7:15 a.m., so I check the time to see if I'm on track to leave on time, and it's 6:50 a.m.

Perfect.

I walk over to the kitchen as I put my earrings in, holding my shoes under one arm. Once both earrings are secure, I drop my shoes onto the floor, not having enough time to care that the *thump* was much louder than anticipated. I reach up to grab my black tumbler from the cabinet above my coffee maker as I ask myself why I chose to put an everyday essential on the highest shelf in the cabinet.

Maybe Winter Break will include a deep clean and organization of my kitchen because I have to get up on my tip-toes to reach the shelf.

Barely balanced, I pour my coffee in the tumbler while simultaneously attempting to slip on my Vans.

As a teacher, you'd think multitasking would be one of my skills, and it was working for me up until now. Unfortunately, I have more work to do until it officially settles into my skill set.

Moving too quickly and working way too close to the

edge of the counter, I go to grab my tumbler, filled to the brim with hot coffee and instead knock it right towards me.

I try to step back to avoid the coffee splashing on me but trip on the shoes, not all the way on my feet, just below me. I fall straight on my butt with a loud enough noise to wake my whole apartment complex.

The fall was ten times louder than when I dropped my phone and my shoes and was also followed by a shriek when the coffee splashed all over me. If my ass meeting the floor didn't wake everyone, my scream definitely did.

I let myself take a moment to thank my past self, once again, but this time it's for choosing my *thicker* black turtleneck today, otherwise the list of things to go wrong this morning would've included second-degree burns.

As I'm sitting on the floor, covered with coffee, the silence surrounding me is a not-so-friendly reminder of how loud I must have been just a few moments ago.

No wonder my downstairs neighbor hates me.

CHAPTER 4

DREW

ABOUT THREE MONTHS INTO DATING, Reed was walking me to class like he always did. He grabbed my hand, the one not holding all my books, and I smiled to myself feeling the warmth of his hand in mine.

As we passed one of the science labs, I noticed his eyes peered inside the window of the closed door. Then, he stopped walking, turned to look at me, wearing his crooked smile that always meant trouble. Without warning, he pulled me into the empty classroom before I had time to protest.

"What are you doing?" I whisper-yelled. You could hear the amusement in my hushed voice. He pulled me into the vacant room, grabbed my books, and threw them on a nearby lab table.

"Shh! Someone's going to hear us," he whisper-yelled back. His face a silhouette in the dark classroom,

"Rightfully so! You're kidnapping me!" He couldn't see my face, but I'm sure he knew I was smiling.

"You wish." His face was so close to mine, I could feel his breath on my lips.

Before I could ask if he had completely lost his mind, he grabbed me by the belt loops of my jeans and pulled me in. His lips crashed into mine as his fingers dug into my hips. He kissed me hard and passionately, not caring that anyone could walk into the room at any moment.

But, the more I wanted to pull away, the more he was like a magnet I couldn't separate myself from. Our kiss became deeper as he eased his hands over the back pockets of my skin-tight jeans. My hands snaked up his arms, and I wrapped myself around his shoulders pulling myself into him even more.

He was kissing me with an intensity he had never shown me before, and I didn't think I was ever going to be able to live without it.

Reed slid his hands further down to pick me up and set me down onto the nearby table as he positioned himself between my legs. His tongue began to explore my mouth, and my fingers found their way up his neck and through his hair.

Suddenly, he pulled away. I thought maybe he heard someone coming in, but when I peeked over his shoulder, it was still just the two of us in the dark, our heavy breathing being the only noise around us.

That's when he caught my gaze and said three words to me that had been looming in the air around us the past couple of weeks.

In a whisper that made my heart skip a beat, he said, "I love you."

I felt tears well up in my eyes, hearing those words said to me for what felt like the first time in my life. I repeated the same words back, "I love you too, Reed."

My eyes had adjusted to the darkness, and I could see the most beautiful smile appear before me. I felt his hand touch the side of my face and then wrap around the back of my neck to pull me into the sweetest kiss. A kiss that sent a kaleidoscope of butterflies off in my stomach.

"You're mine," he said against my lips. "Always remember that."

As our relationship continued to grow, we finished our junior year together and had a summer fit for the movies, aside from the night I spent our anniversary crying in his lap.

We spent most of our time together working at his parent's shop, having picnics at the local park on our days off, seeing movies, getting ice cream, and not being able to keep our hands off each other.

There was one night I heard my phone buzz from under my pillow, knowing it was him on the other side.

"Hello?" I answered.

"I need to see you," he whispered to me from his bed, under the covers.

With flutters in my stomach, just from the sound of his voice, I smiled so big my cheeks were going to start to hurt. I pulled myself under my own covers, so my mom couldn't hear me whispering, longing to feel Reed's arms around me rather than my sheets.

"Tomorrow, silly. I'll ask my mom if I ca—"

"Let me call you back," he cut me off. He hung up the phone without even a goodbye.

Confused, and a little disappointed our conversation ended so abruptly, I put my phone under my pillow.

That was weird, I thought to myself.

A few minutes later, my pillow started to vibrate, another phone call coming in.

Reed parked his truck, with the lights off, down the street, and I met him behind my mom's house at the back screen door. "Tomorrow felt too far away," he said as he pulled his face away from mine to grab my hand.

We ran to his truck, muffled laughter and eager grins on our faces, and, with the windows down and music playing, we drove around under the summer night sky, soaking up every moment together before we ran out of moonlight. We parked somewhere quiet and secluded to make-out under the stars, wrapped up in each other, the adrenaline of no one knowing where we were ruminating in the air around us.

I didn't understand what it meant to have butterflies until I met Reed. The fluttering wings of hope and young love in my stomach were a constant until they shriveled up underneath the cloud of guilt that took over my stomach when our relationship had officially run its course.

The summer faded into our senior year of high school, and we started to talk about what comes next for us because we knew that this was it.

"D, I can't wait for our life together." Reed was taking me home from school one autumn afternoon. Not too far into the school year, he started talking about this dream he had for us. That we would take over his family's shop, two miles down the street from our high school—as if changing oil was really changing lives. I always loved his passion for the work he did there, even if I never completely understood it.

I enjoyed working there with him during the summer, but did I really want to do it for the rest of my life?

"My parents said the shop is mine when I'm eighteen. We can run it together." I looked out the window, trying to not let myself be distracted by the smile on his face.

"What about college?" I asked.

"D, we don't need college." He took one of his hands off the wheel to reach over and give my thigh a squeeze. "Going from high school to a job right away, is like skipping a step."

I could hear the excitement in his voice.

"You don't want to go to college?" I asked, feeling like I had to hide the hope in my voice.

"Why would I?" He snuck a glance my way, but he wasn't looking for an answer.

I answered anyway, "Well, what if you want to do something other than work at the shop?" My eyes traced the trees passing us as we drove.

He laughed, but I didn't think anything I said was funny. It was a serious question, but I guess that was my answer.

The conversation ended there.

January of our senior year came around, in what felt like, a blink of an eye. Reed was now eighteen and took over the shop from his parents. Through a program offered at our high school, his last semester of our senior year could be done working rather than in classes. It became all he talked about, never forgetting to remind me that my job would be waiting for me after graduation.

The winter faded into spring, and graduation grew closer. The more we talked about what came after graduation, the more I found myself wanting to want those things but not being able to.

Reed's blue-gray eyes were so hooked into me, the color once seeming so clear but now reminded me of fog on a winding road, blurring my vision and muddling my sense of direction of where I wanted to go in life.

Anytime I would try to explain to him the doubt I was having, he would hit me with that crooked grin and reassure me that we were ready.

It wasn't until I was out to lunch one weekend with Lacey that I realized that Reed and I were always talking about what *he* wanted, not me.

Lacey had just gotten her acceptance letter to the University of Madison for business, a field I had absolutely no interest in but sparked something in Lacey. It was March, over a full year since the day I met Reed. College acceptance letters were flooding the mailboxes of my peers, but not mine because I was *skipping that step*.

Lacey was so excited as she told me about the business school, the classes she was going to take, her potential roommate, and the dorm building she was hoping to get.

The enthusiasm in her voice was infectious, and I was so incredibly happy for her. We spent the afternoon walking the aisles of T.J. Maxx and Target, looking for potential dorm decor for her.

It wasn't until I dropped her off at home that I felt a pang of jealousy in my chest, and that little ounce of jealousy festered inside me, growing over the coming weeks until I couldn't take it anymore.

I decided that I wanted that.

I wanted to go to college and pick out decorations for my dorm, and pursue a degree I was passionate about.

I wanted that.

I applied to a college not too far but far enough when I got home that afternoon, not telling anyone. I hoped I had enough time to still get an acceptance letter in a few weeks.

I didn't know what I wanted to pursue yet, so I just applied as "Undecided" when it came to my major. It wasn't until later that I remembered my dream had never been to help manage an auto repair shop. I didn't want to answer phone calls or run emission tests.

Ever since I was little, I wanted to be a teacher.

Even though I was being convinced otherwise.

Just applying made me feel like I was in control of my life. It was a feeling I never felt before, and it was a feeling I never wanted to let go of. After weeks of letting Reed tell me what I wanted, I was finally doing something that I knew *I* wanted.

Those few weeks of waiting for my answer, checking the mailbox every day when I got home, gave me some time to prepare for telling Reed that I didn't want to work at the shop, or start our future so soon. I knew he would be mad because he always seemed annoyed when I would bring up feeling a little nervous or uneasy. But, after weeks of being told I was supposed to want different things for myself, I decided I was going to do what I wanted, not what Reed wanted *for* me.

The week before graduation, I decided to initiate a conversation with Reed in an attempt to start the conversation about how we *may* want different things. I found myself scared to bring it up to him, and I didn't know why.

He wanted to spend this upcoming summer working like we did last summer, and he even hinted about getting engaged. I knew I didn't have time for that. I had to use my time to find a place to live, meet with my advisor, register for classes, and find a campus job.

And, we were way too young.

He was taking me home from school, and it took me the first five minutes of the ride to work up the courage.

"So, I've been wanting to talk to you about something," I said, and Reed stole a glance my way. His lips wavered to the side in a slight arch before he turned his eyes back on the road. "I was talking to Lacey a few weeks ago, and she was telling me about her plans for UW-Madison. It sounds super fun, so it got me think—I couldn't even finish my thought because I saw his jaw lock, his grip on the steering wheel tighten.

"Thinking about what?" he spit out with a coldness to his voice that made my blood go cold.

I hesitated, not sure if I should say anything. "I was... thinking of maybe going to college." I couldn't even hide the shakiness in my voice.

He laughed a humorless laugh. "C'mon, Drew. That's not the plan. You know that."

"It's just a little change. I'll keep going to school while you work. It's kind of like what we're doing now, right? Then, we can do all the other stuff when I graduate."

Not even meeting my eyes, focusing on the road in front of him, his words reeking of condescension, he said, "You really think you're built for college? What are you going to do without me?"

I knew he didn't expect me to have answers to his questions.

I knew he thought I would crumble without him.

And in that moment, I thought that I might.

I knew I couldn't keep convincing myself that this was going to work.

The day after graduation, Reed was on his way to pick me up, and my shoulders were heavy with what should have been excitement but instead was overwhelming guilt I'd been carrying for weeks. I didn't have the nerve to bring up our conversation in the car again, and Reed pretended like it never happened.

How could I tell the guy who taught me what it means to be loved that I didn't want to be with him anymore?

Then I thought, how can I love someone who thinks I'm *nothing* without him?

He came to get me at the back door, the same one I snuck out of to see him so many times before, and I couldn't even step outside. I felt protected by the screen between us, feeling like it was shielding me from the disappointment he was about to pour over me.

I told Reed the truth and made a clean break. *I got into college. I saved up enough money. I'm moving into my new apartment next month. This is what I want to do.*

I didn't have to say I was breaking up with him because that went without saying. Choosing to do what I wanted rather than what he wanted for us was the same thing in his mind.

Saying my piece and shutting the door on him, his smile crumpled before my eyes as I shot my loaded words at him. Seeing the confusion, fury, and betrayal on his face made my heart twist. And I promised myself I would never let myself see him again to avoid hurting him—and myself—all over again.

But, the joke was on me because when I left my hometown to start my journey, I would always be reminded of the feelings he, and no one else, made me feel, and I felt the wall I tried to build between us shatter.

Sitting alone in my college apartment, night after night, wanting to feel his comfort and warmth. I texted him that I missed him.

And when I did, he texted back within minutes.

Send me your address.

Within the hour, he was knocking on my door.

Being with him that night reminded me of what it felt to be seventeen and in love. The feeling of no responsibilities, young love, wind in my hair, and his hand on my thigh in the front seat of his truck. That night in my college apartment was my first time, and too many times to count have followed since then, leading us to where we are today—me reaching out when the loneliness trickles in.

At seventeen, if you asked me where I would be at twenty-four, I would have never said here.

Even though there are no more phone calls under the covers worthy of butterflies, the problem of me deleting his number can be easily solved.

It's not like I haven't seen it enough times to have it memorized anyway.

CHAPTER 5
EMMETT

EVER SINCE THIS girl moved in, I haven't gotten any sleep.

I need to give her a piece of my mind.

Again.

And maybe this time, I'll give her the piece that has been thinking about her a little too much.

I rub my eyes, trying to adjust to the darkness around me. I could go back to sleep, see if I can get another hour or so. Or, I could make my way to the bar early.

I wasn't planning on heading in until 9 a.m. or so, but maybe I can catch the delivery guys before they pull in. They come on Fridays, and I don't need them destroying the back room I just spent all week organizing. They always just dump the shit and leave, and it pisses me off.

I roll out of bed, deciding to go with the latter, knowing that Drew will probably wake me up just when I fall back asleep anyway. I'm greeted by the alarmingly cold air around me as I stand. I forgot to close my window last night, when I slithered out of my clothes before passing out, a little too tipsy than I'd like to admit for a Thursday night.

I don't usually drink at work, but the regulars that came

out to my bar last night were feeling the stress that the holidays bring on, and I could tell they wanted a good time. Plus, the holidays always make me feel like I could use an extra drink, so I couldn't say no to the one shot... or the other four. It also didn't help that I got a text asking to meet up with someone I'd much rather never see again.

I head to the bathroom to brush my teeth, grabbing my toothbrush when my shoulders jolt at the sound of a series of loud bangs just above me.

What the hell is she doing up there?

I truly do not understand how someone as small as her can be so loud.

Why is she up this early anyway?

I think she's a teacher or something, but I don't think schools start this early. So I'm not quite sure why she gets up at the butt crack of dawn and doesn't get home until the early evening, sometimes even later.

She is always alone too. It's never any voices I hear up there. Usually just one pair of footsteps—maybe two every once in a while—her dropping shit, and her music, which I can't complain too much about because it's the same type of music I listen to.

I remember around the time she first moved in, about six months ago, I saw her at the elevator and gave her a hard time for listening to her music so loud. It was the morning after I helped Riley move out, and Drew caught me at a bad time. I told her how the last thing I wanted to listen to after a long day of bullshit was the Blink-182 album *without* Tom Delonge.

I don't think she really liked me commenting on her music taste, or anything else for that matter, because she glared at me with those captivating eyes—green with a ring of gold bursting outwards. I had to look away before I lost myself in them.

Bothered and unamused, she went to say something but

then turned as red as her hair and stomped off, saved by the elevator opening to the garage floor we were both heading to, not having a response for me. I was left feeling like these little interactions of ours were going to be fun.

I feel the corner of my lips pull upwards, then roll my eyes at myself for even giving my upstairs neighbor, with lead feet and butterfingers, a second thought.

I haven't been getting much sleep these days. I'm still getting used to sleeping alone, even though I don't miss the person who's no longer there, and Drew always seems to catch me in those moments where I'm quick to anger, not caring if the edge in my tone is offensive or not when I let her know what she did to bug me. It helps me blow off steam, even if she probably thinks I'm a total dick. I could probably be nicer to her about how much noise she makes—she may even try to be more considerate of the noise she is making if I was more polite—but I just don't have the patience.

Plus, I like the reaction I pull out of her.

I glob some toothpaste onto the bristles of my toothbrush, run it under water, and start brushing my teeth, washing away the residual taste of whiskey from last night.

As I stare at the reflection of my dingy black hoodie in the reflection in front of me, the minty taste of my toothpaste making me feel more awake, I hear the shower turn on above me. I leave the bathroom before thoughts of what she's doing just above me invade my brain without my permission.

I head into the kitchen, still brushing my teeth, and check the fridge to see if I can scavenge something for breakfast this morning, or if I have to stop at the gas station on the corner before I walk over to the bar.

I love making meals—especially breakfast—but it's not as much fun making food for one, so I haven't been keeping my kitchen as stocked as I used to.

Just as I suspected, there's nothing but an energy drink I

bought yesterday, but was too busy to drink at work, a few beers, and leftover pizza from a few nights ago,

I'll have to go to the store tonight.

I spit out the toothpaste foam into the kitchen sink and dip my head under the running water to rinse out my mouth as I hear a muffled thud coming from the ceiling above my bathroom.

Leave it to Drew to let the soap bottle slip out of her hands.

Without warning, the thought of her, naked, in the shower pops into my head. I can see the water droplets dripping down her legs, her cheeks flushed from the stream, her red hair damp, sticking to her glistening body. I blink the thoughts away, not wanting to unpack where they're coming from.

I haven't really thought of any girl since Riley and I broke things off a few months ago—besides my upstairs neighbor who I know I don't have any business thinking of that way. I shake my head at myself, making my way back to my bedroom to get dressed for the day.

The apartment has felt a little empty since my ex-fiancé left, but I barely spend time here these days that doesn't consist of sleeping, watching TV, or playing video games. I don't really give myself too much time to think about it.

Riley and I were together for a few years and got engaged a few months before we decided to break things off. I met her after I graduated college eight years ago. She was a friend of a friend and we hit it off when we met at a wedding, seated at the same table, where neither of us brought a plus one.

The sting of her leaving isn't as strong anymore, and I've been through worse... much worse. But, I try not to think about it more than I have to. Riley wasn't too fond of the idea of being married to a bartender, and I had no intention of finding a new career. We both could have compromised, but the fact that neither one of us wanted to spoke volumes.

That's why it pisses me off so much that she had the audacity to text me last night asking if we could talk.

I throw on a black Metallica t-shirt and some black jeans before heading back in the bathroom to deal with my hair. Riley always hated it long, but since she's not here to complain about it, I've let it grow out just under my shoulders. The dark curls can get unruly, but nothing that a topknot can't fix.

I grab my hair and twist it around my finger, making a bun. I loosely secure it, knowing strands will break free throughout the day and wash my face. As I spray on some cologne, I check the time, and see it's only 6:25 a.m. I head back to my bedroom to grab my phone from the charger and lay back down. I spend the next twenty minutes mindlessly scrolling through Reddit, not wanting to leave just yet but not wanting to fall back asleep either.

At 6:50 a.m., I decide that I should probably head to the bar because the delivery guys get there at around 7:15 a.m.

I spend a few minutes typing down some things I want to pick up from the store after work in my Notes app then slide my phone into my back pocket. As I go to grab my keys, my whole body jumps as I hear a huge crash above me, followed by a scream.

Damn. This girl can't keep quiet to save her life.

CHAPTER 6
DREW

I *FINALLY* MAKE it out the door a little after 7 o'clock in the morning, with no coffee, a new turtleneck, and a bruised butt to match my ego.

My apartment is just down the hall from the elevator, so I quickly push the DOWN button and figure I'll get a head start on my emails while I wait.

There is no way I am going to be in my classroom by 7:15 a.m., which won't leave me my normal forty-five minutes of uninterrupted prep to get everything done. I'll be lucky to get to my desk with twenty minutes to spare before I have to go grab the kids from the gym.

Only needing to wait for a minute or two for the elevator, I step in as the doors open and press the button for the garage. The doors slowly close, leaving me in silence aside from the muffled creaking of the rusty, unoiled cables.

Sometimes this thing feels like it's hanging on by a thread.

I hear the ding of the elevator, thinking I'm already arriving at the garage as most of my attention is on an email about the secretary's wish to spread holiday cheer with cookies in the staff lounge. I'll have to add *stopping by the lounge* to my to-do list for when I get to school.

Not even looking up from my phone, I take a step forward expecting a waft of cool air and a clear pathway into the garage. Instead, I walk straight into a steaming presence and an infamous yet delectable aroma of wood with a hint of vanilla. I'm engulfed by the scent as I look up from my phone to see the black Metallica shirt come into focus.

Emmett Ryan.

The thirty-year-old bartender who happens to be my downstairs neighbor, and it is just my luck that our elevator schedules always somehow align perfectly on days I really wish they wouldn't.

It's safe to say, he's not my biggest fan.

I thought my coffee fiasco was the start of my uphill battle because how can my day get worse than that?

I was wrong.

I step back trying to find the words *I'm sorry,* but words never seem to leave the tip of my tongue when his eyes are on me.

I look up, meeting his chocolate brown eyes that are at least a foot higher than mine. He holds my gaze for just a second too long then looks away as he steps around me, not saying a word, just wearing the signature smoldering yet disapproving expression he always seems to have around me.

The elevator doors close, trapping us in together, and my eyes have minds of their own as they follow his chiseled arms peeking out from his short sleeves. Those tattooed forearms crossed, holding a black hoodie across his broad chest, closing him off, and doing something to me. His hair is dark, his shoulders broad, and his face is sculpted with a sharp jawline slightly dulled by the scruff that runs along it, framing his full lips.

"I just can't get away from you, can I?" He says looking up to the ceiling, as if running into me is the equivalent of slamming your hand in a car door. His voice is so smooth yet as sharp as a blade. "Thanks for waking up the whole floor this morning, Drew." He lets out a chuckle, even though what he said wasn't funny. "What'd you do? Start your day by throwing yourself onto the floor?"

I feel my cheeks warm at the sound of his voice. "Excuse me?" I somehow manage to push the words off my tongue, trying to ignore the flick I felt in my stomach when I heard him say my name. "It's not like I did anything on purpose." I look away knowing that if I keep looking at him, my words won't come out.

"I just don't understand how someone as small as you makes *that* much noise."

I scoff. As small as me? He's the one standing at least 6'4" with muscles *begging* to break free from under his clothes. I'm sure everyone looks small to him.

"You walk around your place like you're the only one in the whole complex." His brows form a "V" as he turns his head to face me, his voice is deep and stern. "Some people don't enjoy waking up to banging on the ceiling at 6 a.m."

I roll my eyes at him. "You're being dramatic." I feel myself getting mad, wanting to properly confront him, so I turn my body to face him, not backing down this time. "It was almost 7 a.m. Don't you get up around then anyway?" I put my hands on my hips, ready to say more, but I pause at his now raised eyebrow.

"Oh, so not only are you an unwanted alarm clock, but you're also a stalker?"

All the heat in my body rushes up to my face. "Y-y-you know, that's not, you're the—forget it," I somehow stammer out.

Emmett bartends across the street at a local place that has been there forever. It's one of those bars where the regulars give you the side eye if they've never seen you before, so I've never bothered to see what he's like there, or even outside the four walls of this elevator.

We have tons of mornings just like this, so I know he gets up as early as me.

"Regardless . . . 7 a.m.?" Emmett retorts. "I heard your elephant footsteps way before that." He turns his head away from me, as if I don't deserve his time. "Have you ever tried being considerate of the people around you?"

Am I actually going to let this guy, who doesn't even know me, tell me I'm inconsiderate?

Absolutely not.

But, when I go to protest, I can't get anything to leave my mouth. My lips stay parted, ready to speak, but nothing comes out.

I see him roll his eyes as he leans his head back into the corner of the elevator, smirking at his ability to shut me up.

I cross my arms, looking straight ahead, backing up and shrinking into the opposite corner—trying to get as far away from him as I can in this little space. The tension thickens as we move down the seven stories from his floor to the garage.

I barely even know this guy, and I'm not going to let myself take anything he's saying personally. He's just an angry, lonely douchebag, and he's *not* going to ruin my day.

Each time I've seen Emmett around, there's always something I've done to piss him off.

One of my first nights here, I was up late online shopping for some new books to read during my summer break. It was a Saturday night in June, and I had forgotten my wallet in my car. I went down to get it, and I bumped into him. He was entering the elevator as I was walking out into the garage, and it was an honest mistake. I wasn't expecting to run into anyone considering how late it was, and I apologized quickly.

Wanting to be neighborly, I also introduced myself. "I'm Drew. I just moved in on the eighth floor." I held my hand out, expecting him to shake it but instead he just looked at it, then he glided his eyes back up to mine, keeping his hands in his pockets. He met my eyes with his, and I thought he was going to say something. Instead, he stepped around me and walked into the elevator without a word. I turned around as the elevators were closing to find him inside, leaning back against the wall. Our eyes met again, and just before the doors closed, I heard him say, "Emmett."

That was our first-ever interaction.

That next morning, I ran into him on my way back from the grocery store. We were standing, just like we are now.

I figured he wasn't the neighborly type, so I didn't bother trying to break the silence, even though I wanted to.

As the elevator opened to his floor, he stepped out. Without even turning around to look at me, I heard him say, "If you're going to blast music and wake the whole damn building, at least listen to a better album."

I was stunned to hear his voice directed at me because it was the first time he said more than a singular word to me. I felt all the heat in my body rush up to my face. I couldn't even respond as he turned to look at me as the doors closed. I was left alone in the elevator thinking I pissed off the wrong person. Or, encountered a pissed off person at a very wrong time.

Every week since then, we have had multiple mornings starting off just like this, as well as the occasional afternoon encounters, and even a couple late-night run-ins if I happen to be up past bar-close.

Six months of pissing each other off.

Last week, my door slammed too hard and woke him up; my footsteps made his ceiling creak, and my TV was too loud.

The week before, the timer on my oven went off when he was sleeping; my cabinets closed too loudly, and my "butterfingers" couldn't hold anything for shit.

Each time he comes to me with some stupid reason I suck

as a neighbor, he says his piece, and I'm left feeling flustered and bothered, not even being able to hide it. He *has* to know what he's doing because he does it so well. Sometimes, I think he looks for something to be pissed at me about, just to take his anger out on someone.

Last month, he even commented on the *consistent banging on the wall* and how it kept him up all night. My red face said it all when I tried to respond and couldn't because I remembered that was before I swore off Reed.

Finally, after what feels like hours, the elevator dings, and the doors open. As we step forward at the same time, both wanting to get out of this situation as quickly as possible, our shoulders briefly touch as we walk through the elevator doors.

The spark I feel is quickly negated by the cold rush of air that floods us as we enter the garage.

"All I'm saying is I would appreciate it if you were a little more thoughtful of who's below you." Emmett turns to me with those deep, rich eyes peeking behind a few loose curls. The rush of air that welcomed us to the garage knocked some strands loose from his topknot.

Why am I thinking about what it would be like to untie his hair and run my fingers through it instead of coming up with a way to respond to him?

His gaze burning into mine, The cold air no longer being a match for my red-hot-cheeks, I have nothing to say back, like usual.

I stay frozen in the middle of the elevator doors' path, still a little stunned from that touch, then from the thoughts invading my brain, and now feeling his eyes on me.

He turns to continue walking and creates a bigger space between us, pulling his hoodie over his head, revealing the skin just above his jeans as he reaches up to put his arms through. He heads towards the door that leads him out onto the street.

Glancing over his shoulder, he finds my eyes still on him. The look on his face almost makes me think he is enjoying whatever this *thing* is between us.

He breaks the hold he has on me, turns, and pushes the door open to head out into the December cold—on his way to start his day.

I thought I saw a smirk to match the look in his eyes as he turned away, but I might have imagined it.

Or not.

Maybe he gets off on being a dick.

The echoing tap of his Vans, like mine but twice the size, fade away as I'm left with a familiar flutter in my stomach I haven't felt in a while.

After a moment frozen in place, I shiver the thoughts running through my head away, feeling like I can move again now that his eyes are off me.

I walk to my car and open up the door to get in. The few yards I walked from the elevator give my cheeks time to finally fade back to their natural shade

I don't understand what this guy does to me. He pisses me off yet steals my ability to speak at the same time.

My life consists of holding conversations with angsty, hormonal sixth graders for a living, so what is it about this guy that makes it so hard to say what I'm thinking without all the blood in my body rushing to my head?

I back out of my parking space to leave the apartment complex's garage and begin my drive to school, trying to block out the dirty thoughts of how many tattoos lay underneath his band tees or what it would be like to see a pile of our black clothes next to my bed.

I want to slap myself in the face for even having these thoughts about Emmett because I don't even know where they're coming from, and I know he can't stand me.

Just like how I can't stand him.

I try to drown the thoughts in A Day to Remember lyrics,

opening Spotify and clicking on their Common Courtesy album.

Halfway through my commute, I realize that the lyrics are not doing their job and instead are reminding me of when I tried to make conversation with Emmett in the elevator about his A Day to Remember t-shirt, and he just looked at me as if I had two heads.

"That's a cool shirt," I had said, trying to break the silence in the elevator, obviously not learning my lesson from our prior encounters. I had just gotten home from Open House and was in a good mood after meeting some of the students I would have in my classroom in just a few days.

He looked down at his shirt and then back at me, the look of distaste all over his face.

"What?" I said. Trying to fight the warmth of embarrassment bubbling in my cheeks.

He shook his head and let out a little laugh, one free of humor. "Nothing," he said as he looked straight ahead at the closed doors.

"What's so funny?" I tried not to let the offense I felt translate to my voice.

He turns his head to face me as the elevator halts, opening up to his floor. "The last thing I want to do right now is make small talk with anyone, especially you."

And with that, he turned away from me, walking towards his apartment, once again, leaving me red-faced, flustered, and pissed off with so much to say but no words leaving my mouth.

Safe to say, I haven't been the one to initiate a conversation since.

I turn off the music to stop myself from thinking of Emmett, not wanting to give him any part of my mind. Finally, I see the sign that tells me my commute has ended: *North Shore Middle School*. I pull into a spot in the staff parking lot, and I take a deep breath to refocus on the day.

This day was not going to be ruined by thoughts of Emmett Ryan or Reed Michaels.

No more dwelling on the past and thinking about what could've been with my ex-boyfriend.

And definitely no more focusing my attention on a brooding neighbor I barely know.

Today was going to be a good one.

Today can only go up from here.

I turn off the car and step out into the fresh, frigid air.

No more of this nonsense, I think to myself.

Now that I'm here, I'm no longer Drew.

No longer a let-down of a daughter, sister, or best friend.

No longer Reed's inconsistent lover or Emmett's inconsiderate upstairs neighbor.

I'm Ms. Thomas.

CHAPTER 7
DREW

I LOOP my badge around my neck, grab my backpack in my front seat and head into the building. I have about fifteen minutes to prepare for the day before having to go get the kids from the gym, so I have to haul ass. As I head up the stairs to my classroom, I revisit my mental to-do list from earlier this morning.

One by one, I check things off: making my copies, creating a few slides, and turning my projector on. After a morning like this one, I think coffee is more important than the other stuff, especially because my first cup is currently all over the sweater in my hamper back at home.

I decide I'll have Cole write the learning targets on the board and pass out the morning work when students arrive, rather than taking the time to put it on their desks now.

Cole is my favorite student. And I know I'm not supposed to have favorites, but Cole is an exception because I've known him since I started in the North Shore School District.

I had done my undergrad at the university about two miles away and was placed at one of the two elementary schools in the district for student teaching. At that time, Cole Andrews was in 4th grade, and he lit up the classroom with his bleach-blonde hair, bright blue eyes, and a smile that was contagious. At the early age of ten, he was always kind and willing to help, even though odds were against him.

I smell the comforting scent brewing before me, and I grab my "My Classroom is my Happy Place" mug. My advice to any teacher is having your own coffee maker in your classroom.

Today is Friday, and it is also the last school day before Winter Break. The sun is actually shining, and there's snow on the radar for the afternoon and the weekend, so I'm prepared for my classroom management to be put to the test today. I check the time, and I have five minutes to spare before my day *actually* begins.

The hustle and bustle of the morning didn't even allow me to think twice about how my day started. It's only a few minutes before 10 a.m., but time flies when you don't have a chance to slow down.

The kids are at their Social/Emotional Learning class with the guidance counselor, so I finally have a moment to take a breath.

I clean up some of the miscellaneous papers and pencils that, for some reason, can't stay in the students' desks, and then I finally have a chance to sit.

This morning at school followed a similar pattern as my morning at home. The kids came in buzzing with anticipation for Winter Break, making every transition take double the time they usually do. When everyone was finally in their seats, Cole was about to pass out their morning work when I realized I printed and made copies of the wrong worksheet. My classroom is right across from a workroom, so I quickly printed more and had a student go grab them just to find out the copier was not only out of toner but completely jammed.

Then, when I tried to email the office, I was greeted with a *"No Internet"* message. The announcements came on minutes later saying the Wi-Fi was down for the morning due to maintenance that just couldn't wait until the school was empty over break.

Luckily, I could make my math lesson and instructional activities work with materials I had ready from earlier in the week, and I knew the kids were barely listening to me anyway. I, once again, thanked my past self for creating lessons that would anticipate where the kids' minds would be on the eve of Winter Break.

I like to keep the classroom lively and collaborative, so this morning's math lesson involved the kids chatting and problem-solving together to figure out algebraic equations that used a variety of winter emojis instead of variables. It was fun yet challenging, and the time flew by. Before we knew it, it was 9:30 a.m., and time for them to wrap-up and transition.

My classroom is a perfect parallel to my life outside of it. Choosing a profession where no day is the same is an odd choice for someone who doesn't always welcome change with open arms, but I wouldn't have it any other way.

While my classroom is dynamic, constantly changing depending on the day and the moods of the preteens, my life outside the classroom is consistent and . . . boring, for a lack of a better word. But, not in a bad way. In a way where I know what to expect, and I'm in control.

Control.

Such an odd concept with such different connotations.

On one hand, I *do* have control of my classroom, just like I do in my personal life.

Control of my choices, of my behavior management, of my lessons.

But, on the other hand, I have no control in my classroom.

I never know for sure if my lessons will land or if my students will stay engaged, and usually when I think they will, they don't.

At all.

I have no control over the outside factors that impact these tiny humans, who are still learning how to manage their thoughts, emotions, and actions.

No control over outside factors that impact the inside of our classroom daily.

But when it comes to my personal life, there is a sense of control. Control I've learned I'm capable of holding on to, so I can make the best decisions for myself.

Or at least I tell myself that, especially when I talk myself out of calling my parents, Calvin, or Lacey and instead text Reed.

I have only a few minutes until the students will be back, and we'll have to start with reading. Because sixth grade is students' first year in middle school, students have me as their teacher for all of their core classes, and they go elsewhere for electives and specials like P.E., foreign language, music, and art classes.

The classroom always feels odd when they are all gone, and it's silent. It's nice for a moment, but then it feels weird. The silence always seems so out of place.

So unnatural.

I take the minutes I have to sip on my now-cold coffee and scroll through the Snapchat stories I didn't get to earlier this morning. As I click through the stories, I'm reminded of the thoughts from this morning and close out the app before I begin to dwell. I throw my phone in my backpack under my desk and tell myself I don't have time to let those thoughts trickle in again. No time because the bell just rang, and my students are back as quickly as they left.

Time seems to go by so fast when they're gone.

I hear the footsteps of my students arriving back from SEL, so I prop open our classroom door and meet them as they come down the hall.

I greet all twenty-four students as they file in and have a

seat, making a mental note that they are all here and accounted for.

I move to the front of the room to get started by asking a volunteer to read the learning target written on the board, thanks to Cole. He was, as always, so eager to help when he arrived this morning.

"Addison, thank you for volunteering. What is it that we are going to be able to do by the end of reading class today?"

"'I can identify possible character traits to describe the protagonist of the story.'"

"Wonderful," I respond. "Thank you, Addi. Now, who can tell me our *action* for today's reading class? What exactly are we *doing* as we read our texts today?"

I look around the room to see the hands raise up. "Jack. What is it we are doing today?"

"Identifying."

"Awesome! That is exactly it. We are *identifying*. And, what does it mean to identify, Jack?"

He ponders for a moment and answers, "Kind of like looking for something?"

"Good!" I walk around the classroom, twenty-four pairs of eyes on me as I point at the board behind me with a projection of a slide with a handful of characters from various holiday and winter-themed movies. The Wi-Fi maintenance luckily didn't take as long as the tech department said it would, so I could use the slides I made for this winter-themed reading class.

I made sure to stick with characters students would recognize, but I was also sure to not only use the popular Christmas characters, knowing not *all* my students celebrate Christmas.

"Okay, everyone. I want you to look at these characters and give me a thumbs-up if you recognize at least one of them."

Thankfully, I was correct with my assumption that most, if

not all students, would recognize Anna or Elsa from *Frozen* or Sid, Manny, or Diego from *Ice Age*. I see twenty-four thumbs-up after a quick ten seconds of their eyes scanning the screen.

"Perfect," I say. "So, today, we are going to look at clips from some of these movies and identify character traits for these characters. We'll then identify evidence from the clip to prove our claim."

I see a couple heads turn towards one another and hushed chatting of who's going to be whose partner commences.

Before I can ask students to stay silent until I'm done giving directions and passing out the graphic organizers, I hear a deafening pop from down the hall.

My body freezes.

"What was that?" My student, Marco, asks—a tone of fear in his voice.

I hear the slight whisper as all my students look around at one another and then back at me.

"Ms. Thomas?" I hear one of them say, but I am still frozen. Before I can even truly recognize what the sound was, we hear it again.

How the hell did kids get fireworks into the school?

CHAPTER 8
EMMETT

THERE'S nothing like three horny old men talking about my eighteen-year-old bartender loud enough for the whole damn bar to hear to start my day.

If it wasn't for my red-headed neighbor, I'd be able to get some sleep and not begin the day with my patience as low as the damn ground.

Seeing Drew's cheeks heat up this morning was as good as caffeine to wake me up, but the rush I felt during our elevator ride quickly wore off when I got to the bar, greeted by the delivery guys bringing me everything I *didn't* order.

There is something about Drew that gets me worked up to the point I don't know how to act around her, so I just resort to being an asshole. And something about her hazel eyes and tight black pants linger in my thoughts.

After talking with the good-for-nothing delivery guys for fifteen minutes this morning, trying to figure out where the miscommunication was regarding what I ordered and what I got, I realized I was getting nowhere. Nowhere except for more pissed off. I could tell the two guys didn't care, and it was above their pay grade, so I just took what they brought hoping the holiday crowd wouldn't be too picky with their alcohol this season.

Giving the two guys a hard time definitely did not have the same effect as getting Drew all flustered.

I spent the rest of my time this morning before I opened making the schedule for the next week, assigning the different morning, afternoon, and night shifts between myself and my two bartenders. I took the bulk of the shifts, knowing that the two of them have more going for them in their lives than I do now.

I ended up concluding that I'd have to hire another bartender soon if I didn't want to spend an unhealthy amount of time here. But I decided that that would be a job for another day. I had serious doubts with myself and my patience to deal with the process of finding, interviewing, and training someone anytime soon.

I am finding, with my reaction to these three assholes currently seated at my bar, that I was right in assuming so.

Any other day with these guys talking about Annie's cleavage, I would just give them a look to shut them up, but today I think I might kick their asses.

The former would definitely be the better option, if I want to keep this place in business, so I make eye contact with one of them from behind the bar making my message loud and clear. The next thing I hear from their corner of the bar is a clearing of a throat and muffled voices changing the subject.

It's a quarter past ten o'clock this morning, and I opened up my bar fifteen minutes ago. The usual crowd of regulars is here, starting their holiday weekend off with something strong, wanting to pick up where we left off last night.

Most of them have been coming since my dad bought the place twenty-five years ago, so I'm used to their banter. But today, it took me less than half an hour to already want the day to be over. Granted, *my* day at the bar started about three hours ago, earlier if you consider waking up to my neighbor/unwanted alarm clock, but that's what I get for owning the bar and living below Drew.

"Annie, I'm going to head to my office to do some paperwork," I say over my shoulder as I head into the back. I don't listen for her response, but I hear her making her way over to the guys who are now asking for her to turn up the TV.

Something about wanting to hear the news.

Lenny's, renamed after my sister, was much more fun when my priorities were pouring Seven & Sevens and Captain and Cokes all day while my dad did all the orders, phone calls, and bills that take over my list of things to get done now.

When I was old enough to start working here as a bartender, I always wondered what he did in his office all day. It wasn't until five years ago, when he got to the age where Wisconsin winters became too much for his old bones, that I realized how much he truly did.

He and my mom recently migrated to Florida, spending only the three summer months here in Wisconsin.

At least that was the plan, spending three months here. Truthfully, I don't even remember the last time they've been back for more than a week.

Personally, I think it was more than their old bones that made them want to spend a little less time in these parts.

It does get cold, and they're retired, so—besides me—there's nothing left holding them here anymore. I was at a very different point in my life when they decided they wanted to sell their house and do what so many of their retired friends with adult children were doing, so they had no problem leaving me behind.

I know that being around alcohol is hard for my parents too, and it's not easy to stay away from it when you own a bar, or even just being in Wisconsin for that matter.

And I get it.

I remember thinking I would never take another sip of

alcohol when I heard how Lennon died. I was eighteen at the time, so my sips up until that point had been done illegally, and I held to that promise I made to myself and Lennon, until I was twenty-one and realized she would've totally made fun of me for being such a square.

In my parents' minds, drinking leads to getting drunk, which can then unfortunately lead to drunk driving.

I can't blame my parents for wanting to get out of here and out of this scene, but it won't bring her back.

I shake my head to try and shake the thoughts out, a few strands of hair falling from my now-loosened top knot. I take out the hair tie and quickly re-tie my hair to get it out of my face.

This is the most I've thought of my parents, or Lennon, in months, and I need to get my mind off all of this.

Sitting down at my desk, I grab my backpack and take out my laptop to start thinking up some marketing materials for the new year. When I finish up brainstorming, I move to planning when to do inventory and look at the budget going into the new year. I should probably get those things done soon, with the year ending in just a few weeks.

I go to grab my headphones from my pocket, so I can just zone into the work I have to get done. If I want to be productive for these next couple hours, some Asking Alexandria and A Day to Remember will help me get there.

I reach in my pocket and come up empty, just now realizing that I didn't grab them from my bedside table this morning.

At least the day can only go up from here.

CHAPTER 9
DREW

WITHOUT MUCH THINKING, I find my feet moving towards the door. I peek my head outside into the hallway to find my colleague, Rita Torres, the other sixth-grade-teacher, across the hall doing the same. She's a woman old enough to be my mother and is always there to listen to me vent, sitting with her nurturing expression, nodding her head.

We make eye contact as we hear a third pop followed by screams and the sound of a single pair of footsteps running down the hall, perpendicular from ours but out of sight.

We hear the sound of doors swinging and slamming shut echoing through the parts of the hallway we can't quite see. It's all happening so fast—I can't make my brain function fast enough.

Our two classrooms are the only ones before the hallway bends to where most of the seventh grade classrooms and the guidance counselor's room are. On the other side of us is a doorway leading to a staircase.

I see a look of utter fear in Rita's eyes.

It's a fear I have never seen before.

My heart stops and complete terror cascades over me as I

come to the conclusion that my worst nightmare is coming true.

Before my mind can even process, my body takes over.

It is my job to keep these twenty-four students safe.

The staff has had the training for this before, but this cannot fucking be happening.

In our ALICE training, the first thing they tell you is the sooner you understand that you're in danger, the sooner you can save yourself. A speedy response is critical—seconds count.

So, in a matter of seconds, I give my mind no option but to catch up with my body.

This is not a drill.

This is not a joke.

This is for real, and I have to fucking do something.

There's a shooter.

There's people screaming.

There's a shooter, and he's fired three shots.

And he's just down the hall.

I muster up the strength to move through the horror that is beginning to close in on us and close and lock my door before shutting off my classroom lights. I see through the window of the door, before pulling down the shade that covers the glass, Rita doing the same. Her eyes never leave mine until we both pull down the shade, no longer being able to see outside into the hall.

I turn to look around the room at the worried faces waiting for me to tell them what to do. Some are frozen, some are looking around the room, some have tears in their eyes.

And it's silent.

Keep it together, Drew.

Keep it together.

ALICE is an acronym, standing for the five options to combat the situation. You don't have to go in order, but I need to go through our options and choose what the hell we are going to do—and I have to do it fast.

"A" stands for, "Alert—recognize the alert."

Done.

And we have to get out of here.

I look around and make myself think. We are on the second floor, next to the window. The window faces the blacktop behind the school. The stairs are right outside to the left, to the right is the hallway where we heard the shots and footsteps running down.

We can make it if we go down the stairs.

They lead right outside to the blacktop.

But wait. Which way was the shooter going?

Oh my fucking god. Shooter.

There's a fucking shooter.

Is he going to turn down this hallway and head to the stairs?

Is he planning on entering every classroom?

Who is he?

Why is he here?

I shake my head at the influx of questions that have no clear answers. I realize there is no way to know, beyond a shadow of a doubt, that it is safe to evacuate. I can't take a risk that would put any of my students in danger. There's no way to know where that scream came from or when the next—

POP!

Shot number four.

We all freeze.

I feel tears starting to well up in my eyes, but I squeeze my eyes shut to stop them from fully forming. My insides feel like they're about to explode, but I have twenty-four pre-teens looking at me for what to do.

I *need* to stay calm. I need to be thinking clearly.

The "L" in ALICE stands for "Lockdown."

We need to barricade the door.

Studies show that shooters often don't attempt to get into locked or barricaded doors.

But then again, I'm not putting any trust into this armed person following a common pattern, not after they walked into this school and put the lives of kids and teachers at risk in a place we are supposed to feel safe.

I try to speak but the words don't leave my mouth at first.

I can't believe this is happening.

Five minutes ago, we were talking about identifying character traits.

It's the day before Winter Break.

We were going to watch *Frosty the Snowman* after the assembly to end our day.

This is a place for *children.*

This isn't supposed to be happening.

"We need to barricade the door."

The words finally leave my lips, but they don't feel like mine.

The shocked, confused faces of my students continue to stare. No one moves. All the pieces of my heart—all frozen in fear—right in front of me.

"Now. Now, please. Guys, you have to move." My husky, unfamiliar whisper is the only sound in our room. "You have to be quiet, but you have to move. We can do this. We'll be okay. We can do this." The words pour out of my mouth but still don't feel like mine.

I need to keep them safe. I need to protect them.

The door is locked, but I am putting nothing up to chance.

Slowly, a few of them begin to move. Cole, Marco, Jack, and a few others help me block the door with desks and chairs.

I go to grab my phone out of my pocket to silence it and call 9-1-1, but it's not there.

Fuck. Where did I put it?

Suddenly, we hear over the school's intercom, "Shooter is on the west side of the building, second floor." And, seconds later, we hear three consecutive shots, closer than the ones from before.

In our training, administration explained that communication was key to such a quickly-changing situation. Luckily, they have eyes on whoever this person is.

POP! POP! POP!

Screams fill the classroom right across from ours.

There are too many obstacles in front of the door for me to even try to see who is hurt.

Those obstacles—trapping us in but keeping us safe.

Did Rita not lock her door?

As the screams echo, I grab on to whoever is closest to me, ushering all the students to move to the corner that is most hidden from the door, huddling against the wall, gripping onto each other as if to stay grounded.

The screams are followed by ear-piercing silence.

I push my students back as far as I can into the corner and whisper to them to stay quiet. With tears streaming down their faces, hands covering their mouths, I need them to fade into the silence. I need them to survive.

It's too quiet for a classroom.

I look around to find something to arm myself with.

He's coming.

Whoever he is.

I don't know what to grab.

What is there to protect yourself from a *gun*?

But, he's coming.

Those shots were on the other side of the hallway.

My stomach tightens at the thought of who was in that room.

Rita.

The other sixth graders.

The ones we share a hallway, a lunch hour, a recess with.

I'm too small to cover all my students with my own body. I wish I could stretch myself to shield them all.

Why? Why was this happening?

I turn my body, so I'm facing them, looking at their faces, so scared and so helpless, thinking my face must reflect the same.

On the first day of school, I told them that our year together would be amazing. We would learn so much. Together. We would have so much fun. Together. We would make memories we would never forget.

Together.

I didn't think this would be one of those memories.

I close my eyes and pray to the God I no longer believe in to save these twenty-four faces in front of me. My cheeks are soaked with tears I could no longer help from falling, and I latch on to the bodies in front of me.

We can't stay like this, I think to myself. If the shooter somehow gets in here, we are in the perfect position for the most damage to be done.

I try to tell my students that we need to arm ourselves in case he gets through the door, but all that comes out of my mouth is a series of whispers.

I'm sorry. I'm sorry. I'm sorry. I'm sorry.

I'm distracted by the resounding muffled cries before me when I suddenly hear police sirens approaching outside our windows, overlooking the blacktop and the staff parking lot behind the school. Police cars and fire trucks begin to overflow the lot.

I have a second of relief that turns right back into panic when I hear footsteps running past our classroom, further interrupting the silence and stillness we were drowning in just seconds before. The footsteps rush down the stairway on the other side of the very wall opposite of us now.

Frozen.

Then, I take a breath.

CHAPTER 10
EMMETT

"HEY, boss, you might want to see this."

Annie rarely ever bothers me when I'm in my office. Anyone else would probably leave me alone because they would be scared of pissing me off, but I've known Annie a long time. She is the least bit scared of me and one of the few people who are immune to my bullshit. She handles herself, even for as young as she is.

She wouldn't be bothering me though unless it was something big.

If one of those pervs went too far, I'm throwing them out on their asses. I don't care how long they've been coming here.

I get up without a word and follow her out into the bar where people have congregated in front of the spot where the TV sits. The three assholes are finally quiet, eyes glued to the screen, along with the dozen or so people behind them.

What's going on?

I follow Annie's gaze which is also on the TV and see the "Breaking News" headlines. The whole bar watches in horror as the story unfolds in front of us.

Milwaukee Middle School Shooting:

Suspect In Police Custody

A picture of a kid, no older than seventeen or eighteen, flashes across the screen.

FINN ANDREWS

I see lips moving from the reporter at the scene, but my heart is pumping loud enough so my ears can't hear any other sound.

17 INJURED, 3 DEAD

What the fuck?

What fucking prick gets off on shooting up a place with a bunch of kids and teachers—

Wait, *teachers*.

Isn't Drew a teacher?

———

The rest of the day at the bar, my mind was flooded with questions I had no answers for.

What grade does Drew teach?

What school does she teach at?

Is she okay?

We had never had enough small talk to actually talk about each other's work, so I learned most of what I knew about her through observation and nosy neighbors we shared. I felt a subtle ache of regret that I always gave her a hard time, rather than asking about her day or something.

I know what it's like to live through trauma and wouldn't wish the aftermath of pain to anyone. Knowing that she could possibly be living with what happened today, or *worse*, made me wish every interaction I had with her left her smiling rather than fuming.

I move through the motions for the rest of my shift, anxiously awaiting for any customer coming in with news to report. The few hours following the shooting, there was consistent talk about it, but because of the influx of school shootings in this country, the story's shock factor dwindled off at an alarmingly fast rate, leaving the conversations in the bar to go back to normal by the afternoon.

I call Eddie, my other bartender and best friend, to come in a little earlier than his shift at 5 p.m. because I can't stand being in this place any longer. My mind isn't here, and I feel this intense urge to go home and see if Drew is okay.

Eddie is here by four, no questions asked.

That's what is so great about him—he's there when I need it and doesn't pry because he knows I'll tell him when I'm ready.

I run home, choosing to ignore the grocery shopping I had planned to do after work today.

Drew's car is parked in her usual spot when I get into the garage, and I feel a wave of relief wash over me before I run past the elevator to the stairs.

It may seem weird that I know her car and where she usually parks, but I've been paying attention to her for a while now, more than I'd ever admit to anyone.

Especially her.

I don't have time for the rickety son of a bitch to take its time right now, but when I get to the seventh floor, I stop.

I barely know this girl, I think to myself.

There's no way she wants *me* coming to check on her. Wouldn't that be weird? Knocking on her door out of the blue.

I've never even seen her outside the elevator, and its immediate surroundings.

It's not like we're strangers. We've known each other for six months, but I guess "know" is a relative term. I know she drops things and listens to music loud enough for me to feel like it's coming from a speaker in my apartment, but I don't know the first thing about her.

I don't know if she works at the school that was on the news.

Drew could very well just be home because it's the end of the school day. Maybe she doesn't even know what happened.

Still, I need to know she is okay.

Instead of going up the next flight to her floor, I round the corner and head to my apartment.

My mind is warping with thoughts of what to do, what is appropriate, what is an invasion of privacy. If I just waltz up to her place and knock on the door, that shows all my cards of how much I *actually* think of this girl.

No. I'm being silly, I think to myself.

She's probably fine, and, if not, I'm sure she has people looking out for her.

Or, at least I hope that's the case.

I pull out my keys from my pocket to unlock my door. Just as I put the key in the lock, my next-door neighbors come out of their place.

I live next to a younger couple, probably about my age or a year or two younger. We make small talk here and there, and they don't make much noise or ever bug me, so I'm much more pleasant of a neighbor towards them compared to the asshole I am towards Drew.

"Hey, Emmett," I hear the guy, Evan, say. He's a short, skinny guy, always in athletic clothes. Nine out of ten times I see him, he is dressed for a run.

I turn over my shoulder giving him a quick nod and turning back to unlock my door, hoping he catches on that I'm not in the mood to talk today.

He doesn't.

"Did you hear what happened today?"

That gets my attention.

My hands freeze mid-turn of the key, and I turn to face him before opening my door.

"Crazy stuff. I can't believe something like that happened

at a school," he adds before I can even respond to what he asked.

"Yeah, and it was just a few miles away from here," his partner, Nora, chimes in as she bends down to tie her tennis shoe, her blonde hair covering her face. "And, at a middle school." Her voice is hard to hear because she's bent down a few feet in front of me.

Does Drew work at a middle school?

Does she work close by?

No.

She's fine.

She's home.

And she's none of my business.

Evan crosses his arm and blows out a breath as he leans back on the wall behind him. "So close too. And, to think we know someone who works there." He turns to Nora as she stands. "You ready?" he asks her.

"Wait," I say before they can head to the elevator. "You guys know someone who works there?"

"We're not friends or anything, but yeah she lives upstairs. Do you know Drew? From the eighth floor?"

My heart stops. After talking myself out of Drew having anything to do with the horrible thing that happened today. I'm now finding out that my gut was right.

"Drew teaches at the school where today's shooting happened?" I ask, trying to hide the uneasiness in my voice. I can't believe I even have to specify how it is *today's* school shooting.

"Yeah, she and Nora have talked a few times because they leave around the same time in the morning."

I think Nora is a nurse or does something in the hospital. When I've run into her, she's either in running clothes like Evan, or she's in scrubs.

But that matters nothing to me right now

"I hope she's okay," Nora adds. "I wasn't on call today but

heard the hospital was packed with people who were hurt, and people who were just looking for a place to go to feel safe." She lets out a sigh at the thought.

I see Nora's lips continue to move, talking about how often tragedies strike and how she sees it at work, but I couldn't care less about her right now.

My neighbors probably think I'm a jerk when I turn back to head inside my apartment, not even giving them an excuse or goodbye. I close the door behind me, and the only thing I can think about right now is making sure Drew wasn't one of the ones injured, *or worse*.

If the girl is home, I'll know.

She does have lead feet after all.

I kick off my Vans, take off my hoodie, and grab a beer. I take a seat on the couch, not turning on the TV, and just listen.

I listen for footsteps, music, books falling off the shelves, asses falling to the floor. Anything. My legs bounce with anxiety as I wait to hear something. *Anything*.

I take a few sips of my beer, and I finally hear the echo of footsteps and muffled voices above me.

Drew must have had family or friends bring her home.

More waves of relief topple over me, and I'm surprised to feel a weight lift off my shoulders at the thought that Drew is okay. Feeling a little alarmed with the effect this girl has had on me these past six months, especially today.

I spend the rest of the night busying myself with a few more beers, video games, and ordering my second pizza of the week, not being able to stop myself from listening for any and all noises above me.

My anxiety grows little by little as the night goes on and as the sounds grow fewer and farther between.

I used to find the sounds I heard above me as a nuisance, but I now find myself aching to hear them. Because those noises mean Drew's there. They mean she's okay.

I head to bed at about eleven o'clock because I want to get to sleep pretty early. I fall asleep pretty easily, probably because my mind has been racing all day. My eyes close as I think about the long day ahead of me tomorrow. Lenny's is open tomorrow, but I'm closing the bar for the two following days—Christmas Eve and Christmas Day—so it's going to be a long day.

Drifting off to sleep comes easily tonight—the sleep so heavy that dreams, and nightmares, don't even invade.

I wake up the next morning at 8 a.m. to my alarm, and I feel completely well-rested for the first time in I don't know how long. But I have this odd feeling that something about my morning is missing.

It isn't until I get out of bed and brush my teeth that I realize that it's because no red-headed girl, with a good taste in music and shoes that match mine, woke me up.

And my blissful morning comes to an end as the reality of what happened yesterday hits me directly in the chest.

CHAPTER 11
DREW

I JOLT out of bed to the sound of knocking on my door. The knocks seem to echo in my head, tricking my brain into flight or fight mode, making my heart pound.

Are loud noises going to scare the shit out of me from now on? *Most likely.*

It's December 24th, technically Christmas Eve, but I can't say I'm in the holiday spirit.

The past forty-eight hours have been a complete blur. I've been in and out of sleep, my nightmares not letting my mind or body rest.

I have been too scared to fall asleep because I'm afraid to see the worst day of my life play in my mind, over and over again. I've been forcing my eyes to stay open until they close against my will—before I find myself tearing them open to make the nightmares stop, beginning the painful cycle again.

After what felt like an eternity piled in the corner of my classroom with my twenty-four students, we heard from a bullhorn outside that the suspect was in police custody, and police were sweeping the area.

My students and I stayed plastered in the corner, silence

taking over us, until we heard the announcement that the area was clear, and we could come out.

Walking my students outside into the crowd of people was the most surreal experience. I had walked my students out to that very same blacktop numerous times before, but I knew it would never feel that simple again. I knew this time was being etched deep into my skin, making a mark on my soul.

The sun was still shining as we made our way out the school doors, but the brightness of the day didn't make the darkness of what took place any lighter.

My eyes took a second to adjust after squeezing them shut so tightly just minutes earlier. The air was cold, but it didn't bother me—I would have felt cold even if it was the middle of the summer.

As I walked across the concrete—my arms holding onto a few students who couldn't bring themselves to let go of me— I was bombarded with voices: police, paramedics, reporters, all coming at me.

"What's your name?"

"What do you do here?"

"How many students do you have?"

"Are you or your students injured?"

I have no recollection of how I responded, or if I even did, but the next thing I remember was that I was watching my kids get ushered off by police to contact their families. I didn't realize how much I was relying on the ones holding on to my arms to keep me from falling to my knees. The second the few of them let go, I felt my legs give out below me. A paramedic caught me right before everything went black.

The school sent out an emergency message when everything happened, and Lacey is my emergency contact. She and Tyler came to the school to pick me up once the paramedics checked me out.

I could feel Lacey's warmth the second her arms wrapped

around me, and I instantly felt a small sense of relief. I vaguely remember getting in the car with her, Tyler staying to grab my phone, keys, and other things. He ended up driving my car back to my apartment.

I don't think I ever passed out again, but the car ride home is foggy in my brain. I remember learning my head against the cold passenger side window and closing my eyes. I had done the drive from school to my complex so many times, I knew what turns we were making even with my eyes closed.

Lacey didn't say anything, but she held onto my hand the entire drive. The slow movement of her thumb, back and forth against the back of my hand, lulling me to a sense of calmness.

I don't remember anything after that. Not until waking up to Lacey and Tyler's muffled voices in my kitchen a few hours later. I was in bed, under my covers, so I figured they must have put me there.

I think my mind was trying to protect me from any more trauma, and it tried to block out the hours following what happened.

Lacey heard me rustling in my bed and came in to see how I was doing.

My face was damp with tears, my hair sticking to my face, and my mouth was so dry, I wasn't sure I would be able to talk.

I looked down to see I was still in the clothes I wore to school that morning, but I felt Lacey touch my cheek as she moved a piece of hair out of my face.

"Hi, honey. I'm glad you're awake." I looked up to meet her green eyes, so kind but concerned, and I felt a sense of relief run through me having her there, knowing that I didn't want anyone else by my side—at this very moment.

Lacey has always been my exact opposite.

Confident in who she is, and absolutely gorgeous.

She is four or five inches taller than me, her body still in great shape from years of being a Pilates instructor in college. Her blonde hair falls in loose curls over her shoulders, and she is consistently dressed in pastels to complement her ivory skin and business casual.

She's the yin to my yang, always there to balance me out.

When I'm negative, she's positive. When I'm doubtful, she is full of hope. When I feel like I am falling apart, she is there to hold all the pieces together.

Seeing her the day I needed her the most was like a light at the end of a dark tunnel. She was wearing white trousers and a lavender sweater that enhanced her features perfectly, and I wanted nothing more than for her to wrap the knit material around me.

"What time is it?" My voice cracked as I managed to get the words out. I noticed that the only light in my bedroom was coming from the muted TV and the light shining in from my living room.

"It's about 10 p.m.," she said. "You've been out since we got you home this afternoon. The paramedics checked you out back at the school. You're okay."

All of a sudden the terror struck me as if I was reliving the moments that unfolded twelve hours prior.

"My students? The staff? Is everyone okay? Is anyone hurt?"

I heard Tyler's footsteps make their way from my kitchen to the door frame of my bedroom. I've never had more than one person in my apartment before, so I was a little startled at the sight of him at first.

"Hey, Drew. We're glad you're okay," he said. It was a nice gesture, but I didn't care at that moment.

I needed answers.

Tyler has light brown hair that some would argue is blonde. He has blue eyes and is clean-shaven with a few patch work tattoos on his arms. That night he was wearing an off-white collared shirt opened with a fitted white t-shirt underneath and dark jeans, and was standing in the door with his broad shoulders and long legs.

"Honey, let's get you out of those clothes, so you can get some rest. We can talk about it tomorrow." Lacey turned to face Tyler. "Can you get Drew a glass of water?" She looked back at me before standing up and extending her arm out to me.

Wanting to protest but not having the energy, I grabbed onto her hand.

We walked to my bathroom, and she helped me get out of my clothes and into the shower.

The same shower I stood in that morning, wondering if I should call her.

I let my mind succumb to darkness and the last thing I remember is her closing the glass door as I sunk down into the corner of my shower, bringing my knees to my chest and wrapping my arms around myself, feeling the drops of the warm water on my freezing cold skin.

Lacey stayed with me that night, and the majority of the next day. The idea of a sleepover with my best friend, however, didn't have all the fun and excitement it did when we were young.

The next day, I avoided asking her about anything to do with what happened the day before and instead spent the day on my couch with her, watching the *Twilight* movies and avoiding the elephant in the room. Eventually, she had to head home to get ready for her red-eye flight to get to Seattle. Her parents moved there to be closer to her grandparents, and she was visiting them with Tyler for the holidays.

"Are you sure you don't want me to stay?" She asked as she was putting on her shoes.

"Yes, Lace. I'm fine," I reassured her, even if the sentiment didn't hold much truth. "Thank you for everything." I hugged her tightly, wishing I could stay in her arms longer but knowing it wasn't fair for me to ask her to change her holiday plans.

"I was so scared when I got that call, Drew," she whispered into my hair, her arms tightly wrapped around my shoulders. "I'm so glad you're okay."

When I had to put down an emergency contact, I didn't even hesitate on putting Lacey down. She is so strong and the best friend I could ask for. Putting my mom or dad down didn't even cross my mind. Neither of them ever being there for me like Lacey. I have Cal down as my secondary one, but I don't even know if I put down the right number for him.

"Don't hesitate to call me or text me if you need anything."

"I won't, but seriously you've done more than enough."

"And I'd do it again. Don't hesitate, okay?"

"Okay," I said, giving her one more squeeze around her waist before letting her go.

As I closed the door behind her, I took a deep breath and exhaled it out, as if trying to empty myself of all the thoughts I knew were at risk of boiling over at any moment. But, instead of dealing with them, I told myself that I would be okay on my own.

That was yesterday, yet it feels like days have passed.

As my heart rate levels, and I breathe out the thoughts I want to bury so deep down they can't be found, I peel myself out of the sheets and walk towards my door. The initial adrenaline from the knocks has faded, and they no longer sound so loud.

I hope to the higher powers that it isn't my mom or dad on the other side of the door, making a surprise visit out of obligation. They both called me yesterday, making sure I was okay and asking if I needed anything. I told them each that I was fine, and I just needed some time alone as I processed what happened. I let them know I would keep them updated and left it at that. Then, each of them talked to Lacey who assured them of everything I had just said but obviously didn't mean much to them coming from me.

It couldn't be Calvin because I don't think he knows I moved from my last place.

Cal texted me saying he heard what happened and wanted to check to see how I was doing. The text was from a number I didn't have saved, proving that the number I had for him wasn't even his anymore. It just further proved how little we have talked over the years.

I was surprised he even knew what school I taught at.

I know it's not Lacey at the door because she is across the country, and she would have let herself in with one of my two spare keys, the other key just being in my junk drawer.

I find myself feeling very uneasy as I unlock the door and twist the knob, having no idea who it could be.

As I slowly swing the door open just enough to see who's on the other side, I see a face that I haven't seen in what feels like forever.

Reed.

I couldn't hide the shock on my face at seeing him, of all people, here in front of me. The person whom I haven't heard from in weeks and who hasn't reached out even once since that November night.

I open the door a little more, revealing myself in the pajamas I haven't taken off in two days, unwashed hair, dried tears trailing on my face, and skin pale, like I've seen a ghost.

I feel this intense rush of emotions as I feel his eyes scan over me, taking in the image before him, most likely not recognizing the person he once knew inside and out.

I feel my vision blur as he just looks at me with tenderness that washed away the tightness in my chest I've had since Friday, December 22nd.

The worst day of my life.

He reads the expression on my face as a plea to help my

knees from buckling, and he steps forward wrapping his arms around me.

He whispers into my hair, "I'm so sorry, D."

I let him hold me up, keeping me steady, feeling the warmth of him unfreezing me little by little as the moments pass. I slowly bring my arms up from my sides to cling around his waist, and I feel his lips press against the top of my head as his arms tighten.

Then, without warning, my body stills beneath his touch.

It was as if my body realized that it was being held by a stranger, before my mind could even register.

Reed feels my reaction and pulls away, still in the doorway of my apartment. He looks at me, puzzled at my reaction, almost as if he's offended, like I hurt his feelings.

"What's wrong?" He asks, taking a step back from me, separating us just a little bit more.

"What are you doing here?" I ignore his question because I don't have an answer for what is wrong.

All I know is there is not a lot that seems *right* at the moment.

As if my words were a slap, Reed looks at me with what is *definitely* offense.

"What do you mean? I'm here for you. I saw the news and thought you'd be happy to see me." His words contributed to my feeling of a stranger in my home.

"You could've texted or called," I respond. "I'm not really up for visitors right now."

Reed scoffs. "Not up for visitors? Is that all I am to you?" He lets out a chuckle as if my response is funny.

As if this is all an inconvenience to him.

"You haven't reached out in weeks, and now you just—"

"You haven't either." His face was tense. His words were loaded.

I take a deep breath before responding, not in the mood to argue. "Look, I've been through a lot these past two days, and

I still don't even know what I'm feeling about . . ." I couldn't say the word. *Shooting.* "About what happened. I just need some time."

It was like the words I was saying were in a different language.

A language Reed didn't understand.

"Time? Time for what? Yeah, what happened sucked, but you're fine. You weren't one of those teachers he was aft—"

My face must have changed because he stopped talking before he finished the sentence.

"What are you talking about?" I said, my voice uneven.

"Haven't you seen the news?" His face loosened just a bit, with a slight look of concern.

No. No, I haven't, I think to myself.

I want to tell him that I've been too busy sleeping or in a state of fragmentary blackouts, but my face must say it all. Reed takes another step back, finally aware that he is making this situation worse.

"I should probably go." I wasn't even listening to the words coming out of his mouth. The only thing on my mind was needing to see what the news was saying about what happened Friday. "Let me know when you—" I shut the door and walk over to my living room. I go to grab the TV remote but can't bring myself to turn it on.

Do I really want to know?

Yes.

Can I handle finding out alone?

I don't know.

I put the remote back where it was on the couch and sit down. I think about calling Lacey, but I don't want to bother her. The thought of asking Reed to come back to tell me what happened quickly crosses my brain.

No.

Maybe it's too soon to find answers to my questions.

The school sent an email to staff about taking Winter

Break to rest and recuperate. The district even gave us an extra two weeks after break to allow everyone to recover from the trauma.

Trauma.

I can't believe I lived through trauma.

No, I can't believe I'm *living* through trauma.

For me, this is anything but over.

The district is offering services and recommending places to get help, but I don't even think I'm there yet.

I think I'm still in a state of shock.

I'm going to give myself some more time before I fill in the blanks and relive the worst day of my life.

Needing to get my mind off all of this, I walk over to my kitchen and bend down to open the cabinet under my sink. I pull out glass cleaner, all-purpose spray, microfiber cloths, and any other cleaning products I have stored away. I stand up, go grab my phone and connect it to my living room speaker to listen to some music.

I sweep the floors, vacuum my area rugs, scrub the shower, wipe down the kitchen surfaces, change my sheets, and load the dishwasher with the few plates and mugs that have been harboring in my sink since when Lacey was still here.

Hopeful that it's at least early afternoon, I check the time and see it's only been an hour. Feeling accomplished yet defeated at the same time, I flop onto the couch and close my eyes. I listen to my music playing at a pleasant volume around me, too afraid to let myself be in silence. One of my favorite songs comes on: *All Downhill from Here* by New Found Glory.

The lyrics I know by heart fill my apartment, making me feel a sense of familiarity and comfort, and I let my mind focus on the chorus.

The tightness in my chest from Reed's surprise visit this morning begins to release, and, for a moment, I can just let myself breathe. That is, until I feel the thoughts I've been trying to keep away creep their way into my temporary solace.

I force my eyes open to not let myself go back to those feelings in the classroom. I don't let my mind show me the tears streaming down faces, or the hands covering the noiseless screams, or the footsteps running down the stairs. I don't let my mind recall the echoing pops, or the screams across the hall.

I jolt up, getting off the couch as if walking away from it is the same as walking away from the thoughts that were just invading my brain. I tell myself that taking a quick shower, brushing my teeth, and putting on clothes for the day will make me feel better, so that's what I do.

It didn't work.

I tell myself making something to eat will make me feel better, so I swing open my fridge, and I'm greeted by a half empty bottle of wine, expired orange juice, and leftover taco meat I know I won't be eating.

That didn't work either.

I grab the Tupperware of ground beef and chuck the whole thing in the trash, grab my keys, slip on my shoes, and head out to go to the grocery store.

As I'm waiting for the elevator, I'm reminded of Friday morning when I was waiting in this exact spot, thinking my biggest problems were not having enough prep time that morning because I was too busy thinking about the past and spilling coffee all over myself.

How silly are those thoughts now?

The ding of the elevator brings me back to reality, and the doors open. I step into the empty cab and let out a deep sigh.

I push the garage level button and lean back onto the wall opposite the doors.

My mind floods with thoughts of the last time I was in the elevator, and *who* I was in the elevator with.

Emmett.

How I wish my biggest worries were being too loud when I got ready. How I wish his disapproving eyes on me were the only thing that made me wish I was anywhere else. How I wish he was *here*, in this elevator, crossing his tattooed arms, stealing glances my way with those warm, rich eyes, helping me forget the last forty-eight hours.

Wrapped up in my thoughts, I don't even notice when the elevator pauses at the floor below me.

The doors open, revealing no one waiting to get in.

I don't think much of it until I arrive in the garage, wishing I was hearing the echoing of footsteps, coming from Vans twice my size.

CHAPTER 12
EMMETT

WHEN I WAKE up this morning, well-rested again, it feels oddly quiet in my apartment. No loud thuds or screams, but I'm still finding myself distracted by thoughts of Drew, which remind me of what she must be going through right now, which leads me to think about Lennon.

When Lennon died, I never thought I would outlive the suffering I felt every day. I wouldn't survive the agony I felt at every waking moment, and I remember longing for someone who understood the pain.

My sister died twelve years ago, and sometimes it feels like that much time has passed. Other days it feels like it was yesterday.

Grief works in such odd ways.

I remember my therapist explaining it to me as a balloon in a box with a button. The button was the grief, and when the balloon was big enough to push it, that is when you felt it. When my sister died, the balloon was blown up so big that it barely had room to move in the box, so the grief button was being held down.

All morning, all day, all night.

But, as time went on, the balloon began to deflate—more

on some days than others—and the button wasn't being pushed as often. The balloon is still there, but it's small enough now so it only hits that button occasionally.

Hearing a phone ring in the middle of the night never means good news because good news waits until the morning. Bad news, heartbreaking news, life-changing news comes in the middle of the night.

I recall drifting off to sleep, the time being somewhere just after midnight. It was a Friday night, and the stress of senior year was put on hold for the weekend. My dad gave me the night off from the bar, and I used it to play video games until my eyes were red-rimmed.

I remember thinking that it was weird to be getting a phone call to the house this late, and the mumbling from my parents' bedroom down the hall was all I could hear in the realm between awake and asleep.

My mom was the one who answered the phone because my dad was still at the bar. What started as inaudible whispering quickly transformed into a wail. I don't remember how I got out of bed and ended up kneeling next to my mom because of how fast I moved. The phone was dropped between her feet and her head was in her hands, and I was no longer the least bit tired.

It all became a blur when I picked up the phone from the floor and said, "Hello?"

The words, "Lennon," "hit," "tree," and "drunk," were swirling in the air as I hung up to call my dad at the bar. I have no memory of the phone call I had with him or getting to the hospital, but, the next thing I knew, I heard the doctors tell my parents that she didn't even make it out of the car. She had died on impact, but there wasn't a drop of alcohol in her system.

It was as if my life could have ended there, my parents' cries being the soundtrack to my demise. It was a living nightmare standing there in the hospital, watching them wrap their arms around each other and let out tears so filled with sorrow that the sobs were silent. My own eyes were blurry with the tears I refused the let fall—I had to be strong for them.

My life didn't end there, not even close, and I know that now—along with the fact that it wasn't my job to stay strong for my mom and dad. Arriving at this took a lot of therapy and understanding my feelings surrounding what happened, but, in some ways, a part of me never left the hospital that day.

I often wonder what it would be like if Lennon was still around. Still here. Still *alive*.

Would she be proud?

Would she be happy?

My parents have their own ways of coping with the loss, and both cope in private. We don't talk about Lennon much, and I don't share that part of my past with anyone, not even Eddie. I talked about it with Riley once, but I could tell she was uncomfortable, so I changed the subject.

That should've been another clue that we were never going to work out.

———

I've been laying here in bed for the past two hours, and it's still only 9 a.m. With the bar closed today and tomorrow, I have two days to myself.

I feel the button press, washing me with grief.

I grew up celebrating Christmas Eve and Christmas, but after Lennon died, my faith died along with her. I couldn't believe the God I learned about in Sunday school was the God that took her away.

My parents are in Florida, my sister is dead, and my friends are all visiting families of their own with significant others.

I have two days.

Alone.

I roll over, not even interested in scrolling on my phone or turning on the TV. Instead, I muster up the motivation to get myself out of bed and do something with the day.

As I walk to the bathroom, I remember the grocery shopping I was going to do on Friday that I never got to because of everything that happened. It's Sunday now, and, even though it's Christmas Eve, most stores are open until at least early evening.

The stores will probably be packed, but the busyness might keep me distracted from thinking about Lennon, *or Drew.*

I quickly brush my teeth, tie my hair up, and pull on some jeans and a t-shirt. I grab my phone to check the list I typed up on Friday. I add a couple other things before heading out the door, and I find myself half-hoping that I'll run into Drew. Not to give her a hard time, but because I only recently realized the place that she's come to have in my routine, and my brain, over the past six months. It's like she snuck her way in and found her place, leaving me feeling like she's always been there.

I hope the flush in her cheeks doesn't disappear after what has happened to her. Same with the sparkle in her eye and the slight catch of her breath when she spots me.

Living through a trauma changes a person, and I hope the glimpses I got of Drew, and the person she is, are still there. I want her to be okay, selfishly and empathetically. I've experienced feelings so big and so hard to understand, and no one deserves that. Especially a teacher who went to work with no intention of having the worst day of her life.

I head down the hallway to the elevator and push the button. It lights up, and I hear the grating noise from the metal parts pushing and grinding against one another as the car makes its way to my floor.

One day, that cable is just going to snap, I think to myself.

Just as I hear the ding that tells me the door is about to open, I realize that I forgot to grab my jacket, and my car is going to be freezing from not driving it the past week. Before the doors can open, I jog back to my apartment to grab it.

CHAPTER 13
DREW

AS I CRUISE through the aisles of the grocery store, for once thankful for the hustle and bustle of the crowd grabbing last-minute items for their Christmas Eve dinners, I'm too happily distracted with the world around me to focus on the war going on inside my head.

Growing up, there was such a different atmosphere depending on whose house I was at. At my mom's, there was an abundance of fruits and veggies and nothing that had over three grams of carbs. Dinners were colorful and full of protein, and dessert was a once-a-week kind of thing.

At my dad's, it was paralleled with a near-empty fridge and take-out boxes overflowing the garbage and recycling bins.

I decided that when I moved out, I would take the best of both worlds and live a healthy, yet balanced, lifestyle, sticking to only two nights a week ordering out, plates with every food group, and dessert being an every-night occurrence.

But today, I've grabbed a new holiday coffee creamer to try, a box of blueberry Pop-Tarts, and two pints of ice cream: one chocolate-y and one fruity. I need one for both moods.

I decide to peruse the freezer section, knowing full well I

will not be bothered to cook a full meal anytime soon and settle on the classics that I know I love: Jack's frozen pepperoni pizzas, Tyson chicken strips, and microwaveable breakfast burritos. All can be made with the kitchen appliances I have, allowing me to forget the chore of cooking for the foreseeable future.

No need to be balanced for the time being.

Everything in my cart is an example of a temptation I try to keep out of my home. But, I tell myself that my favorite foods, no matter how many grams of sugar or carbs, will help make me feel better.

Even if it is temporary.

I feel my phone vibrate, hoping it will stop after one. When the vibrations continue, telling me it's a phone call rather than a text, my stomach drops, hoping it's not either of the parents I was just thinking about. I pull out my phone to see a picture of Lacey laughing with a glass of wine in her hand, a picture from a dinner we had to celebrate her getting her first job out of college. My hesitation to answer the phone fades away. I touch the green circle on the screen. "Hey, bestie girl."

"Drew, honey! I'm so glad to hear your voice." Her voice, so inherently pleasant and kind, is exactly what I didn't know I needed right now. "What are you up to?

"Nothing much," I respond. "I'm just grabbing some stuff at the grocery store. How was your flight?"

"Good! I got in super early this morning, and I'm already spending my time trying to get a word in while everyone talks about how *amazing* Sal is," she explains. Sal is Lacey's older brother who has always shined in the spotlight, even at Lacey's expense. Having brothers, mine younger and hers older, with names that rhymed is something we bonded over when we first met on the school bus back in kindergarten. She sat next to me on the first day of school, getting on at the stop right after me. We exchanged how her house and my house were both gray, and how my brother's name was Cal and hers was Sal. These two things in common, and we decided it only made sense we become best friends, and it's been that way ever since.

It's crazy to think how easy life seems when you're five, bonding over the color of paint and a shared phonemic awareness skill and then subconsciously deciding that this person would be your person for the rest of your life.

"You're amazing, Lace. You know that," I reply, meaning every single word. "Tell everyone I say hello."

Lacey's parents moved to be closer to her grandparents when she went to college, her and Sal both staying here to go to college in Madison, Sal being two years older than us.

"Of course! You should come out with me next time I come, it would be nice for you to get away, you know, from everything." The cheeriness in her voice fades slightly when she says that last part.

While I know that she means well, I feel the weight get heavier on my chest as the brief bliss of forgetting what happened to me teased my brain into thinking I could have a normal conversation with my best friend.

"Yeah, maybe. So, what's up?"

"Oh, right! So, I fly back later this week, and I was hoping we could grab lunch, just you and me. I know you're still on break, and I have off until after the new year."

It's been months since Lacey and I sat down, just the two of us to catch up, but the thought of it right now makes me nauseous. The only thing to catch up about is the last thing I want to talk about, not to mention my run-in with Reed this morning and my grumpy neighbor. Those three things being the only *new* things to discuss, and Lacey doesn't need me dumping any stress on her.

"Um, yeah maybe," I manage to get out after a little hesitation. "Text me when you're back."

"Oh my gosh. Awesome! Yes, will do!" Her excitement

and slight tone of surprise tells me she had a clue as to what I was thinking and didn't expect me to somewhat agree. After a brief pause, she continues, "Promise me you're doing okay?"

"I'm okay," I tell her, feeling my voice lose confidence.

Am I okay?

Maybe if I say it out loud enough times or enough people tell me that I am, I'll feel like it.

"I have to go," I quickly add before she can ask if I'm *really* okay. "I need to get in line to check-out if I ever want to get out of here."

"No worries. I'm sure the Christmas Eve crowd is crazy!" I can hear voices on her end. "I have to run too. Mom's yelling for me to help her with brunch." I smile knowing exactly how Mrs. Anderson's voice gets when she needs Lacey to do something. "Don't forget to text me, okay?"

"I will, Lace! Now go help your mom."

She laughs in her carefree sort of way, and my world is a better place because of it. "Okay, love you, bye!" The phone clicks before I can tell her I love her too.

I put my phone into the back pocket of my jeans and glance up at the signs for what else is in the aisle I'm in. I didn't come with a list, which is always a bad idea, yet I can't find it within me to care.

With Lacey's voice still fresh in my mind, I slowly push my cart down the rest of the frozen aisle. My mind starts to take me back to this morning and my encounter with Reed, and I feel an odd rush of guilt wash over me.

Why didn't I tell Lacey?

She was on the phone, asked me how I was doing, and I just lied and said I was okay. Reed and Lacey are the only two I have as constants in my life, even if one is way more reliable than the other. And the reliable one is always there for me to complain about the *un*-reliable one.

I guess that is until recently.

I start racking my brain for the last time I talked to Lacey about Reed, and I come up empty. I didn't tell Lacey about what Reed said to me about my teaching job a few weeks ago, or how I deleted his number for *real* this time. Those are things a *normal* person tells their best friend.

I come up empty, with no recollection of a personal conversation with Lacey, or anyone else for that matter. Conversations didn't go far with Reed, and the only other person outside of work I've talked to is Emmett, if you can even consider our encounters as conversations.

My cheeks warm just at the thought of Emmett, and then warm even more at the realization of my reaction to thinking about him.

He's the last thing I need to be thinking about.

Bringing my mind back to what matters, I think about how Lacey and I have drifted so much that I don't remember the last time we talked like we did when she would visit me at my off-campus apartment, or when I would spend the weekend with her in Madison. She liked Reed just fine in high school. At least until senior year when she told me that if Reed was making me feel guilty for following what I wanted to do then our relationship never meant anything. Ever since then, she's lovingly advised me against the relationship I continued with Reed through college and up until now, but she never made me feel like she was judging me for it.

My fingertips graze the top of my back pocket, but I stop myself from grabbing my phone again. I know Lacey would drop everything if I called her back, but I can't. She's with her family, preparing Christmas Eve brunch. It's not fair for me to dump that all on her. Lacey and I probably wouldn't even have had that phone call just now if it weren't for the—

I stop mid-step, gripping the metal cart's handle, feeling the skin covering my knuckles strain. My body starts to freeze, feeling as if I'm inside the freezers surrounding me.

No.

This can't happen.

Everyone's telling me that I'm okay, and I am.

I'm okay.

It doesn't matter that Lacey and I have drifted apart or that I didn't tell her about Reed. What matters is she is in my life, and I was lucky that she was there for me in the time I needed her the most. I'm okay, and I'm lucky.

Right?

I manage to uncurl my fingers from the handle, reaching for my phone once again. I decide to not bother Lacey with my spiraling thoughts and open my messages to start a new thread.

I type in a number that isn't saved into my contacts, but I know all too well. I send something short and sweet–apologizing for my surprise this morning and letting Reed know I appreciate him thinking of me. I click send before I can think myself out of it, and I slip my phone back into my pocket. I half-heartedly hope to feel it vibrate with a text right away, but nothing comes.

Before leaving the freezer section, I assess my cart and find that I need one more thing: Eggo waffles. While homemade waffles are *much* better, the kind that you can just put in the toaster will do for the next few days. I cross the aisle and open the door to all the frozen breakfast options. A slight fog appears as I open the door, the water vapor chilling my cheeks.

I spend way too much time contemplating on grabbing the normal waffles or the minis and end up choosing to get a box of each. I throw the boxes in my cart and close the freezer door, and I am met with a face I recognize, yet feel like I'm seeing for the first time.

CHAPTER 14
EMMETT

I'M not sure how long I was watching her ponder her frozen food choices, but I couldn't pull my eyes away. I haven't seen Drew since Friday morning, and I barely recognize the girl in front of me.

Rather than the flushed cheeks matching the color of her hair tied back leaving two pieces that frame her face perfectly, I see someone who has been through an unspeakable tragedy. Sadness in her eyes in the form of red rings that somehow accentuate the green in her hazel eyes.

She looks beautiful in a beautifully tragic way.

I take a few steps towards her, knowing that I'm probably the last thing on her mind, but I want to get a closer look.

I've seen her numerous times before, but there's this unfamiliarity to her that is pulling me in—the way her clothes are hanging a little looser, her hair missing its shine, her dark lashes even darker from the tears.

I find myself on the other side of the freezer door she has open, and, as she closes it, she meets my gaze. We lock eyes for a moment until she breaks the hold she has on me.

I watch her tuck a piece of hair behind her ear, evading my eyes, and I bend down a little to try to meet her gaze again, wanting to hook into those eyes again. "Nice to see you, Drew."

I see her shift on her feet, looking as if she's ready to grab her cart and go, but, for some reason, I don't want her to. I'm really not quite sure what else to say aside from telling her the truth.

It *is* nice to see her.

It always made me feel worse when people walked on eggshells around me after Lennon died, but, being on the other side, I understand how it feels to not know how to help someone who probably doesn't even know what they need.

"Nice to see you, too." Still avoiding my eyes, an uneasiness in her voice as if she doesn't quite understand why I would be talking to her.

I take a step closer. "I heard what happened." She freezes, and I can tell I struck the nerve. I pause, not knowing if I should say anymore or give her an out.

Instead of either of those, I ask, "How are you?"

"Why do you care?" Her voice has an edge, almost like the bark of a dog being cornered. "It's none of your business."

I should have expected this. I've never been anything but rude to the girl, and now I'm approaching her as if the past six months have been filled with pleasantries.

I assumed that she would say she is fine and maybe excuse herself from the interaction, but I didn't think she would get defensive.

"You're right. I'm sorry." I take a few steps back, thinking I've crossed a line, not wanting to make her any more uncomfortable. Then, as I go to turn, I hear her say something.

"No." She shakes her head and brings a hand to her forehead. "I should apologize. That was out of line." She brings her hand down, letting out an exhale—one she has probably been holding onto for a while. "It's just been a rough couple of days, and I'm not used to *you* of all people being so, I don't know, nice? I guess I didn't know how to respond properly."

Guilt hits me in my chest because I'm seeing the impact our interactions have had on her, making her feel on edge when she is around me, as if she doesn't know what to expect.

I can't really blame her for feeling that way, and I don't want her thinking that anymore. And I don't want her thinking she has to apologize to me either. "No, please don't apologize. I can't imagine what you're going through." I take a slow step forward as if I move too quickly I'll scare her away. "How are you doing?"

I watch her look at the different boxes and containers in her cart as people walk next to us, up and down the aisle. People who are completely oblivious to what she is going through.

It takes her a few moments to respond, and this should feel awkward. This should feel weird, seeing each other outside the elevator, under these circumstances.

We barely ever have a conversation that doesn't leave us both hot and bothered, me usually hot, her usually bothered.

But, it doesn't.

It doesn't feel awkward.

Drew glances up from her cart for the first time since she looked away from our initial glance and meets my eyes with a peculiar face.

Is that a surprised look? Shock?

"Um, I'm sorry. No one's asked me that since—" she pauses before letting herself say the word—*shooting*. "Since before what happened." She exhales then continues, "I've been told everything's fine, that I'm okay, and I should take some time to recover. But, no one's asked me that."

I don't know what to say because her words rang so true in my mind and took me back to the day we got the call that Lennon's car was found wrapped around a tree filled with three friends she was driving home from a party.

I remember thinking how damn ironic it was that Lennon

was the sober one, being responsible, driving her drunk friends home, and then she was hit by a drunk driver. All the girls were rushed to the hospital, Lennon being the only one who didn't even make it out of the car.

The next week, being in a daze of disbelief and depression, everyone—my parents, the doctors, friends, teachers—told me that everything would be okay and to take time to recover.

They said I had to learn to live with the trauma.

"Honestly, I'm not great," she says, eyes still glued to mine. An unmistakable sadness in her voice.

"Honestly," I hold tightly to her gaze. "I didn't think you would be." My eyes never leave hers as I take one more step closer, only the distance of her cart between us now. "And, that's okay."

I watch her react to my words, seeing her shoulders release tension and her jaw untighten. She opens her mouth to say something, but then her lips close before anything comes out.

I want her to know that it's okay to not be okay, because her reaction is telling me that no one has told her that before. By not saying anything, she's telling me more than she could express with words.

"Did you have more shopping to do?" I ask.

She shakes her head. I don't know if she's telling the truth or not, but I decide to take her word for it.

"I was just about to check-out," I reply, gesturing to my basket that is nowhere filled to where I need it to be, but that can wait for another day. "Do you want to head the check-out lines with me?"

She nods. And before she can change her mind, I pull her cart towards me and lead her down the aisle towards the self-checkout. As she walks next to me, she's quiet, but again, it's not awkward.

Being in her company feels… *right*. I can't explain it, but I like it and don't think I've ever felt it before today. All the other times I've been in her vicinity, I was always just thinking of a different way to ruffle her feathers, to make her cheeks turn red, to see her stomp off, to make the air around us feel anything but right.

I scan my items as she rests up against the handles of her cart. When I finish scanning my few things, I go to grab her items.

"Oh, you don't have to do that," she quickly intervenes.

"I know," I respond. I give her a little smile and go to grab her plethora of frozen meals, Pop-Tarts, and coffee creamer. She quickly turns away, a familiar pink coming to her cheeks. It's then I realize that I don't think I've ever smiled at the girl.

Without another word, I throw all her stuff in the two reusable bags I find under the junk food. I quietly chuckle to myself seeing that even her grocery bags match her aesthetic: black.

I go to pay with my card before she can reach into the fanny pack across her chest for hers.

"No, no. Please, I can pay for my stuff."

"Drew, don't worry. You chose the same things as a ten-year-old with a twenty dollar allowance. I got it."

Before she could protest anymore, I swipe my card, feeling a flutter in my stomach at the thought of being able to do this for her, and I'm not sure why. Do I like doing something nice for her? Providing for her? Spoiling her?

I get a little embarrassed I'm even having these thoughts, so I ignore the dip my stomach does and grab our bags.

Relax, it's just junk food, I think to myself.

We walk our way through the piles of people checking out their supplies for their holiday dinners and gatherings, bagging their groceries, making small talk with those around them, spreading their holiday spirit that seems to halt before getting to Drew and me.

We make our way to the exit, Drew walking next to me as

I hold our bags with one hand and push her empty cart with another.

Again, I'm pleasantly surprised with how I feel when she's around me, not worrying about how to push her buttons, just making our way towards the parking lot.

When I approached her in the freezer aisle, I wasn't quite sure what I had in mind. I didn't have the intention of talking to her, but I also didn't *hate* the idea of her catching me staring. When I saw her perusing the frozen waffles, it was like I was seeing her for the first time because in front of me was a shell of a person I've seen so many times before.

All the other times, her cheeks were pink with fluster, her voice high and agitated when she managed to get her words out, her eyes bright and enticing.

Today, her skin shows barely a hint of its normal color; her voice is small and shaky; and her eyes are full of sorrow and things that can never be forgotten.

Walking out of the store, side-by-side, feels like the first time the presence of each other is more than accidental or bad timing, and Drew seems more comfortable as the minutes tick by, not all seeming like she is in a rush to get away from me.

As we walk out the automatic doors, I push the cart back to the line of unused ones at the grocery store's entrance, and Drew reaches for her groceries hooked around my arm.

"Thanks," she says as she gives me a soft smile. A smile as pure as the fresh snow around us, warming me up despite the winter air.

The corners of her lips then droop, her lack of understanding showing in the way her eyebrows slightly come together when I don't reciprocate her action by letting her take the bags. "Where's your car?" I ask.

Now she gets it, she rolls her eyes, giving me a small smirk, even though it doesn't yet reach her eyes. The upturns of her lips give me hope that she will make it through this mess she's in.

This time, as she speaks to me, there's a playfulness to her voice I don't recall hearing before.

"I can carry my own groceries, Emmett."

"Where is your car?" I ask again, pausing just a touch between each word, and adding a playfulness of my own. She shakes her head letting out a small chuckle I would've missed if I wasn't watching her every move so closely.

"Seriously. You've done more than enough."

"Drew."

"What?" Her eyes find mine again.

"Don't make me ask again."

And with that, I'm reminded why I give this girl a hard time. Her cheeks heat up, making my heart stop, telling me she's not a shell. She is the same girl that wakes me up before my alarm or in the middle of the night with her inability to move around her apartment without making noise. The same girl who catches me in my dullest moments where I walk away after pestering her about things that seem so miniscule now.

"Over there." She turns her head away from me, but I can see her smile is spreading up to the corners of her eyes. I spot her car, the one I subconsciously check for in the parking garage whenever I leave or get home from our complex.

We step out from the awning covering us from the snow that must have started to fall during the time we were in the store.

I walk a few steps behind her, thankful for her choice of black skinny jeans today. I feel heat spread across my chest at the sight, thankful my thoughts and emotions don't show on my face. Then I instantly want to slap myself for even letting that cross my mind right now, so I politely divert my eyes as we walk to her car, admiring how her red hair contrasts against the snowflakes falling instead.

When we get to her car, she opens the back seat behind the driver's side for me to set her bags of groceries down. I bend in to put them on the floor behind her driver's seat for her and then stand back up and move out of the way so she can close the door.

We meet face-to-face, and I'm stuck as if petrified just by looking at her directly in the eyes. Something about being in her close proximity, the natural light of the winter day allowing me to see freckles on her cheeks and nose I never noticed before, captivates me to the point I feel my feet have rooted into the concrete.

I'm not sure how to end the interaction. I have to tear my feet from out below me and take a few steps back. I find myself so gravitated towards her, wanting to count each freckle powdered on her face, but I don't want to do something that will freak her out.

We barely know each other after all.

She stays put, hand on the driver's side door handle, maybe trying to predict what I'm going to say. I leave her with the words I would've wanted to hear when I was in her shoes. The words I would've wanted my friends to say instead of, "It's going to be okay," or, "I know what you're going through."

The words that would've shown me that what I felt was valid enough to be expressed. The words that would've saved me from trying to heal in isolation. The words that would've shown me someone wanted to listen.

"If you want to talk about it, you know where to find me."

CHAPTER 15
DREW

I DRIVE HOME from the grocery store not really sure how to feel, listening to Paramore's *Hard Times,* as I drive through the flurries of snow.

Do I feel better? Worse? The same?

What I did know is that the last person I ever thought I'd want around was the person who was somehow there when I needed it.

And I didn't push him away.

It wasn't until I got home to my apartment and started putting my groceries away that I remembered Reed coming over just a few hours ago. That he said all the wrong things just a few hours ago. That me closing the door in his face—again—was just a few hours ago. I check my phone to see if I missed it vibrate, but there's still no response from the apology text I sent after I got off the phone with Lacey.

Lacey.

I should tell her what just happened, give her a quick call back. She would love to know that my grumpy neighbor felt bad enough for me that he approached me at the grocery store. He probably could tell I was about to fall apart because he treated me like I could crumble at any moment.

It should have been humiliating. More so than the times he made comments about what he heard going on up here or out-right told me he had no interest in talking to me.

I finish putting my groceries away, trying to distance my mind from what just happened. I head into the living room to find something to watch on the TV. I turn on *Breaking Dawn Part 1*, picking up where Lacey and I left off yesterday and distract myself with the problems of the characters in front of me, rather than my own.

After about an hour, my stomach starts to growl. It's been almost two days without a solid meal, but I can bring myself to eat something of substance. I check the time, and it's about one o'clock. I could make lunch, or I could turn on *Breaking Dawn Part 2* and continue to distract myself. I go with the latter, grabbing a blanket and making myself comfortable.

The movie is about thirty minutes in when I feel my eyelids begin to get heavy. I fight to keep them open, focusing hard on the screen in front of me, but the darkness takes over.

———

My eyes snap open, and I'm covered in a cold sweat. The blanket I covered myself with a few hours ago is now wrapped around me so tightly, I feel like my limbs are adhered to my body. I try to unwrap myself, but I'm shaking, my heart pounding in my ears, and it takes me a second to register where I am, what day it is, and what is happening to me.

My mouth is dry—my throat coarse. I try to take control of my breathing, but my chest is heaving up and down so fast. I can't get the air to my lungs.

I peel my arms from my sides to pull the blanket off of me, feeling a trickle of liquid coming from my palms.

Blood.

My fists were clenched so tightly, I broke skin.

I slowly push myself up with my arms, still trying to control my breathing, and I swing my legs back below me so I'm in a sitting position. My apartment is now dark, the TV is no longer making a sound, and I tell myself I have to regain my composure.

I steady myself on my coffee table in front of me and slowly stand up, grabbing my phone from the couch and connecting it to my speaker to play some music. My fingers shake as I try to click the right buttons, until Hayley Williams' voice finally breaks the silence. I breathe along to the beat of the music playing and slowly make my way to the bathroom where I am met with a reflection of a person on the verge of falling apart.

I turn on the sink and dip my head under the running water for a few sips, trying to relieve the dryness in my throat. I could tell that if I tried to talk, my voice would be hoarse and cracked.

How did I lose my voice in my sleep?

I haven't checked the time, but I fell asleep just after the opening scenes of *Breaking Dawn Part 2*. When I finally woke up, the movie and ending credits were long over.

I must have been asleep for about three hours, longer than any nap I would've taken before all of this. But why is my body more strained and tired than it was before?

I walk back into the kitchen and glance at the time on my oven. It's a little past 4 p.m. now, and I have to find a way to stay busy—and awake—for the rest of the day.

Grabbing some coffee grounds and a filter to put a pot on, the smell reminds me of the morning, waking up well-rested and ready for the day, but it will be serving a different purpose today.

While I wait for the coffee to brew, I grab the box of Pop-Tarts I put in my pantry and pull out a foiled package. I open it up, slide one out of the packaging, and break it in half before taking a bite, the sweet frosting and tangy filling making me feel much better almost immediately after swallowing.

The coffee is almost done, so I reach into the cabinet above for a mug and set it on the counter. I head over to my bookshelf, taking a look at the To Be Read shelf and pick a book that will keep my attention, and my eyes open, for the next few hours. It's a 300-page thriller, recommended to me by Lacey. I throw it on the couch as I walk back to the kitchen to grab my coffee.

I spend the rest of the evening reading, getting through the first thriller in a little over three hours, liking it, but not loving it.

I get off the couch for the first time since I sat down to start reading and walk back over to my shelf to grab another thriller to read in bed.

Once again, I keep my eyes open until I can't bear the weight of my eyelids any longer. I fight to stay awake to get to the climax of the story, but the words are starting to blend together on the page. I end up falling asleep around nine, knowing I won't get any rest.

———

Christmas Day is uneventful which is sad to say about a holiday that is known for happiness and cheer. I spend the day celebrating by myself with some online shopping, scheduling a grocery delivery for tomorrow, eating more Pop-Tarts, and watching two of my favorite Christmas movies: *Elf* and *Home Alone*.

Most of the day is spent on the couch, occasionally looking out the window at the piles of snow that formed overnight. It's sunny, and the light peaking in automatically brightens my mood. I can't remember the last time we had a Christmas Day with piles of snow *and* sunshine in Wisconsin.

I also spent a solid amount of time trying to focus on my book to avoid the itch I had to scroll through my phone. I've been avoiding social media since Friday, along with the texts from my parents. I only grab my phone to open Lacey's text: *"Wishing you a merry day!"* She followed it with a GIF of Snoopy and Woodstock putting ornaments on a Christmas tree.

I responded to her message with a GIF of SpongeBob in a Santa hat, and we've been going back and forth about the family drama she's witnessing in Seattle.

I finish the thriller I started last night with still half the day left, so I spend the rest evening plummeting into a love story of Hades and Persephone, needing a change in genre. The fantasy-romance has me so wrapped up in the story, I reach the last two chapters and wonder how the author is going to finish up the story in less than fifteen pages. When I get to the last page, I find that it is because she doesn't, and this is just the *first* book in a series.

Leave it to me to buy a book that is part of the series and not even know it.

Now, I have to wait to read the next book and find a time this week to venture out amongst all the people returning the gifts they're probably opening right now, to get the rest of the books.

CHAPTER 16
EMMETT

THE PAST TWO days have been extremely uneventful for me. With Lenny's being closed, along with most other establishments, I've had to make myself busy inside the walls of my apartment. I've caught up on a couple shows I wanted to watch, played some video games, cooked a few meals, and tidied up my apartment. I did a few loads of laundry that have been piling up, called my parents, and got ahead on some of my paperwork for the bar.

Overall, I've been productive, and I'm feeling accomplished, but I still have this nagging feeling that there's more I could be doing.

Drew has also been home the past two days, and I know because I could hear her make her way around her apartment, dropping a few things along the way and playing music at almost all waking hours. For once, I didn't mind the noise she made. It gave me a sense of relief and normalcy.

Except for yesterday afternoon.

I was laying on the couch while watching TV when I heard screaming. But it wasn't the kind of shriek you hear when someone trips or stubs their toe, I've heard plenty of those come from upstairs.

It was the kind of screaming that makes you freeze.

The kind of screaming that says the person is scared.

Scared of what they're seeing.

Scared for their life.

I paused the TV when I heard it, at first not sure if it was coming from the speakers or somewhere else. It took me a moment to register that the noise was stemming from my ceiling, the source being right above me. I didn't know what to do, didn't know why it was happening, didn't know if Drew was okay. The scream was followed by silence, and I told myself it was nothing to worry about but still felt a little unsettled.

I unpaused the show I was watching, brushing it off, but then, about twenty minutes later, I heard it again. This time, I heard creaking and scratching as if the legs of her couch were moving back and forth. That's when I realized that she must be asleep, trapped in a dream, screaming for her life, tossing and turning trying to escape it.

It's a feeling I know all too well.

The first few nights after Lennon died, I'd wake up in cold sweats with my heart pumping out of my chest. I had the same nightmare every night for I don't know how long. I was running down a dark street, chasing headlights that were getting further and further away. I would wake up screaming Lennon's name, aching to reach her. My parents had to put a rug under my bed because I would move so much in my sleep, the legs of my bed started making these large indents in the hardwood floor.

My therapist explained to me that nightmares after a trauma are an intense expression of the body working through the traumatic experiences it's been through. They can also represent a breakdown of the body's own ability to process what has happened to it.

School shootings are becoming such a norm in the daily news, and it's incomprehensible how nothing is being done about it. I saw an insane statistic of almost six hundred and fifty mass shootings happening within a year with fifty-one of those happen at schools.

And here we are again, adding another to that already unsettling number.

The day the shooting at Drew's middle school happened, there was coverage, but it's like the news stations move onto the next hot topic once the commotion of it all is over.

It's incredibly heartbreaking and completely unfair.

These teachers shouldn't have to make the choices they are put having to make. I'm surprised more don't leave the profession because of these types of risks.

I have so much respect for teachers, my grandma had been a music teacher for her entire working life, and I think it's crazy that teachers always get the short end of the stick. Not to mention the possibility of a fucking asshole being able to not only buy an unnecessary gun, but also walk right into a school with hundreds of innocent kids.

I read that the kid was only eighteen, but that didn't stop him from having a twenty-one-year-old friend buy it for him.

I should have used the stories of the classroom I heard from my grandma to make a connection with Drew, but I was always too selfish or pissed to have a polite conversation with her.

She was probably already stressed from the job, and now, with all of this, she has to decide if she's going to go back. I honestly don't know how someone could after this. I know I wouldn't be able to.

It's so soon after the shooting, the wounds from that day still being so fresh, I wonder if she's thought about it. That day will be etched into her bones, becoming a part of who she is, but I hope she doesn't let it take over. Drew doesn't strike me as someone who has gotten through life without having to work for it; she seems strong.

But I still can't help but worry.

I had not felt helpless like I did when I heard Drew screaming in a while. I felt like there was *something* I should have done.

I didn't know what though—still don't.

I don't know what she needs, how to help her, or if she even *wants* help.

I ran into the same internal struggle when I wanted to rush up to her place the day of the shooting—wanting to see if she was okay but feeling like it wasn't my place.

My heart hurts at the thought of her going through something like this alone. I can't imagine how scared she must have been in her classroom or how she must be feeling now.

Until I could confirm Drew was awake, I kept the TV paused and just kept listening, hearing her screams a few times each hour she was asleep. My fist clenched at every one, and I would wince from the pain I heard in every outcry.

After a few hours, I heard footsteps and music playing again, telling me that she was awake.

I felt like I could breathe again.

I'm not sure if she went to sleep that night or not, but I didn't hear the screams again. If I would have, I don't know if I would have been able to stop myself from running up the steps separating my floor from hers.

CHAPTER 17
DREW

TO SAY I have not been sleeping well would be an understatement because to not be sleeping well, I would have to actually be falling asleep. The past two nights, I have been staying in a state of being asleep, but not deep enough to get any rest, waking up more tired than I was the night before.

I don't know how long I can keep this up, but I have no intention of letting myself revisit the place my mind took me last time I fell into a deep sleep.

While still lying in bed, I reach under my pillow to grab the remote to turn off the TV in my bedroom. It has been playing through season three of *New Girl* for two nights straight, and I know I will be picking up where I left off when I get back in bed tonight. I connect my phone to the speaker in my living room. The latest All Time Low album begins to play as I get myself out of bed.

I go through my morning routine of brushing my teeth, washing my face, but *not* changing out my pajamas. It's not like I have anywhere I need to be for today, and my oversized t-shirt and shorts, that barely cover my butt, are appropriate for the day I have planned of sitting on my couch and starting the daunting, time-consuming feat of watching all of the Marvel movies in chronological order.

I head into the kitchen to make some coffee, throwing out the old filter and grounds, letting a few yawns out as I do so, and I realize my garbage is about to overflow. Today is Thursday, and I'm pretty sure I haven't taken out my garbage since this time last week. I pull the bag out by the strings and tie it up. My apartment is only three doors down from a garbage chute, so I quickly dispose of the bag, hoping I don't run into any of my neighbors in my current attire.

When I'm back in my apartment, my coffee is ready for me. I grab the same mug I've been using and washing and using again from the sink, and fill it with coffee before adding some of my holiday creamer: Frosted Sugar Cookie. I bring the mug to my lips to find the perfect blend of bitterness and sweetness and then sit back on the couch.

I hear my phone buzzing on the other side of my wall in the bedroom, but I have no intention of looking at it. Instead, I queue up *Captain America* and turn off the music playing as I press play. I watch the opening scenes and sip on my coffee.

As the movie plays, I am reminded how this is probably the most boring movie of the MCU. Last time I watched it was in theaters with Lacey, and she still makes fun of me for being the kind of person who falls asleep in a movie theater.

I try to power through it, finishing my coffee and covering myself with a blanket, but I feel my eyelids getting heavy despite the caffeine. My brain is not staying entertained with the scenes playing out on the screen, so I sit myself upright, not wanting to doze off and decide that this movie can be video wallpaper while I read, only needing to pay attention to the exciting parts. I take the blanket off my legs before getting up to walk over to my bookshelf.

Before Friday, my plans for Winter Break were a rotation of sleeping, reading, and watching movies. Those three things are *my* version of self-care which is what teachers are always reminded to do during breaks. Safe to say, I've been doing two of those three things religiously because they are also perfect for keeping my mind off of what happened the day before break.

Unfortunately for me, I am actively trying to avoid the other, even though it was what I was most looking forward to spending my break doing.

As I round the couch, a few steps away from my bookshelf, I hear my phone buzz a few more times in my bedroom, and I'm starting to get a little curious as to why it's going off so much. I head to the bedroom to grab it and find that my school and the district sent a handful of emails out.

I sit down on the edge of my bed and open up the notifications. The first one is an email containing a notice from the superintendent that will be sent to families later today. It's a notice about the school being closed for the two weeks following Winter Break to allow for the school and surrounding community to *recuperate*. They had let staff know about this, but they were now officially telling families too.

The next email is from my principal highlighting ways teachers can *cope*, and the last three are from HR and contain resources about how to *recover*.

Recuperate, rest, cope, recover.

All things we need to do after what happened to us.

After living through what we lived through.

After a school shooting.

This is not how I planned to spend my Winter Break.

I scroll through the links, but the titles alone give me a visceral reaction.

"Coping in the Aftermath"

"Crisis Management"

"Survivors: what happens now?"

I feel my heartbeat quickening, hearing the thumping in my ears. My chest starts to feel tight as my lungs strain to fill with air.

This can't be a normal reaction, and I can't keep burying these feelings. It's no wonder they keep trying to claw their way out.

But, against my better judgment, I close out the email app and throw my phone on my bed because I don't know if I can face these feelings alone.

I find an ounce of relief but still feel anxious and unsettled, ignoring the realization in the back of my mind that I have no control over when I'm brought back to that place—these feelings getting stronger the more I push them away.

I walk back into my kitchen hoping that making myself something to eat may settle these feelings. I open the freezer, the slight flurry that greets me helps my adrenaline further subside. I reach in, grabbing two frozen waffles before putting the box back and closing the door. I walk over to the corner of my kitchen with my toaster and drop the two waffles into the slots, pulling the little lever down, watching them disappear between the heating metal.

I head back into my living room to turn up the TV. Not that I'm even watching *Captain America* anymore, but I want to be surrounded by more noise. I'm momentarily distracted by Captain America and Red Skull's fight scene, when I hear a sudden pop behind me. All of a sudden, my heart jumps into my throat, and I throw myself to the ground, the noise sounding all too familiar.

I squeeze my eyes shut as I'm all of a sudden back in my classroom thinking of all the ways I could contort my body to cover as many of my students as possible.

I'm frozen.

Can't move.

Can't think.

Can't breathe.

I don't know how long I'm there, a few minutes at least, frozen on the floor of my living room. Then, just beyond my palms plastered against my ears, I hear three quiet knocks on my door. I squeeze my eyes tighter, balling my hands into fists, bringing them together at my chest, reopening the cuts that were beginning to heal, scared to breathe.

From the other side of the door, I hear a level voice.

"Drew?" My knees squeeze up further into my abdomen. "Are you okay?"

I don't move.

I can't find my voice.

I can't find my breath.

"I heard a loud noise. It sounded like a fall." A pause. Then again, "Drew?"

The voice speaking to me is clear and monotone, almost like he doesn't want to alarm me. I hear the doorknob twist slightly, and my chest feels like it's about to explode. My body is paralyzed in fear as I realize I forgot to lock the door when I came back from throwing my garbage away this morning.

"Drew? It's Emmett. The door is unlocked. I'm going to slowly open the door and come in, okay?"

Eyes still clamped shut, body still glued to the floor, I hear the whisper of footsteps walk through the entryway, through the kitchen, getting closer to me. The smell of burning waffles ruminating in the air.

"Drew, it's okay." He pauses, probably looking around. "I think your toaster popped your waffles out. It must have caught you off guard." His voice is just a few feet above me as he explains the scene to both himself and me. I hear his voice again, and it's closer. He must be kneeling next to me. "It's okay. You're in your apartment." He doesn't try to touch me, but I can feel his presence around me. "You're safe."

I slowly uncurl my fists and lengthen my body from the fetal position I was in. I let my arms spread from my body, and my palms sting as the air meets my reopened wounds. I set my hands down on the floor to stop them from shaking as I peel open my eyes and push up from the floor to rest on my elbows. My eyes prickle a little as my tears meet the air and as I adjust to the light.

"Can you stand?" Emmett asks. His voice is tender and nurturing—two words I never would have used to describe him until today.

I feel his eyes on me, concerned and burning into me like he has no intention of looking away. I slowly nod once, pushing my body up a little more so I'm in a sitting position.

Emmett reaches his hand out to me to help me stand, but I hesitate a moment. My eyes are cloudy, and my brain is foggy. I'm unsure of how I should be reacting or responding at this moment. But I take his hand anyway, the warmth of him taking over me as if it was injected into my veins.

He closes his hand around mine, and I don't know if he doesn't notice the cuts in my palms or chooses to ignore them. Regardless, the relief I feel is almost instant. I feel my lungs fill with air again. My heart beat begins to slow. My body releases the tension it held during those moments I was brought back to the only time in my life I felt true fear.

Fear for my life.

Fear for the ones I love most.

As I stand, I feel Emmett's other arm slowly wrap around my waist to help me balance. It's like every move he makes is slow and calculated, as if wanting me to feel his movements before he makes them. As if he's scared I'll see him as a threat.

He helps me take the few steps to my couch, ushering me to sit. His eyes never leave me. I sit, and he follows, his hand still gently holding mine, his arm never untangling from around me. My breathing is still a little fast—my heartbeat still slightly filling my ears.

Then, without a word, Emmett takes a deep breath in, and I turn to meet his gaze. Without even thinking about it, I copy his lifted chest and open mouth with a deep breath of my own. I fill my whole body up before matching his exhale and letting it all go. I feel my mind clear a little more.

We do the same thing two more times, still without exchanging anything aside from our gazes, still in his arms.

After I let out a final exhale, feeling like I can breathe normally again, he asks, "Are you okay?"

I don't even take a second to think before saying, "No."

His lips slightly curl and the worry in his eyes begins to fade as he moves the arm from around my waist to brush the hair from my face, tucking it behind my ear. My cheeks tingle as his fingertips linger.

"And, that's okay," he says.

CHAPTER 18

DREW

AT SOME POINT—I'M not exactly sure when, or if it was happening so slowly I couldn't *tell* it was happening—I melt into Emmett, his embrace, his warmth, his presence, as we sit on the couch. My head found the place between his chin and his shoulder, and the hand holding his found his chest. Both of his arms were around me, pulling me into him.

Captain America ended sometime between my toaster popping and him coming up here, but the quietness surrounding me is tolerable when he was around.

I feel *safe*.

I let myself sink into the moment, letting my eyes wander his bare forearms, captivated by the intricate lines and shading, alluring canvases of black ink.

Without warning, my body, so overwhelmed with fatigue, relentlessly relaxes, my eyes falling shut before I can protest.

———

Hours later, the sunshine invades my bedroom through the uncovered window begging my eyes to open. The brightness is intense due to the reflection bouncing off the brand new snow mounds lining the streets. The clouds are scarce, revealing the light blue sky after a few days of gray, swollen clouds.

It must have snowed all night, ceasing sometime early this morning.

Wait, morning?

Is it the morning?

Is it tomorrow?

I sit straight up and look around to see I'm in my bed but don't remember getting here. My apartment is empty, the living room TV on at a low volume, the lights off.

When did I fall asleep?

I rack my brain, trying to remember what led me here, and the series of events that unfolded yesterday morning comes back to me.

Holy shit.

Emmett.

Last thing I remember, we were on the couch. I must have fallen asleep, but, that doesn't explain how I slept until *tomorrow*. I got out of bed around 8 a.m. yesterday, and Emmett must have come up an hour or so after that.

When he heard me fall to the ground.

When he found me frozen to the floor.

When he helped me to the couch.

I don't know how long we were there, but there's no way I actually slept until tomorrow.

I glance at my bedside table to see my phone on the charger.

Did I put it there?

Either way, I check the time—8 a.m.

Holy shit. Again.

I slept until tomorrow.

I'm still in the pajamas I woke up in yesterday, but I don't remember walking to my bed. I don't remember anything past my head slowly falling on to Emmett's chest. I must have fallen asleep, and Emmett must have carried me to bed.

But I can't even begin to think about how embarrassing that is, or the flutter teasing my stomach because I am too stuck on the fact that I slept for almost twenty-four hours.

Twenty-four hours without a single nightmare.

Twenty-four hours where my body sunk into my bed.

Twenty-four hours undisturbed by my mind.

Twenty-four hours of rest.

I was running on empty because there is no other way I would have been able to sleep so hard for so long.

I make my way to the bathroom to brush my teeth, shower, and get dressed in clothes other than pajamas or lounge wear. I put some coffee on and take a seat on my couch while I wait for it to brew. A woodsy, vanilla smell still lingering on the cushions.

Emmett, this gruff, angst-y guy, dressed in all black, with tattoos and a permanent scowl. Every time we were in the elevator together, I was left thinking how he couldn't get away from me fast enough.

Now, I'm left thinking how he showed me a side of him yesterday that was patient and protective.

And it definitely was not patience or protectiveness I experienced from him before.

Ever.

These had to be traits he learned through his own experiences, through his own hardships, maybe even through his own *trauma*.

He knew what to say.

He knew what to do.

He was *there*.

My stomach growls, pulling my attention from Emmett back to reality. Proud of myself for waking up with an appetite, I throw a frozen pizza into the oven, but instead of setting the timer, I make a mental note of the time—8:30 a.m.

Not the best breakfast choice, but at least it's better than grabbing the last Pop-Tart package.

I walk into the living room to turn up the volume of the TV a little more, so the voices of Nick, Jess, Schmidt, and Winston are loud enough to make out what they are saying, rather than just a mumble in the background.

Emmett must have seen the show in my "recently watched" because I know it wasn't on when Emmett was here. The episode has about ten minutes left, so I tell myself to check the pizza when it ends.

As I watch, knowing almost every line, my thoughts begin to wonder about yesterday. Is it normal to have the reaction to the toaster that I did? Probably not. Is it healthy to be too afraid of my reaction to set a timer on the oven? Again, probably not. Should I be keeping myself awake long enough to the point I pass out on my neighbor and sleep twenty-four hours? Once again, probably not.

When the next episode begins to queue up, I check the pizza and see it could use a few more minutes, but when I open the oven, a wave of heat envelops me, filing the air with the smell of baking crust, melted cheese, and a slight scent of oregano. I don't have the patience to wait because my stomach is eating itself. I grab an oven mitt to pull it out, not being able to wait for the edges to crisp up.

I didn't realize how hungry I was until I went to grab another slice of pizza to find that I had already finished the whole thing.

Now, I'm back on my couch, reading a book (that I double-checked was *not* part of a series) that isn't piquing my interest as much as other books I've read this past week, The sun is high now, telling me it's the afternoon, and I hear my phone buzz for the first time in a few hours.

Thinking it is likely one of my parents texting me with the intent of making themselves feel better, I pick it up to clear the notification.

But, to my surprise, I see it's from Emmett.

Wait, I don't have his number, I think to myself.

I look to see a past message, dated to yesterday, sent from me to him.

All it says is *Drew.*

He must have texted himself to have my number, and I'm not sure if I should be flattered or frightened… What I do know is I am definitely flustered at the fact that our relationship of neighbors who butt heads and who only recently saw each other outside of the apartment elevator has escalated to the point where we have each other's number. I find myself smiling with anticipation as I look at the message from today.

> Hey, it's Emmett. Hope you got some good sleep. How are you feeling?

There he goes again, saying the right things and asking the right questions. I realize, after re-reading the text once more, that the difference between Emmett and Reed, or Emmett and Lacey, or Emmett and my parents is that Emmett, even practically being a stranger, has never once *told* me I'm okay. Or *told* me I'm fine.

I know they all mean well, but they don't know. They don't understand what it means to be okay after going through something only fit for nightmares. The word has a completely different meaning to me now.

Yes, I'm lucky to be alive.

Yes, I'm lucky to have gotten out of there unharmed, but living through a trauma doesn't make me feel okay or fine *or lucky.*

It makes me feel infuriated.

It makes me feel helpless.

It makes me feel broken.

But no one has asked me how I am. No one has asked me how I'm feeling.

No one besides Emmett.

CHAPTER 19
EMMETT

IT SOUNDED like Drew got up around eight o'clock, showered, and went about her day. All of which I was happy to hear . . . Literally.

I hope she ate something too.

The movements ceased for a few hours this morning, so I thought maybe she was napping, but then I heard something like a remote or maybe a book fall, which told me she was doing something to keep her mind at bay.

When I was in her apartment yesterday, it was the first time I felt like I gained a glimpse of who she was—what she liked, what she did, and how she spent her free time.

I felt her fall asleep on me, and I didn't want to move. I tried my hardest not to disturb her because I wasn't sure how much sleep she's gotten since I heard her screaming on Christmas Day—three days ago.

I haven't heard anything like that coming from up there since then, which makes me assume she hasn't been sleeping at all.

Those kinds of nightmares don't just stop.

When her breathing steadied and tension in her body released, I knew I couldn't risk moving and waking her up, so

I just looked around—taking in her space, taking in her breath, taking in what I felt having my arms around her.

It's hard for me to describe how I felt when I heard her fall to the floor, but I didn't even hesitate when I heard that thud.

Finding her in that position, glued to the floor, her knuckles white, her eyes squeezed shut, I felt this immense crack in my chest as my heart broke for her. I wanted nothing more than to take the pain away, wanting to do anything I could to make her feel better.

Instead of running towards her, taking her into my arms, and never letting go, I slowly walked to her, making sure she could sense my every move. I felt like I was approaching an injured fawn, too scared to move but could bolt at any second.

When she took my hand, I wished I could absorb the struggle. I wished I could stop the battle in her head, the battle I knew all too well.

The battle between wanting to forget and wanting to heal.

After about an hour, I carried her to her bed. I didn't want her to wake up, but I also didn't want her to feel embarrassed for falling asleep on me, so I figured leaving before she opened her eyes was the best way to avoid that.

I would have stayed all day—not having anywhere else I would rather be—but my better judgment convinced me otherwise.

When I hooked my arms under her legs, pulling her onto my lap, her breathing didn't even shift. I figured she wouldn't be waking up anytime soon.

I felt this strange twirl in my stomach carrying her into her bedroom, and I couldn't figure out if it was a good thing or a bad thing. What I was doing felt intimate, but a little invasive. Drew and I are getting to know each other more and more, but under circumstances that are anything but ideal. I feel like we're connected on a level I don't quite understand, but I'm not sure she feels the same.

I placed her down carefully on her unmade bed and pulled the covers over her, hoping the state of peace I saw on her face was the same state of peace her mind was in now.

I found her phone in the kitchen and texted myself, so I could save my number in her phone. I'm not quite sure of the support system she has, but one more person can't hurt.

At least that is what I told myself.

I can't help but be a little selfish when it comes to this girl.

I plugged her phone into the charger by her bedside and then went back to the kitchen to clean up, hoping that by getting rid of the mess it would help alleviate any extra stress when she woke up.

When I got back to my apartment later that morning, I was surprised with myself. I acted so much on instinct that it almost felt like an out-of-body experience. I tried to only do what Drew needed—whatever I could do to make her eyes open, her shoulder drop, her knuckles uncurl, her breathing steady . . . and we barely even talked.

I don't think she said anything the whole time I was there.

When we sat down on the couch, and I took in a deep breath, she mirrored me. She understood what I was saying without either of us saying a single word.

I rack my brain for a time I felt a connection like that with anyone else, and nothing comes to mind. I can't think of a time—even with Riley—where I felt *responsible* for shielding someone from all the things that darken us.

Yet, I didn't even hesitate with Drew.

Then again, Riley never shined as bright as Drew.

And I don't like seeing Drew's light so dim.

When Riley left, I thought it would feel like when Lennon died. I thought I would have no choice but to welcome the ache in my chest and the dull pain in my stomach when I thought about her packing up her things and never coming back.

I thought I would wake up in cold sweats grasping for the figure that resembled Riley in my dreams—going through the day with a sense of uneasiness that made even the simplest of tasks difficult.

But, to my surprise, none of that ever happened. Instead, I felt a sense of freedom and empowerment, as if the eggshells I had been walking on for the entirety of my and Riley's relationship vanished. My bed didn't feel empty, it just felt bigger. My place didn't feel lonely, it just felt quiet. My life didn't feel upended, it felt like it was *mine*.

It didn't feel like the aftermath of losing Lennon, and I didn't spend much time missing Riley like I thought I would.

It's early evening now, and Drew texted me back a little while ago, thanking me for yesterday and letting me know that she was feeling very well-rested.

The conversation dwindled after I sent a message reminding her to let me know if she needed anything, to let me know.

She just "liked" my message, showing me she received it but not having more to say.

CHAPTER 20
DREW

"CAN you believe I just spent an entire week watching my family hang on every single word my brother said?"

Lacey has been doing a bulk of the talking since we sat down for lunch, giving me all the details about her trip to Seattle, work, and her girlfriends from college and what they're up to.

We decided to hit up a spot that has a Happy Hour starting at 3 p.m. with a wine-by-the-glass special, so we finished eating lunch about half an hour ago, and now we are just continuing our conversation over a glass of wine.

This restaurant is in the same parking lot as a few other stores, including a Barnes & Noble. If I feel up to it, maybe I'll walk over there before I head home. I would like to start the next book in the series I started, and I'm sure they have it.

"Actually, I can." I laugh. "What's he even up to these days? Still with that girl from our high school?"

"Absolutely not," Lacey scoffs. "And I know that because my grandma kept saying how *'that girl just wasn't good enough for our Sal.'*" She laughs a humorless laugh as she picks up her glass of wine. "In reality, I think that girl was smart, and *she* dumped *him*. Sal seemed down anytime someone mentioned it, so I think there's more to it than he's leading on." She takes a sip of her wine. "He needs to be single for a while anyway."

I grab my glass to take a sip as I listen to her continue. "Anyway, enough about Sal. He's been the topic of conversation for far too long. What's been new with you?"

I freeze mid-sip before setting my glass down, feeling my hands get a little sweaty. Lacey must be able to sense my change in demeanor because she rephrases, "I'm sure it's been nice to be home! How have you been spending your Winter Break?"

I rub my hands on my thighs, the fabric of my leggings alleviating the moisture. I feel my brain beginning to spiral. Do I tell her about Reed? If I do, that'll lead to when she called me after it happened, and I didn't tell her. That will then lead to the grocery store which will probably somehow lead to the toaster incident, and if I bring that up, that will lead to having to talk about Emmett and what's happening with my once-grumpy neighbor turned person who keeps seeing me in my worst possible moments who I also can't get out of my head.

"Oh, you know, reading, watching movies, cleaning. Nothing too exciting. How's Tyler?" I try to change the subject, not wanting Lacey to notice that the nonchalant, calm demeanor I am trying to project is nowhere near what is actually going on in my head.

Lacey takes another sip of her wine, trying to find my eyes that are now glued to anything but hers.

"He's good," she says with a hint of concern. "But I want to talk about you." She reaches across the table opening her hand. I slowly bring a hand from my lap to grab on to hers and feel my thoughts begin to slow down. "Seriously, I'm worried about you. Do you want to talk about what happened?"

I inhale and somehow manage to meet her eyes, "Honestly, it's been hard." I feel my voice quiver and a familiar sting in my eyes. Lacey squeezes my hand, telling me, without words, she wants me to continue and that she is there for me. "Well, for starters, Reed showed up at my place the day after you left. He and I haven't talked in weeks, and he just showed up expecting me to fall into his arms." I shake my head and let out a breath already feeling a weight lift off my shoulders by telling her.

"Wait, are you guys still, like, together?"

I take my hand back to grab my wine glass. I take a sip before answering her question. "Not really. We haven't talked since November, but he said he saw the news and wanted to make sure I was okay. It was a nice gesture, but–"

"But nothing." Lacey's brow furrows and her voice has an edge. "You don't have to justify how you felt about him showing up."

"I know, but then he mentioned what happened, and, I don't know, I just couldn't talk about it." I feel the familiar tightening in my chest at what we are alluding to. "Either way, I felt like an asshole for closing the door on him. I texted him an apology later that day, but I guess he and I are back to not talking."

Lacey nods, still holding on to her wine glass. She doesn't say anything, but I can tell she wants to. I take another sip of wine, realizing it is the last one. I set my glass down and let out a sigh.

"You do know you don't owe Reed anything, right?" Her words catch me slightly off guard. "You don't need to apologize for dealing with… what you're dealing with."

"No, I know that, but—"

"But nothing, Drew." She sets her glass down before reaching across the table asking for my hands again. I reciprocate her reach, and she takes both my hands in hers. "You have been letting Reed have this hold on you for too long. You don't owe him for dumping him in high school, and you most certainly don't owe him an explanation for not wanting to talk to him after what happened at your school." I see her eyes begin to cloud and feel mine do the same, thankful that she is acknowledging that day but still talking around it.

"Drew, honey, I saw you that day," she begins. "I saw what it did to you. I saw what you looked like after walking out with your students, and Reed, of all people, has no right to make you feel guilty for not being ready to talk about it."

No. No, I can't talk about this.

I pull my hands away from hers and wipe the tears starting to fall. "Lace, no. I can't talk about this. I don't want to talk about this."

"Okay, okay. I'm sorry. You're right. I just hate seeing him have this hold over you." She leans back, letting go of my hands. I notice she wipes the corner of her left eye and then looks at me sympathetically. A few beats of silence pass before she says, "So, aside from this run-in with Reed. What else have you been up to?"

I take this opportunity to change the subject and begin filling her in on the books I've been reading, letting her know I finally read the thriller she recommended. I tell her about my plan to watch the Marvel movie series, per the MCU order, and we laugh about how I could barely get through the first one—reminiscing about when we saw it in theaters.

I strategically leave out the toaster incident that happened during the end of *Captain America* because I want to avoid talking about Emmett, but I accidentally slip that I can't keep my TV above a certain volume level because it upsets my neighbor, and that grabs her attention even more.

"Wait, is this the same neighbor you see in the elevator? Who made fun of the music you listen to?"

Leave it to Lace to remember that tiny detail I don't even remember telling her. I probably mentioned pissing off my grumpy downstairs neighbors in one of our text exchanges over the past few months, but I didn't think she would keep track of it.

"Yeah, that's Emmett. He lives below me, and he is the grumpiest, most frustrating man I've ever met. And, he hates me." I flush, remembering how I caught him staring at me at the grocery store or how he stayed with me in my apartment until I fell asleep. "Well, sort of hates me." I divert my eyes.

"Um, what do you mean 'sort of' and why are you blushing?" I take my hands and press them against my cheeks to cool them down.

"I'm not blushing. It's just the wine."

"Don't you dare. Spill it."

I sigh and decide to give her the abridged version of when I ran into him at the grocery store, only explaining how he was nice and polite compared to times I ran into him before that. "But, no, I know what you're thinking and, while he is hot, tall, and tattooed, with a possible sensitive side, he is nothing more than my downstairs neighbor."

"If you say so," she responds with a smirk. And I know very well there is no truth to those words of hers.

Thankfully, Lacey senses that this conversation about Emmett—most likely by the way I was stuttering and turning red from both my frustration and confusion about him—can be left alone for now. She changes the subject back to when she and Tyler first met, sneakily hinting at how they were former enemies, competing for the same college, turned lovers. We end up reminiscing on the last time we were at this restaurant a few weeks after she met Tyler.

We end the lunch smiling, but I can't get what she said about Reed out of my head. I feel a sense of doubt that I haven't had since the last time she and I argued over my relationship with Reed, and I hate the fact that the doubt found its way back into my gut.

As we walk out of the restaurant, she grabs my hand. We walk hand-in-hand to our cars parked next to each other.

"I'm here for you, Drew. Always." She pulls me in for a hug. I feel some of the dull pressure in my chest that I have come so accustomed to begin to alleviate the longer I am in her arms.

She whispers into my ear, "And, I'm here when you're ready to talk about it." She pulls me in even tighter before letting go and giving me a smile. As she opens the car door and climbs into the driver's seat, she turns back to me and says, "Oh, and make sure you get out of that apartment more, okay? Maybe you'll run into someone hot, tall, and tattooed with a mysterious sensitive side."

I can't help but let out a laugh at her quoting what I said about Emmett as she winks at me and closes the car door, giving me a wave through the window before pulling away.

I'm left thinking that maybe staying out of the apartment may be good for me after all.

CHAPTER 21
DREW

I CRUISE through the romance section at Barnes & Noble, looking for books two and three of the Hades and Persephone series I started by mistake but now am greatly invested in. I'm glad to be here in the early evening, avoiding most of the crowd.

Seeing Lacey really upped my spirits, and I feel a pep in my step I have not had in a while, but it doesn't cancel out the anxiety of being outside the familiar space of my apartment. With my headphones in, listening to Stand Atlantic's album, *Pink Elephant*, I focus on the colorful shelves in front of me, occasionally finding myself distracted by books I'm not looking for but might still be coming home with me.

Being out feels different now.

I have this sense of anxiety hanging over me when I walk around in a crowd of people, unaware of what those around them are going through. I feel like running errands and being out and about should feel *normal*. I never had an issue with it before, but my idea of normal is no longer reality.

It was a *normal* day when someone decided to bring a gun into a middle school.

It was a *normal* day when someone took away my students' sense of security.

It was a *normal* day when my life was changed forever.

I find the next two books of the series and tear myself away from the shelves before I leave with more than I came for. I get in line at the check-out, taking one of my headphones out, and listen to a chaotic mix of Bonnie Fraser's vocals and cashiers asking for phone numbers for Barnes & Noble memberships.

When it's my turn to check out, I give my books to the cashier. I'm only half listening as she tells me how much she *loves* this series and how, if I come back, I *have* to let her know how I like it. She is young and enthusiastic, probably just working to earn the extra holiday pay, and I think I would appreciate her small talk on any other day.

But today, I just want her to give me my books and let me be on my way.

"Are you a Barnes & Noble member?" she asks as she scans the books' barcodes.

"No, but I have the educator's discount." Her enthusiasm withers away at my mention of being a teacher.

"Did…" she treads carefully, avoiding my eyes and staring at the screen in front of her. "Did you know anyone?"

My face or my hesitation must show her my confusion because then she adds in a whisper, "From that shooting?"

Instantly, and without warning, I'm brought back to my classroom. Terror and gunshots making my ears explode. My eyes fill up with water as my throat goes dry. I feel my entire body tense. My chest tightens around my heart, making the beat of it quicken.

I need to move.

I need to get out of here before I'm trapped.

I don't even care if I look crazy, don't even care if I'm making a scene. My breathing is getting shallow, and my lungs are screaming for air. I find the will to unglue my feet from the tiled floor and run out of the store as quickly as I can, sprinting to my car, tears falling from the corners of my eyes, trailing down my cheeks and down my neck.

I finally find solace in the driver's seat.

This isn't healthy.

I can't be brought back to this place at any given moment.

I need to face this.

I need to overcome this.

I grip the steering wheel with my hands and lightly set my head down, touching my forehead to the cool leather. I stay in this position and wait until my heartbeat returns to normal before turning on the car and making my way home.

I'll buy the books online.

———

I pull into the garage, park my car, turn off the ignition, and take a breath. I cannot wait to be back in my own space. I head to the elevator, empty-handed and overwhelmed.

My mind is racing with all the thoughts I have been pushing down. All of the thoughts I need to face because I know I'm no more than a second away from freezing at any given moment, or losing my breath and not being able to get it back—the adrenaline pumping through my body making me feel like my heart will burst from my chest.

I can't live in this state of being so wound up, I could explode at any moment.

The elevator dings, and the doors open. I step in, almost immediately feeling the sense of relief I have been chasing since leaving the bookstore, but I'm no longer alone.

"Fancy seeing you here." Emmett takes a step towards me, pushing himself off the elevator wall. He smiles at me as if seeing me has just brightened his day.

He is in his usual attire of black jeans and a black hoodie, and if I was feeling like myself, I may have commented on how he stole my look, seeing as I am dressed in the same fashion: black leggings and a black sweater.

I force a smile back, but I know he can see through it.

"Everything okay?" he asks, eyebrows tightening with concern.

I sigh, stepping through the doorway, forgetting to push the button for my floor. "I will be." I lean back against the wall, closing my eyes and taking in a breath.

I hear the click of a button being pushed and then feel Emmett take a step closer to me, matching my position. The doors make a creaking sound as they close, and I feel Emmett's outer arm brush up against mine, but the touch doesn't go away. His hands are in his pockets, but his arm stays gently pressed against mine, and it overwhelms me with stability. I begin to feel like his slight touch is strong enough to hold up my entire body.

I exhale, my head falling to the side, resting against his arm, only finding the space just below his shoulder because he is so much taller than me.

Without another word, the cab rides us up, making me feel even more grounded as the bottom of my shoes press against the floor of the elevator. I don't move from the position we're in, and neither does Emmett. Not until the elevator stops, and I open my eyes, bringing my head back to its upright position as the doors open.

I push myself off the wall and take a few steps out of the elevator, assuming this is where we part. The realization of resting my head against my cranky neighbor in the same elevator he has told me I'm the worst person to live below hits me hard, and I feel the blood rush up to my cheeks.

I don't even turn around to say goodbye, instead wanting to get out of there as quickly as possible, I pick up my pace heading for my apartment. Without a word, Emmett takes one large step to match my three small ones, and he walks next to me as we exit the elevator and head to my front door.

As we walk, his hands are no longer in his pockets, and the outside of my hand skims against one of his, sending heat to my skin that touches him, making me blush even more.

My mind is racing as we walk. I feel Emmett stealing glances my way as we make our way down the hallway, not knowing what look is in his eyes because I keep my head down. I don't want to risk looking up at him and showing him the shade of red my cheeks are.

I keep my eyes on my feet as I walk, but I think I like being the product of his gaze. My body definitely is having a reaction to it.

"Hey, D."

I look up for the first time and feel the blood that was congregating in my face drain, as if I'm seeing a ghost.

Reed's smile crumples when he sees Emmett at my side. I watch as Reed's glances shift between my face to Emmett's, having to look a few inches up to meet Emmett's eyes. Reed is tall compared to me, standing at six feet, but I'm only five-three, so most people tower over me. His frame is slender, his flannel filling him out more than his actual body. His brown hair always looks tousled and falls on his forehead, just above his blue eyes. He's wearing a black knit hat and a black and gray flannel over a black Carhartt t-shirt. He has his work boots on and blue jeans, and his hands have their usual tint of black from working underneath cars all day.

Emmett on the other hand, standing at least six-four, makes Reed look *small*. His features are sharper compared to Reed's round face and button nose, and Emmett's look is nothing like Reed's. Emmett's hair is twisted in a bun on the crown of his head with a few curls framing his face. He's wearing black skinny jeans with Vans, and a black hoodie with the design of the Grim Reaper skateboarding with the words "SK8 or DIE" on the back.

Trying his hardest to hide his surprise *or distaste* from seeing Emmett, Reed turns his eyes to me. "I came to see if you were feeling better. You were super out of it when I was here a few days ago."

"You didn't text me back," I say.

"So? I'm here now. You're okay now, right?"

This is exactly what I don't need. I feel myself getting worked up again, the same way I felt at the check-out at Barnes & Noble today, or how I felt looking at the resources the district sent me. I'm starting to feel my chest tighten and my heart beat faster, but I try to swallow the feelings because my fists clench at the thought that he is here. Again. And he is *telling* me how to feel.

How is it that butterflies used to overtake my stomach around Reed? Now, I have a pool of anger bubbling.

"Hey, man. I'm Emmett. I'm Drew's neighbor," Emmett interjects, and he extends his hand to Reed who does not take his eyes off me. Emmett has to move in a little closer to me to try and meet Reed's gaze, so his arm crosses in front of me, putting a minor barrier between Reed and me.

Reed pretends there is no one besides us here. "You busy? I thought we could hang out," Reed continues. Emmett drops his arm but keeps his closeness to me.

At this moment, I don't know what comes over me, but I feel myself fuming, words piling in my throat, ready to projectile vomit at that statement.

"Yeah, I'm busy." I grit through my teeth, even though I'm not busy at all. I don't want to be anywhere near Reed right now.

"C'mon, Drew." Reed takes a step closer to me, and I feel Emmett tense at my side, his gaze shifting between me and Reed. "I miss you, D." His smirk makes my stomach twist as he grabs my belt loop. He uses two fingers to wrap around the material and tug at my hips, trying to bring me closer to him. It is a gesture that used to make me swoon, but right now, I feel like I want to throw up.

In the corner of my eye I see Emmett's hands turn to fists —knuckles white.

Something comes over me. I push Reed back and he has to steady himself on his feet. "Hang out? You mean fuck?"

His mouth drops open at the harshness of my tone, and his eyes widen. I have never given him this response before, not in all the years we have known each other.

I feel Emmett's mood shift too, all of a sudden focusing on me, and me only, and what I'm going to say next.

"Because that's what we do? Right, Reed? That's all we've done for the past five years. Because we aren't in a relationship." I feel all the blood rush to my head, making my temples pound. "I don't owe you an explanation as to why I seemed so 'out of it.' You don't even know me. You don't know what I'm going though, and you sure as hell don't get to come here and tell me that I'm *okay*." My voice is slowly growing in volume. "Do you really think I'm okay, Reed? Do I *look* okay?"

I pause, long enough to allow him to ponder my question but not long enough to answer. "Do you think I'm okay after hearing *gunshots* across the hall from my classroom? Do you think I'm okay after *begging* my students to help me build a *barricade*?" I am now yelling to release almost everything I've been holding in, and I don't care who hears. "Do you think I'm okay after *praying* to a higher power I don't even believe in to *stretch* my body enough to *shield* my kids in case the *shooter* got through the fucking door?"

The words pour out of me as if they've been on the tip of my tongue, and I can tell I have made Reed uncomfortable, but I do not have the energy to make *him* feel better about what I'm saying—what I'm feeling—when I don't even know how to do that for myself.

I find myself huffing and puffing after letting out the words, and Reed is frozen, still in front of my door, so I leave him with a few last words.

"Now, can you please move out of our way?"

CHAPTER 22
EMMETT

I FOLLOW Drew into her apartment. I can tell she still has steam blowing out of her ears from that interaction. I can't tell if she wants to be alone, or if she wants to talk, but I did notice that she told that guy to move out of *our* way.

I'm not sure, if she does want to talk, if she wants to talk to me. I stay put just inside the door, but I close it behind me to make sure that prick doesn't try to come in. He took a second to register once Drew unleashed all of her feelings on him, and I would have felt bad for the guy if he didn't completely bring that upon himself.

Drew had to ask him again to move, and when he finally stepped out of the way of the door, his face changed from surprise to disbelief, like he couldn't believe she had the audacity to not want to see him. Drew paces in her kitchen, back and forth, head down, arms crossed. I don't know what she's thinking, but I can't believe the kid just showed up unannounced like that, expecting to be invited in for...

For whatever it is they do.

I shake the thought away as Drew stops, in the middle of the kitchen, and turns to face me.

"I'm sorry," she says.

"What?" I ask, completely puzzled. "Why in the world are you sorry?"

"When we got in the elevator, you were headed to the garage. Were you on your way out?"

That's what she's thinking about right now?

"Don't feel like you have to stay," she adds. "I mean, you're welcome to, but I understand if you have somewhere you need to be." She steps closer to me.

I smile at her. Smiling has never been so easy when it comes to her. I feel like it is getting easier and easier to *feel* my emotions, raw and real, when she is in my vicinity.

Before I lose the nerve, I ask, "Can I buy you a drink?"

The walk over to Lenny's is quiet, no awkwardness and no talk of the incident outside her door, and it's nice.

Seeing her red hair in the moonlight, giving it a depth I've never seen before, has my mind running in circles that I doubt I would have been able to string together a sentence anyway.

It is a little after 5 p.m., so it is already dark enough to be the middle of the night. The light from the full moon accentuates the gold rings around her irises, almost making it look like her eyes are glowing, and I can't help but steal glances her way as if I can't see clearly unless I'm looking at her.

I wanted to be at the bar by five, but I guess that is one of the perks of being the boss: no one can tell you you're late.

I'm not sure if Drew knows where we're headed, so when we get closer to the door of Lenny's, I walk a few steps ahead of her to get to the door. The bar is on the same side of the road as the apartment complex, about a quarter mile down the street.

"I've never been here before," she says. "This is where you work, right?"

"This is the place." I feel heat creep up my neck, for once being the one whose body has a reaction I can't control, but there is no way it is enough for her to notice. I can't help but feel something at the thought she knows that little tidbit about me, even if it's not *exactly* true.

"Hey, boss!" Eddie shouts from behind the bar as we walk in. The group of regulars at the far end raise their drinks to me. I give them a wave, placing my hand on Drew's back to lead her to the less crowded end of the bar, the familiar smell of worn-in leather and whiskey filling our nostrils.

I can tell her eyes are on me as we walk through the Happy Hour crowd that will disperse when it ends in less than an hour.

I like to keep the light at Lenny's down, lit mostly by dim overhead lights and neon signs lining the walls—no light coming in due to minimal windows. Music is always playing —either my playlist or one of the bartenders'. The actual bar takes up most of the place, but high top tables and a few booths line the outside perimeter.

With everyone back to work after the holiday, the place is packed tightly for the half-priced beers, hard seltzers, and house wines.

I pull out the chair on the far end of the bar, and Drew hops up, her feet hanging because she is so short. We are right next to the back door that leads to my office, giving us a little area of our own. It is loud enough to know it isn't just us, but it is quiet enough for me to only focus on her.

"What can I get you?" I grab a towel from underneath the bar and wipe down the space in front of her before setting a coaster down. I throw the towel over my shoulder and place my palms on the bar, leaning in closer to her.

"Boss? Are you the manager or something?" Her eyes avoid mine as she takes in her surroundings.

"Or something." I clear my throat. "I'm actually the owner."

Her eyes wide, finally meeting mine.

Is she impressed?

"So yeah. Safe to say you're the boss."

I chuckle. "I guess so. My dad bought the place when I was five-years old, so I've been coming here forever. When he owned it, he called it Larry's. Very creative . . . for a guy named Larry." She laughs, and it's my new favorite sound.

"When my sister and I were old enough to work, we spent most of our time here."

"How did you end up taking it over?" she asks, resting her elbows up on the bar, balancing her head in her hands. She is looking at me as if I'm the most interesting person in the world, making my stomach flicker.

"My parents spend nine months out of the year in Florida, so I took it over from my dad around five years ago."

"What about your sister?"

I pause before answering, my smile slowly fading.

My instinctive response is to change the subject, but there is something about how Drew is looking at me that makes me want to open up myself to her.

I shy my eyes away, looking down at the ice bin below me. "My sister died a while back."

I can't bring my eyes back up to look at her, worried that the bomb I just dropped ruined the good thing we had going, not talking about the stuff that makes us sad.

I feel one of her hands over one of mine, my eyes finding their way to hers again.

"What was her name?"

Realizing, while I've thought about her plenty lately, I haven't said her name aloud since my last therapy session a few months ago.

I exhale. "Lennon."

CHAPTER 23
DREW

I FINALLY UNDERSTAND why Emmett and I can say so much to each other without opening our mouths.

"What was she like?" I ask, wanting him to feel the same ease with me as I do with him. Wanting him to share the part of him that is real and raw.

I see his face brighten as he recalls memories of his sister.

"Lennon was always the life of the party. Center of attention—all eyes on her." He lets out a chuckle. "She was two years younger than me, and I spent my time during her short life being her biggest fan. She could brighten up any room she walked in."

Emmett's smile is contagious, and I love seeing this side of him. I find myself wondering if his protective instinct I've seen hints of is from being an older brother.

"She sounds wonderful." My hand, still placed over his. "I'm so sorry for your loss."

"Thank you. I really appreciate you asking about her. I feel like everyone in my life just *forgot* about her." I see the sadness in his smile trying to overwhelm the happiness.

"So," he says, ending the conversation for now, slipping

his hand out from underneath mine to clap his together. "About that drink?"

"Do you have a White Claw?" I ask, sitting back in my chair.

"I have Truly."

I stick my tongue out in disgust letting out a fake gag. "Truly?! Those are the worst hard seltzers! I'll take a vodka club with a lime, please."

I can tell he's amused by my declaration of my least favorite hard seltzer brand on the market. "Is that your drink of choice when you go out? A double, I assume?" he asks, grabbing a glass and filling it with ice.

He moves with an ease behind the bar, like it is second nature, not even having to think about what he is doing.

He grabs the vodka bottle and pours two shots without even having to measure—not waiting for me to hear if I actually wanted a double, but it's a rightful assumption after what he just witnessed in front of my apartment.

"On the off chance I go out, yes. Either that or a lime White Claw."

"Interesting. I feel like I'm learning a lot about you lately." He tops the glass with the club soda from his bar gun, grabbing a straw at the same time.

He sets the drink down in front of me on the coaster he set out when I sat down, catching me staring at him as he works. I blush a little, not only because he caught me but because I like the way he looks here.

In his bar.

He moves with a rhythm of experience, and he looks like he is in his element. Smiling, surrounded by people who respect him, in a place that he owns.

A place he named after his sister.

The smell of the alcohol, mixed with the glass of wine I had earlier with Lacey, allows me to release my inhibitions and ask, "And aside from my drink choices, what else have you learned about me?" I take a few sips of my drink, carefully watching him as he grabs a glass from the sink to the left of him, drying it with the towel he had hanging over his shoulder, placing it on the stack of glasses at the end of the bar.

I like that he chose a spot near the back. It is secluded, and I can put all my focus on him.

"You like to read."

"Did I tell you that?"

"No, but I saw the bookshelves in your apartment, and I've seen you come home with Barnes & Noble bags a couple times, so I assume you go there to buy books."

"Great assumption. If you were one of my students, I would praise you for using your context clues."

He laughs, and I'm a little surprised with myself for talking about my job with such ease.

"I was actually there today. Barnes & Noble that is," I add, taking another sip of my drink, not warning to expand more on my prior comment.

"No good ones to bring home today?"

"It's kind of a long story."

"Good thing I have no other place to be for"—he pauses and checks his wrist that doesn't even have a watch on it—"the rest of the night." He wears a proud grin at his cheesy joke. I give up and let him have a laugh.

Emmett listens to my every word as I tell him about what happened as I was checking out at the bookstore earlier today. He doesn't say much aside from a question here or there, asking to understand the whole picture.

"And the worst part? I didn't even get the two books I wanted."

"What books were you there for?"

"Well, I have this annoying habit of reading a book I don't know is part of a series, so I was there to get the next two of a series I started." I slide out my phone from my back pocket and pull up the picture I saved to my camera roll, my way of creating a book-shopping list. "See? And look how pretty the covers are." He leans in to glance at my phone, a little confused, probably not relating to only choosing books with appealing covers. "I was so excited to have all three on my shelf. I'll probably just order them online."

He leans back, amused. He doesn't say a word, but I see him smirking at me

"What?" I ask.

"Nothing," he says. He clears his throat. "I think it's cool that you read. I'm not much of a reader, but I like hearing you talk about it."

I blush, wanting to keep this conversation going. "So, what else have you learned about me?" I take a few more sips.

"Well, I'm glad you asked." This time smiling with his teeth, and I feel like I just witnessed a blue moon. "If we're talking more recently, I learned that you have the meal choices of a picky teenager, seeing as your grocery cart contained freezer waffles and pizzas. You also have bad taste in Pop Tart flavors.

"But before learning all that, I know you own multiple pairs of the same exact jeans, some looking more worn and faded than others, and your music taste ranges from pop punk, to punk rock, to dad rock, which I assume depends on your mood. Also, you do this thing with your nose when you're nervous or deep in thought." He flares his nostrils while scrunching up his nose, showing me a habit I didn't even know I had.

Not knowing how to respond, my widened eyes and my crimson cheeks not helping me hide what I'm thinking, I feel like I'm about to fall out of my chair.

"And, you have an asshole boyfriend, no offense," he adds, this time with a wink that sends butterflies flying in my lower belly.

Damn.

I'm in awe. This guy probably knows more about me in the six months we've known each other than my whole family *and* the asshole boyfriend.

Ex-boyfriend.

"Wow," is all I can say.

I take a couple more sips of my drink, not sure if releasing my inhibitions more and asking questions I don't know I can handle the answers to is the best idea. But, also not really caring because this is the most relaxed *and normal* I've felt in days.

"You're definitely someone I like learning about." He sets his hands on the bar—on both sides of me—leaning in closer but just a little. His rolled up sleeves put his sculpted, inked forearms on display right in front of me.

"Ex-boyfriend." It comes out of my mouth before my mind can stop it.

Emmett cocks his head to the side, still looking at me.

"Reed is my ex-boyfriend. We broke up when we graduated high school."

"You broke up in high school?" I can tell that clarification made him more confused. "How long ago was that?"

"I graduated almost five years ago," I explain.

"So did he not get the memo, or?

"Well, living alone, I get lonely, so he comes over every now and then." I'm not really sure why I'm explaining this all to Emmett, but I'm finding the more I'm around him the more I feel like he sees the real me, the one I've been trying to hide, so I might as well tell him the things I don't share with anyone besides Lacey. I feel like this connection between Emmett and I is mutual . . . Even though I still feel embarrassed explaining the relationship Reed and I have.

"You guys have known each other for a long time, huh?" Emmett asks, and, for the first time, turns away from me to grab a bottle behind him.

"Yeah. He was my first love, taught me all there was to it, and he was always there for me. My parents were never really there when I needed them, but Reed always was." I notice Emmett paying a lot of attention to the drink he is making in front of him, more attention than I think he needs to based on my prior observations.

Why is he avoiding my eyes?

I continue, "I think he was trying to do the same now, but I wasn't ready to hear it.   I guess I'm the asshole for screaming at him like I did."

Emmett sets a new glass down on the bar with a tad more force than what is needed, making me jump a little. I notice a sharpness to his face, an intensity in his demeanor that was not there a second ago.

I can tell he realized how the noise made me react, and the sharpness slightly fades, but I can tell something I said upset him.

"Don't you dare feel bad about what you said to him. He had no business telling you that you seem 'out of it,' or *touching* you when you didn't want him to." The words seem to burn as they leave his mouth. I remember how the same intensity I feel radiating from him now is what I felt when he was standing next to me when I was telling Reed off.

Emmett doesn't even know all the details of Reed and my relationship, yet he is still saying the same things Lacey was saying earlier today.

What am I not seeing?

"What kind of prick thinks he has the right to ask for *anything* from someone who has gone through what you've gone through?" Emmett doesn't even seem to be talking to me now. He seems to be just talking, releasing the thoughts he must have been holding on to since we made our way over here.

"Emmett," I try to bring him back to me, "don't worry. I'm used to it—used to him. You don't have to worry about me." I try to subside the anger that is bubbling in him, not wanting him to waste any feelings on Reed. I feel a wave of warmth at the thought of Emmett looking out for me.

But, when my words leave my mouth, it is like everything Emmett and I have been through together the past few days disappears, and before me is the angst-y, brooding stranger in the elevator who wants nothing to do with me.

"Let Eddie know if you need anything else. Drinks are on the house. I'll see you around." Without another glance, he heads straight through the door that leads to the part of the bar that's for employees only.

And with that, I'm alone.

CHAPTER 24
EMMETT

HOW CAN Drew *defend* that son of bitch after he pushed her so far to the edge that she had to deal with those horrible thoughts and feelings she was having about what happened to her—*before* she was even ready to let them surface?

That guy doesn't know her—*understand her.*

He doesn't know what she's been through.

How too loud of noises bring her back to that day in her classroom.

How her mind and body were so tired following what happened she slept for a whole day.

How it's okay for her to not want to deal with other people telling her that she's okay. Or it's all going to be fine.

How it's okay for her to cope with what happened to her how *she wants to,* and she does not have to answer to anyone.

I'm pacing back and forth in my office, all of these thoughts clouding my vision.

I am livid.

I feel like my skin is heating up by the second, so I take my hoodie off and throw it over the chair by my desk.

The fact that this girl, this strong, courageous girl, lets someone like *that* dictate when she can feel lonely or not.

How a guy like *that* probably taught her that love has to be earned or that you have to do everything you can to keep someone loving you.

That's not what she deserves.

After a few minutes, I feel myself calming down, and my thoughts become clearer.

I have been saying it for months now.

This girl does something to me.

Especially now. I feel so *responsible* for her.

Not in a creepy, controlling way because I know she can handle herself—I saw how she stood up to that guy.

It's in more of a protective way. Again, I know she can hold her own, but I feel protective over her because I don't want anything to dim her light.

I don't want anything to make her sad or scared or feel like she's not strong.

She spends her days teaching a bunch of kids, probably not being paid enough, and she went through an unspeakable tragedy that some would argue is "part of the job."

I think she's amazing, and I want her to feel that way.

I want to be the one who protects her from anything or anyone that makes her feel otherwise.

I feel the guilt rush into my stomach when I realize how I just shut down and walked away from her. Drew was talking about Reed and their history, and, while it pissed me off how she gives him too much credit, I just walked away.

Fuck.

I rush back out to where the two of us were smiling with one another no more than ten minutes ago.

But Drew is gone.

I round the bar to where Eddie is talking to some regulars.

"Hey, Eddie. Did you see the girl I was talking to? Where'd she go?

"Sorry, man. She must have left." I turn to head towards

the door hoping I can catch her on the street. But before I can, I hear Eddie ask, "Hey, you never bring girls to the bar. Who is she?"

I can hear the eagerness in his voice. He's probably happy to see that everything that happened with Riley didn't leave me incapable of ever talking to a girl again.

Eddie never liked Riley.

I've known Eddie since college, when we roomed together freshman year at Whitewater. We both were getting some bullshit degrees just to say we had one. He came to work for me when my dad handed the place over, and Eddie's been the closest thing I've had to a best friend since Lennon died. He plays drums for a local band, splitting his time between band practice and here.

Eddie never liked how Riley refused to come to Lenny's or declined his invites to come see his band. She always used to say it was because she wasn't part of "that kind of crowd," but he didn't like how she seemed to look down on us.

When I proposed to Riley, Eddie acted like he was happy for me which I'm sure wasn't easy for him. A few nights after the proposal, it was just he and I closing up Lenny's, and he asked me if Riley was the woman I really wanted to be with.

I couldn't look him in the eye when I said yes.

He wasn't surprised when I called him not too long after that night asking him to be the boss for a few days while Riley and I moved her stuff out of my apartment and unknotted the parts of our lives that had become so intertwined. I knew Eddie would be my friend forever when all he said was, "Sure thing."

I thought for sure I was going to hear, "I told you so."

"She's my upstairs neighbor," I yell to him as I round the corner of the bar and make my way to the door. I don't even need to turn around to know that he's wearing his shit-eating grin.

"Sure she is," I hear him say.

"Shut up, Ramirez," I shout in his direction as I run out the door.

The sky is clear—the moon still shining—and there's no snow falling but it's definitely chilly. I didn't grab my hoodie from my office before running out, so I'm just in a t-shirt.

I can see my breath as I turn to make my way to the apartment complex. The burn in my lungs from running in the cold is nothing compared to the guilt I have about leaving my conversation with Drew like I did.

I get to the garage and check for her car out of habit. It's there—thankfully—so I run over to the elevator door and press the button. This time having no hesitation about find her.

It dings almost immediately, telling me that I got here just after someone else got in—just after the doors closed.

The doors open, and I'm met with my new favorite view.

There's nothing like catching Drew by surprise.

I'm thankful for the gust of wind from the garage for pushing her hair from her face, showing me her effortless beauty. The way her eyes—slightly widened—find mine. Her heart-shaped lips, slightly parted, make my heart stop.

She doesn't say anything, and neither do I.

I step into the elevator, moving to find my space next to her, close enough to feel her but not close enough to touch.

The elevator doors close, and I lean to push the button to my floor.

We start our way up. The only sound is the cart trudging along, the unoiled wires straining as we pass each floor.

Not knowing what else to say, but wanting to break the silence I know gets to her, I say, "Hey," while looking straight ahead at the closed doors in front of us.

"Hey," she says, doing the same.

I turn my head to face her, and I notice the redness in her

cheeks has faded since when I initially caught her off guard, except for at the tips of her cheekbones and across her nose, highlighting the clusters of freckles across that skin.

I wonder to myself if it's a reaction to me or a reaction to my drinks.

I'm not sure how much she drinks on a daily basis, but these past few days have probably kept her from sleeping and eating like she normally does so it is possible it's the latter.

Before I can say another word, the elevator spews an ear-spitting screech and drops, causing a gasp from both of us.

I hear the emergency brakes lock us in place as the lights shut off, heart pounding, my stomach in knots.

I turn to see Drew's head between her knees, covering her ears, trying to fuse into the bottom corner of the elevator.

Instinct takes over, and I push the Emergency Call button on the elevator, hoping that someone knows we're in here.

I grab my phone and check the time to see it's already 6 p.m. Maintenance guys usually wrap up their days around now, but I tell myself that there has got to be someone there who knows we are stuck. I tell myself that someone is going to do something, and it is not a priority to scream or call out.

My priority is to make sure Drew is okay.

The screech of the elevator was followed by eerie quietness, but when the light in the elevator cab shut off, any buzzing or movement ceased, making the silence unbearable.

My mind is racing as to what I should do to help Drew. My first thought is to help her to her feet, but we can't go anywhere. How will that help?

Before doing anything, I announce to her, "I'm going to kneel down next to you." Making sure I don't alarm her anymore.

I never should have left her at the bar, bringing her there and leaving her to walk home alone.

Why didn't I keep her smiling across from me?

I see her chest rising and falling at one hundred miles per hour.

I need to slow her breathing.

I sit down next to her and start inhaling and exhaling like I did in her apartment, but after three or four breaths, I don't see her following me like she did before.

"Drew, sweetheart, can you hear me?" Very slowly, I move my hand and place it on her back. She flinches at first, but then, as if pushing a button, her breathing starts to slow.

I exhale a breath of my own.

Our breathing, in and out, being the only sound in the elevator, and I know it probably is not loud enough for her.

Not knowing how else to break the silence, I pull out my phone and click on my Spotify app. I scroll through my recent listen and find *California* by Blink-182.

The Blink-182 album *without* Tom Delonge.

We listen to the first two songs, "Cynical" and "Bored to Death", just breathing and letting the music fill the silence in the air. Once I heard her breathing steady, I took my hand off her back and set it down on my leg. Without moving any other part of her, she reaches her arm towards me, her fingertips wrapping around mine, fitting so nicely.

After the third song—"She's Out Of Her Mind"—ends, Drew slowly lifts her head, her eyes hooking into mine. It is dark, but she is close enough for me to make out her features.

"Did I say something wrong?"

What?

"At the bar," she clarifies.

"No, no, of course not." I keep one hand still locked with hers but reach with my other hand to find her cheek. "Please don't think that." I move the loose hair that fell from her clip and tuck it behind her ear. Her cheeks feel warm under my touch.

"Then why'd you leave?"

I pause. Not sure how to say what I want to say. I feel myself wanting to look away from her, but her eyes are holding mine so tightly.

Then, I remember: this is Drew.

The last thing she needs is someone walking on eggshells around her or saying things that hold no meaning.

"I… I was mad that you were disregarding how that prick talked to you. I got pissed that you didn't see how selfish he was being towards you."

I notice her eyes start to glisten, filling with tears that I would do anything to stop. My hand is still cupping her cheek, and she places her hand over mine.

I continue, "You said *you* were the asshole for saying you needed space to not be okay. And that's not true. You have every right to not be okay." Some of the water welling up in her eyes escapes, cascading down her face. "When I heard you, describing what happened during the—" I stop myself, not wanting to say the word in case she wasn't ready to hear it.

"Shooting."

I guess she is ready.

Damn, she's strong.

"Yeah, the shooting." The word being said to her rather than coming from her mouth causes a slight flinch. "I wasn't sure if you were ready for those words to come out. It felt like he *pushed* you to explain yourself when he had no right to. Like he pushed you to speak about it before you were ready, and that's not fair to you."

As I say my piece, the tears begin to stream down her face, and I can't help but take her face in both of my hands, using my thumbs to wipe each and every one away as they fall, and she closes her eyes. My forehead leans in to meet hers, and I close my own eyes.

All of a sudden, the lights pop on, and we feel the elevator vibrate back to life, moving back up to the seventh floor as if the past minutes never happened.

The doors slowly open, showing me we have arrived at my stop. I slowly stand, helping Drew up as I rise and push the CLOSE DOORS button.

"What are you doing?" she asks.

"I'm taking you home."

CHAPTER 25
DREW

I OPEN up the door to my apartment, Emmett right behind me, and we walk in. I leave the TV on pretty much 24/7 now to avoid any moment of silence, so we're greeted by the episode of *New Girl* where Winston steals his girlfriend's cat because she was cheating on him.

I take off my shoes and start walking to the couch. Hearing no footsteps behind me, I turn around to see Emmett is still in the doorway, waiting for an invitation.

On the surface, Emmett and I are still getting to know each other, so it makes sense. But I think today has been a turning point for us. We are still in the early stages of *whatever this is*. Friendship, maybe? We have shared these intense moments lately, but it is understandable that there is still a level of uncertainty as to where we stand with one another.

Emmett has seen me at my absolute lowest, yet he knows exactly what I need without me having to say it.

"You can come in." I see him take a step towards me. "But take your shoes off."

He smiles and complies, shutting the door behind him.

I sit down on the couch, and Emmett walks over to take a seat next to me.

We sit, watching the TV, shoulders touching, eyes facing forward.

"Have you seen this show before I ask?"

"*New Girl*? No, but I've listened to it a few times." I turn to find him smirking at me, reminding me that this *is* my downstairs neighbor who always finds a reason to complain about how loud I am.

But I like seeing this side of him.

I smile back, feeling my cheeks blush.

"You do that a lot."

"What?" I ask.

"Blush."

"Yeah, it seems to happen around you a lot. I think it's because you always seem to find me in my worst moments."

He smiles at my admission but it's a sad, knowing smile.

"So," I begin before he can make my cheeks turn any more red, "I feel like you know a lot about me, but I know nothing about you."

"Go on."

"What's your favorite Pop-Tart flavor?"

He lets out a laugh, one capable of making my butterflies fly. "Out of all the things you could ask me, that's your question?"

"You mentioned I had *bad* taste in Pop-Tart flavors at the bar, which is very much untrue, so I feel like it's only fair to know what flavor *you* like!"

"S'more."

"Disgusting," I deadpan.

He shows a face of fake-offense. "You cannot tell me S'more is worse than *blueberry*!" He gives me a playful bump on the shoulder with his.

"You should be embarrassed. The fruity flavors top any non-fruity flavor!" I bump back.

"Well, I think you're wrong."

"Oh, yeah?" I spring off the couch, go to my pantry, and pull out the last silver foil package, and sit back down.

I rip open the Pop-Tarts, sliding one out and breaking it in half. I hand one half to Emmett while taking the other half for myself.

"Cheers," I say, holding up mine to clink with his.

He nods at me and then takes a bite.

He chews once before saying, "Absolutely not." He hands me over his half.

"Whatever. More for me!"

"Is this what you consider a meal? No wonder you're so short, all the sugar stunted your growth," he says with a mouth full of dry pastry and hardened frosting. He looks like he is actually struggling to finish chewing before swallowing, and I find it absolutely hilarious to watch.

I stick my tongue out on him, happy to have the sugary pastry all to myself.

"I can't believe they even market them as breakfast, they're a dessert!" He shakes his head at me, but his lips are stretched wide, showing me a grin that tells me he's enjoying this as much as me.

Emmett turns to look at me. "Breakfast is the best meal of the day with arguably the best food choices, and you're telling me you'd rather eat *this*?" He takes the two halves from me, one in each hand.

"Hey! Give those back!" I reach for his hands, but he stands up before I can reach him, holding them high above his head, almost touching my ceiling.

Looking down at me, laughing at my struggle, he says, "Let me show you a real breakfast."

I freeze, arms still up in the air, realizing my chest is pressed up against him, only reaching just below his.

I bring my arms down. "That sounds like a loaded request."

He chuckles at my insinuation. "No strings attached."

"Okay, but it's nighttime, and breakfast is in"—I look past him at my oven clock—"over twelve hours."

"Sweetheart, haven't you ever heard of breakfast for dinner?"

CHAPTER 26
EMMETT

I HAVEN'T HAD ANYONE, let alone a girl, in my apartment since Riley left. The place is mostly for sleeping, making food, and showering, but I do pride myself on my cleanliness. Bringing Drew here, without knowing it was going to happen more than five minutes ago, doesn't bother me.

Our apartments have an identical layout, so I don't waste time showing her around. Instead, I walk us into the kitchen, and tap a spot on the counter as my way of telling her to hop up.

She complies, backing up into the counter, hoisting herself up with her arms.

"Do you know how to make waffles?" I ask. Not letting my hands linger on her legs, even though I want to.

"I know how to put frozen waffles into the toaster. But that's also *not* as easy for me these days." I sense the hint of humor in her voice when she mentions this, leading me to believe she is trying to make light of a situation that has probably been heavy on her mind.

"Well, my waffles do not require a toaster."

"Wait, you cook?" I'm standing directly in front of her, and I am able to see her eyes widen at the realization.

"Don't act so surprised."

Despite my asking, she looks dumbfounded.

"No offense, but I took you for the kind of guy who orders pizza six out of seven nights of the week."

I laugh at the assumption, not wanting her to see the left-over pizza in my fridge—from two different places—that is definitely no longer in the window of time to be safely consumed.

"I actually really love to cook. I'm pretty good at it too."

Drew cocks her head, eye-to-eye with me, as if challenging my last statement. "Prove it."

She is sitting in front of me, knees at my stomach. I put my hands on the counter, arms on each side of her thighs, enclosing her in, leaning into her challenge.

"Watch me."

We stare into each other's eyes, our lips just a few inches away. I think I see her sneak a glance at my lips, but it might have just been a blink.

My mind is moving at a million miles per minute, trying to read her mind, hear what she is thinking, hoping I'm having the effect on her that she is having on me.

It has been a week and a half since the shooting, yet so much has happened in the past ten days. I feel like I've known Drew on a level I don't know anyone else. I am slowly coming to the realization that I don't want to know what days are like without her. I want to learn about her, protect her, help her heal however she needs me to.

Wondering who is going to break this intense eye contact first, I tell myself to let her make the first move. I want her to feel like she is in complete control of whatever happens, or doesn't happen, because that is what she deserves.

To my surprise, she initiates the initial movement,

bringing her forehead to mine, only having to make the subtlest incline because we are already so close.

My skin warms at the touch of hers, and I close my eyes, breathing in her citrusy, sweet scent. I inch my hands from resting on the counter closer to where the backs of her legs meet my counter, resisting any urge to grab her legs and wrap them around my waist.

I want to feel her.

Feel all of her—whatever she is willing to give me.

The good, the bad, the inside, the out.

Then, breaking the bond between us, I hear her stomach growl.

Blood rushes up to her cheeks, turning her head and bringing her head back upright to find my eyes.

"So about those waffles . . ."

I give her a wink. "Coming right up."

I pull out flour, sugar, and baking powder from my pantry before getting milk, eggs, and butter from the fridge, and then return to my place in front of Drew to bend down for two mixing bowls, a whisk, and the waffle iron from the cabinet below where she is seated on my counter. I use my hands to usher her legs to the side, looking up to catch her looking around my place, probably trying to make similar observations I made when I was in her apartment. I grab what I need and close the cabinet, letting her legs swing back to where they were. When I stand up in front of her, she looks back at me.

"Can I do anything?" she asks.

I preheat the oven to a low temperature. "You're doing it. I like an audience."

"Emmett, are you a control-freak or something?"

I laugh out loud. "Not at all." Or at least I didn't think so, until now. I have never had someone join me in the kitchen. "Okay, okay. You can hold the bowls."

"That's it?" I hand her the two bowls. "Actually, that's

probably a good idea. I'm a pretty shitty cook." She grabs the bowls from me, setting them down in her lap. "You got it, boss."

Now it is my turn to get flustered. All the blood in my body eases into my chest and up my neck at the sound of playfulness in her tone.

I love this side of her, I think to myself.

I plug in the waffle iron and grab the larger mixing bowl from Drew so I can whisk together the flour, sugar, baking powder.

As I measure the ingredients, pouring them into the bowl, I sneak glances towards her. She is watching me as I move, rather than looking around. It is the same way she watched me at the bar.

Both in the kitchen and when I'm at work, my movements are natural, not even having to think about what I'm doing or my next move.

I turn to her and say, "Small bowl, please."

She hands me the bowl she is holding in her lap with a smile, as if proud of a job well-done.

I pour in the milk, crack the eggs, and whisk them together.

"Do you want to do the next step?"

As if asking her to disarm a bomb, her smile disappears.

"I don't want to mess anything up."

I let out a chuckle because she is so damn cute. "I trust you."

She hops off the counter, shrinking back to her stature of being a foot shorter than me, and she finds a place next to me, facing my work area.

"What do you need me to do?"

"Pour this mixture into that one while I melt the butter," I direct, pointing from the small bowl to the big bowl.

"That's it?"

"I can't release *all* the control."

She laughs and follows my direction, doing a wonderful job. Once again, smiling at her job well-done. I put the butter into a small bowl, and put it in the microwave.

I hand her a utensil to scrape the residual mixture into the large bowl and pay extra attention to the timer counting down on the microwave, not wanting the beep to catch her off guard.

Before the microwave hits zero, I open up the door, grabbing the butter and gently whisking it.

"Anything else?" she asks.

"Nope." I stand behind her, never moving too quickly, and gently put my hands underneath her arms, lifting her up as I turn, setting her back on her spot on the counter.

The waffle iron is hot and ready, so I begin scooping out cups of batter into the center before closing the iron. Each one is going to take around two minutes, so I decide to use those moments to close the space between me and Drew and ask her any question that pops into my head.

I lean on my elbow resting on the counter space next to her, the waffle iron between us.

"What's your favorite movie?" She turns to face me, looking a little confused.

"Um, I don't know. Probably *Scream*?" she says it as a question, not sure why I changed the subject so fast. "I also like the Marvel movies. What's your favorite movie?"

"You'll have your turn to ask your questions once this light turns red and I put the next scoop of batter in.." I point to the waffle iron. Catching on to the game I'm making up as I go, she nods, ready for my next question.

"What's your full name?"

"Drew Kathryn Thomas."

"What's your favorite color?"

"Black."

"Of course it is. Favorite band?"

"Escape the Fate."

"With Craig Mabbitt or Ronnie Radke?"

Her eyes are wide. "You listen to Escape the Fate?"

"Not your turn."

She rolls her eyes, my stomach flicking in as a response. "Both."

"Favorite author?" She thinks about this one the longest.

After a few moments, she says, "Either Scarlett St. Clair or Tessa Bailey, I can't choose."

"I'll let that slide, even though a favorite usually means one," I reply. She laughs and gives me a light push on the shoulder. Not wanting to waste any of my time, I quickly ask, "What's your favorite scent?"

"Yours."

This stops me in my tracks. Stunned by both her answer and the realization that she wants to let me in.

Wants me to know her.

And damn, do I want to.

Before I can respond, she gives me the most mysterious glance with a smirk on her face. Mysterious because I don't know what is going through that unpredictable brain of hers.

Out of the corner of my eye, I see the light on the waffle iron turn red, telling me that my two minutes is up.

Finding a confidence I only feel in her vicinity, "What is my scent, Drew?" I break our gaze, pushing myself off the counter to take the fresh waffle out and put it on a baking sheet before placing the sheet in the oven to keep warm.

I scoop more batter in, closing the iron, starting the timer again.

"No, no, no," she says. "It's my turn."

CHAPTER 27

DREW

I HAVE SO many questions running through my head.

So many things I want to know about Emmett.

Yes, so little time.

Instead of returning to his spot at the counter he was leaning on before, he closes the oven beside me and steps to stand in front of me, hands resting on the counter right next to the side of my thighs this time, ready for my rapid-fire of questions.

His face is so close to mine, I can barely keep my thoughts straight.

"W-what's your full name?"

"Emmett Theodore Ryan."

"Where did you grow up?"

"Baraboo, Wisconsin."

"Favorite hobby?"

"Watching movies."

"Marvel or DC?"

"Marvel."

"Who's your favorite Marvel character?"

"Iron Man. Also my favorite movie. I'll give you a two for

one with that one." He winks at me, and my heart somersaults.

"T-thank you," I somehow manage to say. "Um, drink of choice?"

He thinks about this one for a moment.

"Old-Fashioned, bourbon, sweet."

"Why?" I glance at the waffle iron, still no red light.

"That's what my dad always used to order."

"Hmm . . . favorite animal?"

"Dog."

"You're good at this." And with that, the light blinks red. "That was way less than two minutes!"

"Sorry, sweetheart," he says before pushing himself off the counter, no longer close enough for me to watch his lips move. "I don't make the rules."

I'm pretty sure that's exactly what you did with this game, I want to say, but I can't manage to get the words out. My body is having so many reactions to his words—flutters in my stomach, goosebumps on my arms, and my cheeks are giving all the thoughts and feelings I'm currently having away.

After four more waffles, and two more turns, each, of getting to know the little things about each other, it's finally time for our breakfast-for-dinner.

I watch as he takes the warmed waffles out of the oven and plates from the cabinet above him, setting a waffle on each one.

"What is your topping of choice?"

While I could just say I'm fine with the basics like butter and syrup, occasionally going for something a little more crazy like jelly, I go with the truth and my number one choice. "I like whipped cream."

"Whipped cream?" he walks over to his refrigerator, and I'm waiting for a comment about how I eat like a child. But, to my surprise, I hear him say, "You're my kind of girl," as he opens the door to the fridge.

And I thought I felt butterflies with Reed?

That's nothing compared to what I've been feeling tonight.

Emmett bends down to take a look at the shelves on the refrigerator door. "You're in luck." He pulls out the red and white can and walks back over to me. "I picked some up last time I was at the store." He dolls up our plates, giving us matching smiley faces of whip cream for the both of us, smiles that don't even measure up to the one on my face. "You're the first person I've met with the correct taste in waffle toppings." He leans his head back to spray some of the whipped topping into this mouth, keeping his eyes locked with mine, a liveliness to them that makes the brown even richer.

He tucks the whipped cream can under his arm and grabs the plates, forks, and napkins, nodding his head to me to follow. "Come on."

I hop off the counter, letting him lead the way.

Our apartments are basically the same layout except where I have my bookshelf, he has a little breakfast nook with a table just big enough for two. I take the seat opposite of him, feeling the butterflies' wings get overpowered by the hunger my stomach won't let me ignore any longer.

I take the first bite, the first home-cooked, non-frozen, non-processed meal I've had in almost two weeks and almost faint as the rich, fluffy, buttery piece of a dream hits my tongue.

"These are amazing!"

"I'm glad you like them. Glad I could make them for you."

"I'm pretty sure I will need you to make these for me every day for the rest of my life." Taking another bite, "Yeah, no, I'm *positive* I need you to make me these every day for forever."

He lets out a chuckle. "I'd be happy to."

Even though I'm piling on the dramatics pretty thick, just

wanting to express to him how good these waffles are, I can hear a bit of truth in his voice. As if my request is actually something he would want to oblige.

We each finish our first waffles, and Emmett stands, grabbing my plate. I go to stand, but he stops me. "No, you sit. I'll get us another."

He comes back this time with another whipped cream smiley face, only this time one with buck teeth and eyebrows.

I laugh at the sight before digging in.

As we each take our bites, the conversation is light and surrounds how breakfast-for-dinner became a staple in his household.

"My sister was a picky eater, but she loved pancakes." He sprays a little extra whipped cream on the last section of his waffle. "It became one of our weekly dinners."

"Did she like whipped cream on her waffles too?"

"She was a butter and syrup person, and the kind who liked a pool of syrup."

"Soggy pancakes?"

"I know, disgraceful."

My brother used to do the same thing, and I feel an ounce of sadness settle into this blissful atmosphere I am currently surrounded by. Instead of heading down that road, I keep the conversation light and ask, "Do you like pancakes or waffles better?"

"Waffles." Emmett doesn't even hesitate. "But it was Lennon's world growing up, and I didn't mind living in it." I can tell I'm not the only one feeling the bitter sweetness of this conversation. The smile is there as Emmett talks, but there is a melancholy hue to his eyes. My heart can't help but feel a little fuller at the thought that he is sharing this story with me. It can't be easy to talk about his sister, and based on how he reacted when I asked about her at the bar, I don't think he talks about her much.

"Another?" Emmett asks after taking his last bite. I look down at my empty plate, and I'm brought back into reality.

"I think I'm going to explode."

"I'll take that as a no." He smirks at me. "Maybe later then."

Heat floods to my cheeks, just when I was able to get them to cool down, at the thought that he wants there to be a later.

I hope I'm not the only one having these feelings, I think to myself as he grabs our plates and heads back to the kitchen.

We clean up the kitchen together, finding a natural rhythm and balance between conversation and me washing the bowls, plates, and utensils as he dries and puts them away. When we finish, Emmett turns off the kitchen lights, and we make the short walk to the living room and sit down on the couch.

He grabs the remote to turn on the TV, and I don't even have to question if he wants me to stay or not.

I can't be the only one thinking that this looks and *feels* like a date, and I'm glowing at the thought of the two of us spending time together getting to know each other's favorite things and middle names,

Today has had so many ups and downs, between seeing Lacey, going to the bookstore, running into Reed, then the bar and elevator.

But right now, I can forget all of it.

I can feel *normal.*

Emmett and I, at this moment, are just two people enjoying each other's company, despite the craziness that led us here. There's a pull between us that has gotten stronger the more time we spend together, and I want to know what it will lead to.

"What do you feel like watching?" he asks, staring at the TV as he scrolls through the options. His other arm finds its way behind me, resting on the couch.

"What do *you* feel watching?" I say in response, glancing up at him. Even seated, I have to lift my chin to look at him. The only light coming from the TV a few feet in front of us, highlights his strong jawline softened by the scruff that he is letting grow a little longer. His long eyelashes and full lips make my heart beat a little faster.

Emmett glances down at me, making me realize how close we are, but how much *closer* I want to be to him. I inch closer, finding how perfect my body fits into his.

"I don't know if I feel like watching anything." The words come out of his mouth as a whisper, one with an edge, different than any I've heard from him before, along with his alluring eyes, making promises that are clear yet left unsaid.

He sets the remote down and brings his hand to the side of my face. I gasp at the warmth I feel rush through my entire body, making my stomach tighten and my heartbeat quicken even more. I feel him looking at the deepest part of me, the part that holds all my fear and everything I want to forget.

Instead of looking away, he pulls me closer, until I feel his breath hitting my lips.

When the night first started, and any other time we've been around each other in the last two weeks, I noticed that he was always waiting for me to make the first move, never testing how far he could get but instead waiting to follow my lead. I can tell that whatever he was holding on to before now is no longer in his grasp.

"You have no idea how long I've waited for this." Before I can react, his lips crash into mine, sending a jolt through my entire body as if he's shocking my system, resetting everything I thought I knew about kissing—showing me what it actually feels like.

One of my hands finds the side of his neck, the other finds his chest, and he is hot to the touch. His lips continue to move on mine, and the kiss warms every inch of my skin.

I never want it to stop.

Emmett brings the arm that was behind me down to my hip, pulling me closer to him. I feel pressure begin to build in my stomach, but the kind of pressure that doesn't make me feel like drowning. Instead, it drives my senses into overload. The hand he had lightly cupped around my cheek slides down to my neck.

Then, our kiss deepens, turning more passionate and eager. I feel his tongue brush against my bottom lip, politely asking for entrance. I comply, and my lower body tightens when his tongue finds mine, making me want more.

My hands find his hair, tied up but loose enough for me to pull out and run my fingers through the curls I've fantasized about more than I would like to admit.

So many thoughts run through my head, so many thoughts of how I want to feel him, *all of him*, everywhere. How kissing him makes me feel all the good things that I haven't been able to think about until right now.

Then, there's a knock on the door.

I freeze, and Emmett pulls away as if we were teenagers caught in the backseat of a parked car. I'm plucked out of the beautiful dream I was in and dropped back into reality. Our eyes meet, and he gives me an apologetic smile that reminds me that whatever happens when I'm with him will turn out fine.

"I'm sorry," he says. His voice is a little shaky, and he's out of breath. I notice a redness running up his neck.

"Don't be," I whisper, wanting to stay in this bubble of ours longer.

"Don't move."

He gets up to see who's at the door, and the second his arms leave my body, the second he's not right next to me, I'm overwhelmed with a feeling of eagerness for the moment I can be close to him again.

I turn to see his face drop the second he opens the door.

"Riley?" I hear him say.

The bubble pops.

Who's Riley?

CHAPTER 28
EMMETT

I JUST GOT off the phone with Eddie, telling him I won't be in today and will be working from home so I can finish some paperwork and make some phone calls to our distributors.

While it's true that I will be using *some* of the day for these things. The other part of my day will be thinking of how I'm going to apologize to Drew for asking her to leave after kissing her on my couch.

Riley came over unannounced, and unwarranted, last night, and it's something I should have expected from her, especially after I ignored her recent texts asking to talk.

I shouldn't be surprised that she feels it's her right to come and go from my life as she sees fit because every other part of our relationship was making sure she was happy, even at my expense. It wasn't until she was truly gone that I realized most of my days with her consisted of making sure I didn't do, or say, something that would cause a fight.

Riley has been blessed with a life free of hardships. Both her parents *and* both sets of grandparents are still alive, and are all still happily married. She grew up never having to worry about things like money or social status, and, through family connections, never had to worry about school or work, leading her to live a life that was *easy*.

I don't want to be with someone like that.

And that's something I didn't realize until I got to know Drew.

I don't want to be with someone who doesn't know what it feels like to be knocked down so far that you have to work your ass off to get back up.

I want to be with someone who is strong.

Someone like Drew.

I knew the amount I thought about Drew, and how much time I wanted to spend with her meant more than I was willing to admit, and I knew there was something growing between us in these last two weeks. But wanting to be more than the neighbor who gives her a hard time hit me hard last night when I kissed her, and it confirmed all the feelings I've had for her since I first saw her.

And I fucked up whatever chance I had.

When I saw Riley on the other side of my door. I was struck with so many emotions. Her blonde hair was shorter than the last time I saw it, and the usual gloss of her lips was in full effect. Her icy blue eyes were looking directly at me, and, for just a moment, I was happy to see her, even hopeful for what she came to say. But that happiness faded as quickly as it appeared, and I was pissed that she came over without letting me know first.

Then, I was nervous about how I was going to explain everything to Drew.

The look on Drew's face when Riley stepped into my apartment was enough to shatter me. The moment just before, I felt her electrifying passion surge through me, making me want her in every way possible.

"What are you doing here, Riley?" I asked through gritted teeth.

She walked through the doorway without an invitation.

"Why have you been ignoring my texts? I want to talk ab—" She stopped talking mid-sentence once she turned towards the living room and saw Drew. "Hi," she said, her nose up as if she didn't even want to acknowledge Drew was there.

"Hi," Drew said.

"I'm here to talk to Emmett. You can go."

I could see the confusion, with a hint of betrayal, in Drew's eyes as she turned from Riley to me.

I walked back over to Drew and whispered to avoid Riley from hearing me as I grabbed her hands to help her up. "I'm so sorry, but I have to take care of this. Do you need me to take you up to your apartment?" Drew tensed immediately. She obviously did not expect me to ask her to leave.

Then, anger flooded over her, and she pulled her hands away from mine. Without a word, she walked past me, past Riley, and out the door, not giving either of us another glance. Riley watched her as she went and then closed the door behind her.

"So, who's she?" she asked, as if she even cared.

"None of your business." I walked into the kitchen and turned a light on. "Why are you here?"

"I wanted to see you. I've been . . . thinking about you, about us. I think we ended things too hastily."

I ran my fingers through my loose hair, the hair that Drew had just run *her* fingers through minutes earlier, and leaned back against the counter

Riley watched me as she walked from the entryway into the kitchen, stopping just a foot in front of me. "You need a haircut," she said as she reached to grab one of the curls framing my face. I caught her wrist in my palm. I didn't want her touch after what it felt like to have Drew's.

But then my eyes found hers.

I felt myself getting pulled in. Getting hypnotized as I felt her caramel irises melt into mine. She slowly took her other hand, the one I wasn't grabbing onto, and found my cheek. I instinctively melted into her hand, and my eyelids slowly closed as I felt the small yet familiar intimate gesture.

It wasn't until my eyes were closed that I realized what I was doing, what I was letting her do. I let go of her hand and pushed myself off the counter to find a spot on the opposite side. I needed to put space between us.

I let out a sigh.

I knew what was coming—I had heard it all before. I had fallen for her tricks time and time again, thinking that because she missed me or wanted me back or told me not to let her go, it would change the fact that we didn't work and never will.

Throughout our time together, I made myself believe that every make-up after a fight meant that things were going to change. Riley was going to become my partner, my companion, the person I could be strong for or the person I could lean on.

She blinded me with her manipulative embraces and distracted me with her lips until we were in bed, making, what I thought was amends, but I was just falling into her trap, and I did so again and again. She knew how to make me forget what I knew deep down, that we were not meant to be. I would forget until the high wore off, and I could finally see straight.

"Riley, we don't work. We never will. We want different things, and I don't think either of us is interested in changing our priorities."

"What are you talking about? Wanting different things? I don't even know what you want."

"Exactly! Because you never care to learn!" My voice began to rise as my patience for this charade plummeted. "You have no interest in even *learning* what I want or being part of the life *I* want to live." My voice grew louder with every word that shot from my mouth, and I didn't even care that the walls of the complex weren't thick enough to keep this conversation between just Riley and me. "I don't want to be with someone who thinks they're too good to come into where I work or for my friends, or who starts a fight over what brand of pretzels I buy, or who thinks breakfast-for-dinner is a stupid idea!"

I saw her look around my kitchen, the waffle maker was still out because it needed to cool.

"And you think your little friend does?"

"Why do you care?"

She scoffed. "You really think I'm intimidated by *her*?"

What the fuck is she talking about?

I felt like I was back in a time loop, not being able to stop her from starting a fight I had no interest in being a part of. "Riley, it's not a competition. You and I are not together, and Drew has nothing to do with you." I try to stay calm, but I'm clenching my fists around the edge of the counter. "I've known Drew for a *fraction* of the time I've known you."

Riley's stature straightened, and she smirked, a smirk bleeding of righteousness, but I wasn't done. "But I know her better than I know you." Riley's smirk disappeared, and she tried to hide her surprise with anger.

"And you think she is somehow better for you than me?"

"Yes! And even better, she wants to know *me*." I shook my head. "Riley, you can say you want me and miss me all you want, but you miss the person I became for you."

I tried to ignore the deep-rooted embarrassment that came to the surface. I'll never forgive myself for letting Riley convince me that I had to change who I was to be good enough for her, and that she was trying to change me for my own good. "You turned me into the type of person that walked on a tightrope to avoid falling backwards into an argument that I had no energy to be a part of." I took a small step towards her. "I don't want to live like that, Riley." She took a small step towards me. "I deserve better."

Then, I took another step, so I was right in front of her.

Her eyes, dry and cold without even a glimmer of a tear, met mine.

With that one glance, I knew my gut was right. Riley had come over that night to play a game that I didn't want to play. She had come to see if she still had the power to chew me up just to spit me out.

I looked away, walking towards my entryway. I grabbed the handle to open the door leading to the empty hallway.

I turned to look at her for the very last time. "*You* can go now."

It's my fault I didn't tell Drew about Riley or the engagement, and that was not something I wanted her finding out like she did. Last night was easy going and fun, like a first date should be. The conversations were light and showed me that there was a real possibility of Drew and I turning into more, and I was hoping she saw it too.

In reality, it's ignorant for me to consider last night our first real date. The day was crazy for Drew between what happened at the store and then with her ex-boyfriend. I left her at the bar right before we got trapped in an elevator. I kissed her on my couch and then asked her to leave. If she used to avoid me like the plague before all of this, I wouldn't be surprised if she found a way to get me kicked out of my place so she'd never have to see my face again.

I've given her trouble she shouldn't have to be dealing with on top of everything else she is going through.

I fucked up the likelihood of her even giving me a chance.

CHAPTER 29
DREW

I'M NEVER TAKING the elevator again.

It just makes me think of Emmett.

Emmett, who has been in the right place at the right time so many times, but then kicked me out of his apartment after kissing me.

And he kicked me out for another girl.

Who was she?

Did he have a girlfriend?

How could I be so stupid and assume he wanted what I wanted.

Wanted to know me, wanted to spend time with me, wanted to see where this thing of ours could go.

When I got back into my apartment after storming out of Emmett's place, I kicked off my shoes and took my phone out of my pocket. I connected my phone to the speaker in my kitchen and turned on some music, so I could distract myself from how stupid I felt. I didn't turn the volume up too loud though.

I didn't want to piss off my *neighbor*.

Because that's all he is.

My rude, angry, downstairs neighbor.

I found a punk rock playlist on Spotify because I needed something a little harder, a little edgier, a little angrier, to match my mood.

As I went to click the first one I could find, I heard a muffled voice, a *familiar* muffled voice, coming from below me. It only took me a second to realize who the voice was coming from, and I had never heard it in that kind of manner.

Who is this woman? And why was he yelling at her?

I found myself kneeling to the ground, trying to make out what he was saying, to no avail. Then I realized what I was doing and stood up, shaking my head at myself for being so stupid, and headed to the bathroom to shower.

I needed to wash Emmett's smell from my clothes, his kiss from my lips, his touch from my skin. What he was doing down there was none of my business.

Aside from that moment, I didn't hear any other noise from Emmett's apartment the rest of the night.

I turned on the shower and undressed, finding my naked reflection before me, riddled with the lingering feeling of Emmett's hands on me, even if it was just over my clothes.

My skin pebbled at the coolness of my apartment, for once thinking maybe sixty-five degrees was too cold after feeling what it felt like in Emmett's arms.

I listened to the water running, and closed my eyes. The drops of water hitting the shower floor behind me mixing with the music that was playing from my kitchen allowed me to focus on the noises around me rather than the thoughts in my head, or the tingle on my skin.

My mind then struck me with unexpected thoughts.

When Emmett and I were alone in his apartment, when he pulled me in, when he kissed me, there was no noise around us. No TV background noise, no music, no anything. Just the silence surrounding us with the sound of our breathing.

I turned away from the mirror before me and got into the

shower, feeling the warmth fall over me, but not comforting me like Emmett did.

As I felt the water fall onto my skin, I thought to myself, *how did I get here?*

The same thought I had two weeks ago.

I'm brought back to that Friday morning. Back to before I went to school, and my biggest struggle was whether or not I should text Reed.

Whether or not I should call my parents or my brother or Lacey.

Whether or not I needed someone to make me feel less lonely.

So much has changed since then, and I have to let myself feel it. I have to let myself deal with what happened because I'm not always going to have someone come to my rescue.

Emmett won't be there the next time the elevator stalls or my toaster goes off. He won't be there when I'm consumed with fear, those moments so intense they steal my breath and hold it hostage.

I washed my hair and my body and rinsed everything that I didn't want to take with me into tomorrow. I got out of the shower and into bed that night, ready to feel what I've been pushing down deep inside me when I woke up the next morning.

It was time to actually click on the link.

———

It's been a week since I last saw Emmett, but it has been a good week. I've started my journey of uncovering the memories from that day in my classroom, the memories I've tried so hard to ignore.

I'm finally ready to admit that I'm in—what professionals call—the "aftermath" of a tragedy, and I'm on the road to recovery.

After coming home from my evening at Emmett's, I fell asleep to *Captain Marvel*, finally picking back up with watching the Marvel movies in chronological order.

The next morning, I woke up from a sleep free of nightmares, so I went into the day feeling like I accomplished *something*.

Even if it was just making it through the night.

My heart, on the other hand, still needed some rest, and I felt like staying in bed after the emotionally-draining day I had before was in order.

I moved on to Marvel movie number five, *The Incredible Hulk*, playing it in the background as I looked through the resources that my school district sent staff. I skipped movies number three and four on the MCU list (*Iron Man* and *Iron Man* 2) because I knew they would lead me to think about someone I had no business thinking about.

I read about the stages we go through after a trauma like a school shooting, and I read stories of other survivors.

That morning, I made the decision to find an expert, a therapist, to help me through my emotions surrounding what happened. I had never been to a therapist before, but I dove in head first and got lucky when I found Dr. James had an opening for an initial appointment for the upcoming Tuesday —the first Tuesday of the new year, the day we would've gone back to school if the district didn't extend the break.

For New Year's Eve, I stayed home, called Lacey, called my parents, even called my brother, and wished them all a Happy New Year at midnight. I had planned to stay up and finish the next Marvel movie on my list, *Avengers: Age of Ultron*, but I was asleep within the first fifteen minutes of the brand new year, hoping that whatever this year brought would be better than how last year ended.

My first therapy session was mostly an opportunity for Dr. James to get to know me and why I wanted to start therapy. Due to the many aspects of my life that needed to be unpacked—the shooting being the priority—we decided to set up weekly sessions, so I have my second appointment with her scheduled for today. I need to log on for my therapy session at noon, grateful for the virtual option which allows me to be comfortable in my own space.

Because we have these extra two weeks in January off before we start the discussions on the best way for staff and students to return to the middle school, I don't have many places to go, which is fine by me. The furthest I've been going lately is a mile or two down the road to get some fresh air.

Since I have about thirty minutes before I have to be at my computer, I grab my headphones and put on some tennis shoes before heading out the door. I walk out of my apartment, walking right past the elevator to find the stairs. I still haven't been in the elevator since the night Emmett and I got stuck.

The night he made me waffles.

The night we kissed.

The night he asked me to leave.

I feel a twist in my heart as I walk past.

I thought I would have heard from him, a text, a knock on my door, *something*, but I haven't even heard him in his apartment.

It feels like he was a ghost, a presence that was there for me when I was at my lowest, helping me get to where I needed but then disappeared once I figured out I had to take my healing into my own hands.

At least I'm used to being alone.

I get back from my walk with a few minutes to spare before needing to login to join my virtual therapy session. I'm a little nervous as I sit down in front of my computer because, the last time Dr. James and I talked, I told her how I had been keeping off of the news and social media and refusing to talk about any details of the shooting with friends or family. She said it might be a good idea to start small going into the next few days, seeing what I feel comfortable with.

The session goes well, but I'm left feeling a little uneasy about my "homework." Dr. James wants me to try reading about what happened or watching some news reports from the day. She said that it might be hard to expose myself to it all, especially because of how deep I buried my memories, thoughts, and feelings about it. It will be anything but easy to learn about the injuries and deaths at the hands of the person who did it, but Dr. James said to try it and notice the emotional and physical reactions that may trigger.

She reminded me that I am safe, even if my mind tries to trick me into thinking I'm not.

Safe . . .

Such a foreign concept to me now.

A school is supposed to be safe.

A classroom is supposed to be safe.

How do we live in a world where students as young as four and five years old have to practice what they would do if someone opened fire in their school?

How do we live in a world where students have to know the difference between a soft and hard lockdown.?

How do we live in a world where students learn how to arm themselves with materials in their classroom?

How do we live in a world where students learn how to stay calm and cry silently in case the intruder could hear the panic?

How do we live in a world where the right to bear arms is more important than the right for children to feel safe at school?

Are we really safe?

After confirming our session for this time next week, I log off. I close my computer, feeling proud of myself for having the strength to face what I'm facing head on and on my own, but I'm still clouded with the anger that has been slowly building about what happened to us that day.

I decide I've had enough healing for today, and I want to spend the rest of the day reading.

I'll get to my homework tomorrow.

Before heading to my To Be Read shelf to start a new book, I put two Eggo waffles into the toaster. I tell myself that I'm not afraid of the toaster popping them out when I least expect it anymore. Even though this is my first time trying since last time. I'm hopeful my mind won't take me back to my class-room when I hear a loud noise or am caught off guard.

As I grab the icy circles from the package and put them in the slots, pushing the lever down to heat them up, I'm reminded of how shitty these waffles are compared to the ones Emmett made.

I check my phone on the off chance I have a text from him waiting for me. It's a silly thought, and I'm aware.

To my nonexistent surprise, the answer is no.

No text from Emmett.

The same answer I've told myself all week when I check my phone.

Should I text him?

Maybe he's giving me space?

But, I'm the one who was wronged in this situation . . . right?

I don't know.

I have no idea what it's like to be in *whatever this* is with someone. Especially someone who isn't Reed. I just always followed Reed's lead when I wasn't sure how to deal with something that came up in our relationship. The only decision I made was the one that ended our relationship.

After a few minutes, my waffles pop out, making me jump, but I take a deep breath in and a deep breath out, and I feel okay.

I slather some butter on both and eat them off a paper towel as I lean back against my counter.

I finish the first one which helps subside my hunger, but I think of how bland and boring it is compared to the ones I had last week. Thinking about that day, I feel myself getting mad at what happened with Emmett, and I lose my appetite, the frustration blinding me from the *other* events that unfolded that day.

I throw away the second waffle and the paper towel, wanting to talk to someone about what happened.

Or, maybe, I just want to talk to someone about something.

Forgetting my better judgment of whom I should reach out to, I grab my phone and type in one of the few numbers I have memorized, even though I swore I never would again.

CHAPTER 30
EMMETT

IT'S BEEN over a week since I've talked to Drew, and it's my fault. I want to see her, want to explain to her what happened, but I doubt she'll give me the time of day.

The past twelve days, I've been in and out of the apartment, working at Lenny's, keeping things running as we enter the new year.

Trying to stay busy.

Today is Tuesday, and I have recently established Tuesdays as my work-from-home days. I get paper paperwork done, make phone calls, and do all of the other behind-the-scenes stuff while Eddie, Annie, and my new bartender, Luke, handle things at the bar.

Tuesday has become my favorite day of the week because it is the only day I get to stay home, uninterrupted, except for the occasional reminder of whom I live below.

Hearing Drew move around her place, her muffled voice as she talks to someone on the phone or something, is about all I get of her these days. And again, I know that's on me.

I find myself a little appalled at the stalker-ish side of me this girl brings out, but I can't help but want to know what she's doing, *how* she's doing, and I don't have the balls to go apologize to her—too scared she'll tell me to fuck off.

I keep thinking, if I don't reach out, I'm prolonging the time where she tells me she never wants to see me again or our few moments together meant nothing, and I don't think I'm ready for that.

It's about six o'clock in the evening, and I'm finishing up with my phone call with my distributor.

"Hey, Dan, one more thing. Is it possible to switch from my hard seltzer cases of Truly to cases of White Claws? Yes. Yes. Same amount but want to try out a new brand. Awesome. Thanks, talk soon." I hang up and make a note to call Eddie to add a special for the Truly seltzers starting tomorrow so we can get rid of them.

And that concludes work for today.

I walk into the kitchen, looking for something to make for dinner, when I hear voices above me. Two voices. More than usual for my upstairs neighbor.

I tell myself to ignore it because it is none of my business who Drew spends her time with even if I do feel a sting of jealousy at the fact that it isn't me. I feel my protectiveness, my possessiveness, over her and her safety surface, but I push it down and quickly remind myself that it is all my doing.

It's my fault she's up there, and I'm down here.

I decide to throw together a pasta with the stuff I have. Tomatoes and spinach that are about to go bad, penne, and some parmesan, setting them all out on the counter and getting to work.

A few minutes pass, and I hear the muffled voices above me become clearer as their volumes increase. I'm about to turn on the stove to put some water to boil when I hear someone yell.

The voice is muffled, but I can make out some of it. "Always . . . Do this . . . all about YOU . . . Wrong with you!"

Is that person talking to Drew? The yelling continues, "Why did . . . . text . . . not how . . . goes!"

Then I hear Drew's voice, loud and clear, "Don't touch me!"

I don't even hesitate.

A cloud of anger engulfs me, and my instinct takes over. Before I know it, I'm at Drew's door. Pounding.

No answer, but I hear low voices behind the door as if someone doesn't want to be heard.

The smuggest face I've ever seen in my fucking life answers the door. Reed looks me up and down, reeking with disdain as if I've interrupted him and whatever he's come here to do.

"We're busy," is all he says to me before going to close the door.

"You're such a fucking idiot," I hear just before I put my foot in between the door and the frame, ready to take control of the situation.

I would know that voice anywhere.

"What the hell, man? Get out of here," Reed declares, but I have no intention of listening.

"Emmett? Is that you?" *Drew.* I can't decipher the tone of her voice. It's not surprise, like I thought it might be.

She sounds pissed.

I push past the prick, ignoring him as he tells me to back off.

I find Drew pacing in her living room, her entire face red. She looks like she's been crying, but there's no sadness in her eyes.

"See, Reed. I told you he was going to come up here." I hear a groan as if this is the biggest inconvenience to him. "I told you my neighbors could probably hear everything."

Neighbors?

Then I remember that is all we are.

"God, what are you so mad for? Quit screaming at me like I did anything you didn't want me to," he throws back at her.

My head looks from left to right, feeling a mix of confusion, anger, and jealousy being in the middle of these two right now. I'm also feeling incredibly out of place as they keep screaming at each other as if I'm not even here.

"You're joking, right? You're fucking impossible!" she yells at him, a tear rolling down her cheek. I've never seen her this mad before. Our encounters never got to the point where she was so visibly pissed off. But she's also crying. This is more than just a disagreement, something happened here.

"I'm impossible? You're the one who can't make up your damn mind!"

"I didn't invite you over for sex, Reed!"

There it is.

"What?" I can't help but intervene now. I turn to Drew. "Are you okay?" I try to grab her face in my hands, but she nods her head and takes a step back so she's out of my reach.

I bring my hands back to my sides and take a second to make sense of the situation I just walked into. Before I can get my thoughts straight, I am walking back over to the entryway where Reed is still standing and grab him by his stupid flannel pulling him up to his toes, so he is eye level with me.

"Did you touch her?" I spit.

The guy scoffs in my face. "Listen, dude, mind your fucking business." He tries to step out of my grip, but I grab him tighter, holding him in place. I want to tell him that Drew *is* my business, but I know I fucked that up.

"Answer the question."

"Look, you don't know her like I do. I know what she wants. I know what she needs." The fact that this guy knows Drew in ways I can only dream of makes me want to tear him in half.

"Are you fucking insane? No means no, asshole!" Drew screams from the living room.

Looking at Reed, hearing how upset Drew is, the smug face in front of me is about to send me into a frenzy.

"She likes playing hard to get." And that's all it takes for anger to blur my vision. His audacity, talking to me as if expecting me to accept this is a misunderstanding or a girl just overreacting.

The nerve of this fucking guy to think that'll make me apologize for interrupting and give him a high five on my way out.

I shove him towards the door. "Get out," I say, trying to act calm but knowing I'm about to explode any second. "Don't you dare bother her again."

"I'm not going anywhere," Reed states as if staking a claim.

I step towards him. "I'm not going to say it again."

He takes a step towards me, not warranting my threat. He looks past me to Drew. "I know you want to, D. You always come crawling back, begging for more."

She stares at him, and if looks could kill…

What the hell was happening up here?

Drew is past the point of anger, and she marches through the living room and kitchen, stopping just before the entryway.

In a voice scarier than the screaming, she says, "Get. The. Fuck. Out."

Reed's eyes widen just a fraction, a look of slight surprise or maybe fear on his face, but he quickly contorts back to his self-righteous expression. "Make. Me," he repeats in her cadence.

I look back at him, and, before I can stop myself, I feel a sharp pain on the outside of my hand as my knuckles meet his face. It's not my place to get involved, but there's no more holding back the rage boiling just under my skin.

Reed falls back a few steps, catching his fall with the door frame. He clutches his cheek with his other hand, and his eyes are black. He's pissed but nowhere near as pissed as I am.

I should've hit him harder.

I reach out and grab him again by his collar. "If you ever touch her again, I will beat your ass into the ground until you forget your fucking name." I use my grip on his shirt to shove him into the hallway. "And you heard her, get the fuck out."

He finds his footing and rights himself, but he's still not leaving.

I take a step towards him, my fists are clenched, ready to swing on him again, but this time, I don't know if I'll be able to stop after just one. The smug look on his face is egging me on, daring me to rearrange it. He's staring right into my eyes, his face tight with irritation. Then, he looks past me as he steps back into the door frame and his face twists into a grin. "Text me later, D." His face finds mine again and winks as he takes one last step back, far enough for me to slam the door in his fucking face.

My knuckles are pure white, my whole body feels like it is going to explode from anger. This guy has no idea what he's done. He better hope I never run into him again.

It takes me a few moments to shake the feelings I'm having right now away, ignoring the overwhelming feeling I have to run to meet him outside and make sure his facial muscles will never be able to contort into that conceited guise again. But I need to focus on what's important.

I need to focus on Drew.

I turn from the door back towards the kitchen to face her. "Are you okay? What do you need?" And with that, tears begin to fall and her face falls into her hands. I hear her trying to speak in between sobs, but I want to grab her by the shoulders and pull her in. Instead I lightly place a hand on her lower back and head her to the couch. "It's okay," I tell her, "just let it out." We sit down on the couch. "He's gone."

Her head still in her hands, her red hair falling over her face. "I'm going to kill him. I'm going to kill him," she repeats over and over again, the anger and betrayal overwhelming her.

After a few minutes, she sits up and rubs her eyes, red-ringed and swollen, and she is still the most beautiful person I have ever seen.

She lets out a sigh before saying, "I texted Reed because I needed someone to talk to." I feel my stomach fill with guilt at the reminder that I was so close to being that person she could talk to. "I thought, after everything he and I have been through, he would be there for me. But—" she flinches at the memory. "He got mad that I didn't want to have sex." I try to hide the fury in my eyes by shaking my head.

I'm not just going to kick this guy's ass. I'm gonna kill him.

"It's what our relationship has been in the past, but I thought it might be good to try doing more than just having sex, but he didn't want to hear it. That's when he—" Her tears begin to fall again. "God, he started kissing me. I pulled away and told him I didn't want to do anything, but then he grabbed me and held me so tight to him, I couldn't get away." Her voice is breaking and her breathing is getting shallower the more she talks. I can feel the anger radiating off her.

She continues, "I was trying to get out of his grip, and I yelled at him to not touch me. That pissed him off which pissed me off." She wipes a loose tear away and sniffles. "He just threw himself on top of me, and for a second I couldn't scream, couldn't move, and he was touching me, touching me everywhere. I wanted to crawl out of my skin." She shudders. "I can still feel him touching me."

The last sentence is barely audible.

"But," she begins again, and this time she is sitting up a little straighter. "I refused to just sit there and let it happen. Not after everything else I've been through. I wasn't just going to freeze, so I pushed him off of me and just started screaming at him." A few moments pass as she replays the conversation in her head. "It's like everything I've been holding in for so long came out, like last time I saw him but much worse." She shakes her head as if trying to shake away the thoughts in her head, remembering when she and I ran into Reed, and he forced her to confront feelings about the shooting. "He never takes me seriously and still sees me as the young seventeen-year-old girl who hung on his every word. But I'm not the young, impressionable girl I was back then, so I told him what an asshole he was for forcing himself on me and how I regretted everything we ever had. I just let it all out."

She takes in a shaky inhale and lets it out.

"He told me that I was stupid to be saying the things I was because of everything he's done for me. All the times he's been there for me." She has a visceral reaction as she tells me this, looking like the words made her nauseous. "He was yelling at me, and I told him to shut up because these walls are so thin, but he didn't care. 'Let them hear what a bitch you're being,' is what he said."

I'm lucky these walls are so thin because I could tell *something* was going on, but Reed is lucky they're thick enough that I didn't hear the specifics of what was being said.

I have to push down the pure fury I am feeling for this asshole. Not only for what he did but for all those horrible things he said to her.

I fucking hate him.

I feel like this wrath within me is going to make me explode, but I need to make sure I am here for Drew.

Whatever she needs.

"What can I do?" I ask through my teeth, trying my hardest to stay calm.

"I need to shower. Need to get his . . . I need to shower."

"Okay. I'll give you some privacy." I go to get up and head home, thinking she probably wants to be alone.

"No," she grabs my arm. "Will you stay? I just—" she pauses. "I don't want to be alone right now."

And with that, I never want to leave.

CHAPTER 31
DREW

I FEEL a sense of relief knowing Emmett is just out in my living room. I know we have some unfinished business between us right now, but it means a lot that he was willing to stay with me after everything that just happened.

He said he had to run down to his place to grab his phone and take care of some things, explaining that he dropped everything and ran up here when he heard the yelling between Reed and me.

By the time I undressed and turned on the water, I heard my door open and close just loud enough to announce he was back without saying he was here.

In the shower, I wash my skin, scrubbing until it's raw. Scrubbing away Reed—wanting any and all remnants of him to circle down the drain.

The Reed I knew—the Reed I *thought* I knew—is gone.

Left in his place is the Reed he truly was all along. The one that Lacey, and even Emmett, could see, but I was too naïve to accept.

My brain floods with memories from the past few years, and I'm struck with the realization that, over time, I became more and more wrapped around Reed's finger, allowing him to take what he wanted, receiving nothing in return, yet always asking him to come back.

Damn.

Reed was right; I am stupid, but not for the reasons he thinks. I was stupid for letting myself get strung along for so many years.

How did I let this happen?

How long has Reed been this person I don't even recognize?

Playing with the part of me that felt guilty for ending things between us all those years ago, tricking me into thinking I *owed* him, taking advantage of the love I had for him those years ago.

I begin to find other times lost in my memories where Reed forced himself on me, subtly enough to see it as lust at the time but enough for me to now see clearly for what it was.

My anger intensifies the more I think about the nights where I wanted companionship or someone to talk to but ended up taking off my clothes and telling myself that *this* is what I wanted. The mornings where I convinced myself that I was content, no longer lonely or empty, even if I still had the feeling that there was something more I needed to feel complete or satisfied.

The tears that stream down my face blend in with the drops of water falling from above, and I let them, feeling like I was not only washing away the lingering feeling Reed left on my skin but releasing the Reed I tried so hard to hold on to, unwrapping myself from around his finger.

I've always been one to hold in my anger. I tend to avoid conflict until everything inside of me boils over into literal form, tears streaming out of my eyes, out of my control.

I turn off the water, immediately freezing without the warmth of the water around me, and quickly grab my towel to dry off.

I slip on an oversized A Day to Remember t-shirt with the

Homesick album cover and a pair of black leggings. I brush through my wet hair before clipping it back and look at myself in the mirror.

I think to myself, *how did I get here?*

Because, the person staring back at me looks tired and worn out. The person before me looks like she's been through hell, yet she is still alive. The person in my reflection has the slightest hint of the person who looked in this same mirror the day her life changed forever.

That day, I was proud of myself because I was happy and exactly where I wanted to be. And that is the person I want staring back at me. Not this fragile, sad girl who lets one guy determine her self-worth, and another kick her out of his apartment.

Knowing that light within me was trying like hell to stay lit tonight, I took a deep inhale and closed my eyes. I let my lungs fill with air, telling myself that I need to set that small little flame ablaze.

Even if it means being alone.

———

Emmett is sitting on the couch and turns to greet me as he hears the bathroom door behind him open, and I know what I have to do.

"Hey," he says to me, a plastic bag on his lap with a logo I'd recognize anywhere. I walk over and take a seat next to him. My eyes sting from how hard I was crying, sure that they're red-ringed and puffy, but trying to ignore it.

"What do you have there?" I ask, gesturing to the bag, delaying the inevitable.

"I bought you something."

I'm caught off guard. "What?"

He hands me the bag, and I pull out the two books that complete the series I've been eager but too distracted to finish. The books with the pretty covers that I've had pictures of on my phone for weeks. The books I've been meaning to order but haven't yet.

The books I told Emmett about.

The matching black covers with dark floral patterns lining the outside cause water to well up in my eyes against my will, making them sting even more. This is a gesture so thoughtful and so kind.

I'm beginning to doubt myself. I feel like I'm high up in the clouds, never wanting to come down, and I want to let myself feel like this.

I look at Emmett, a reassuring smile on my face to tell him I'm happy, not sad, even if my tears deceive me.

"I wasn't sure if you ever got to order them, and I wanted to do something that would make you smile because, well—" he pauses, knowing what he wants to say next but unsure if he should. "I love seeing you smile."

I set the books down on the coffee table, and grab one of his hands with the both of mine. My eyes want to find his, but my vision is blurry from the tears I don't want to let fall.

"I don't know how to thank you for this, and for being there for me these past few weeks, but—"

"You don't have to thank me, Drew." He brings his other hand to place on top of mine. "Especially not after the last time I saw you. I shouldn't have asked you to leave."

I look down, the gravity making the tears escape and stream down my cheek. I take my hands back and interlace my fingers, resting my hands on my lap.

I need to create distance between us.

"Look, I really appreciate what you did tonight. Coming up here to help," I pause, trying to formulate the words to end something that never even officially started. "But, I need some space." His face twists, and I know that's not what he was expecting me to say. Before he can ask for clarification, I continue, "You can't keep barging in here to save me. I know I'm your loud and inconsiderate upstairs neighbor, but—"

"Neighbor?" He throws back at me. "Drew, you're not just a neighbor."

"Yes, I am," I say. "That's all I am to you, and you were very clear about that last time we saw each other." I stand up needing to create even more distance. "And, this"—I gesture between him and I—"this isn't what normal neighbors do, so you should probably just go." I turn to head to my bedroom, knowing that if I turn back, I'll take back everything I just said. I stop in the doorway, hoping he doesn't make this harder and just walks the other direction and back downstairs.

But I hear subtle creaks in my floor behind me, footsteps approaching me, and I feel a warm hand on my shoulder, gently pulling me to turn around.

"You are not just a neighbor," he says carefully.

I turn, pulling my eyes up to find his. "Then who was she?"

CHAPTER 32
EMMETT

DREW DOESN'T RELEASE her eyes from mine, anger still pooling in the warm hazel rings that contradict the coldness she is showing me. One of my hands is resting on her shoulder, but she makes no move to reciprocate my touch. I drop my arm back to my side, and it takes everything in me not to reach for her again.

She must not be able to see that I never want to let go.

She must not be able to see that I want every part of her, even the tears and the anger, and it scares me how those tears, and that anger, make me want to destroy anything and everything that makes them fester.

I don't want to have this conversation with her, not now. I don't want to let Riley ruin any other moment I have with Drew.

But Drew deserves the truth.

I exhale. "Her name is Riley. She's my ex."

"Ex-girlfriend?"

"Ex-fiancé." Drew's mouth slightly opens, as if she was physically affected by the words.

"You were engaged?" She looks hurt, caught so off-guard, and I want to pull her into my chest and tell her I would give those months with Riley back in a heartbeat if it meant I could've spent those months with Drew.

"We broke things off a few months ago. We wanted different things, and I thought I could be who she wanted, but it was doomed from the start."

I see Drew ponder, wrapped up in her thoughts, not saying anything else. She goes to sit back down on the couch, and I follow her.

"What are you thinking?" I ask, trying to bring her down from the whirlpool I can tell is happening in her brain.

"If you broke things off, why did she come over that night?"

I'm not exactly sure what Drew wants me to say at this moment, so I just go with the truth. "She wanted to talk about reconciling." Drew's reaction to my words is apparent, flinching at the words. "But I told her we were never going to work, and it's true." I look down at the floor, my voice growing less confident the more I talk about this. "We wanted different things, but I think we got too comfortable in the rela-tionship, neither of us wanting to start over."

"So, you weren't happy to see her?"

"I was surprised, but not happy," I explain. "For a second, I felt what I thought was happiness, but I was more pissed than anything else. I was mad she showed up, unannounced, and interrupted our night together."

"Why did you ask me to leave instead of her?" I can feel Drew's eyes burning into the side of my head. I can no longer say the edge I heard in her voice tonight with Reed has never been directed at me.

I know I have to meet her eyes, so I do.

And I almost instantly regret doing so.

It feels like a punch in the gut. Her wet hair and freshly clean face. Her features look so soft, but her expression is sharp. This is the last conversation she should have to be having after what just happened to her. But I know I owe her an explanation.

"Honestly, I needed to end things between Riley and me once and for all. Riley has always had a way of pushing me away just enough, so she can reel me back in."

Drew's face softens slightly, and she nods her head as if she knows exactly what I mean.

I continue, "I had to admit to her, and myself, that we were never going to work, and that—" I pause, not sure if I should admit to Drew what I admitted to Riley that night. What I've barely admitted to myself.

"That what?"

"That even though I've known you for a less amount of time than I've known her, you make me feel things she never made me feel."

Drew lets out an exhale she must have been holding on to for a while and doesn't say anything for a minute or two. I watch as she processes everything I told her, looking down at the floor. Her expression slowly begins to soften more, her eyebrows no longer furrowed, her shoulders no longer tense.

Finally, she meets my eyes again, and she says, "I know what you mean."

I let out an exhale of my own because I am relieved to hear her voice, hoping that there's not "but" on the tip of her tongue. "Thanks for telling me," she says. "I know how hard it is to let go of someone you thought you knew."

And this is where we leave the conversation, knowing that I put it all out there, and she still forgives me. Another part of our histories that somehow complement each other, allowing us to understand the other even more.

The brief moment of silence between us is interrupted by her phone vibrating on the coffee table in front of us, making her break away from me to check it.

I watch as she reads the message that popped up, a reminder of some sort.

"Everything okay?" I ask.

"Yeah, everything's fine. It's just an alarm I set for myself."

"Oh, do you have something to do? I can get out of your—"

"No, it's not that. I just—" she pauses, eyes still on her phone. "My therapist gave me some homework, and I wanted to set aside time for myself to do it tonight. It's actually part of the reason I invited Reed over." I fist my hands hearing his name come from her lips. "I wanted some help with it."

She turns to me but quickly looks away.

I'm sure she's contemplating on how to wrestle the hurricane of events she's been through in these few weeks and whether or not I make things worse for her. I'm not sure if she wants me to offer, but I offer anyway because I want nothing more than to be what she needs. "I can help."

Her eyes are looking anywhere but at me, but I see a hint of a smile form on her perfect lips. To my surprise but making my dreams come true, I hear, "I'd like that."

————

We spend the next few hours on her laptop and we read through news articles and watch news reports on what happened at Northshore Middle School at 10 a.m. on Friday, December 22nd. Drew sits with her legs up on the table in front of her couch, her feet crossed at the ankles next to the books I gave her. Her laptop in her lap, and I sit next to her, close, but not wrapped around her like I want to be. There's a distance between us, one that she is sure to keep. The outside of our thighs being the only parts of our bodies to occasionally touch, sending heat throughout my entire body every time.

Drew is tense and nervous, and it takes everything in me not to shut the computer and take her in my arms because I want to protect her. I can see her hands shake as she types or moves the cursor, and my heart aches. I watch as she experiences moments of despair, moments of fear, and moments of anger as the events unfold right in front of her . . . again.

We stick to articles that don't talk about the identity of the shooter or who was hurt or injured, saving that for when she feels ready.

After spending an hour or so reading the different accounts of teachers and students who provided statements and police officers and first responders who were interviewed, Drew says she is ready to read about the shooter.

We find an article about the shooter and his upcoming trial. When she reads the name of the guy her jaw drops. "I know him."

I feel like I was just punched in the stomach.

"What?" I ask.

"He's my student's brother. My student Cole."

Fuck.

This is the last thing she needs.

When will this girl catch a fucking break.

CHAPTER 33
DREW

COLE IS MY FAVORITE STUDENT, and I've known him since I started teaching. I know teachers aren't supposed to have favorites, but it's human nature. I can't help but find a little bit of extra love in my heart for Cole, especially knowing all he has been through at such a young age.

As a student teacher, I was placed in his fourth grade classroom, and he was one of my favorite parts of the day.

There was something about him that made the classroom a little brighter. He was always willing to help others, stand up for those who needed it, and show kindness to anyone he crossed. It's hard to believe he had the upbringing that he did.

Cole and his older brother, Finn, were raised by their grandparents after tragedy struck their family. When the boys were six and twelve, their dad took his alcohol and patterns of abuse too far, and their mother died at his hands.

Finn was there when the situation unfolded, so their father then turned to him, seeing him as the only other person who would know what he had done and needing to keep him quiet.

Finn never told anyone that his mother didn't die from

natural causes, even though that is all it might have taken for police to look just a little further into the case. How she died didn't come out until years later, and it was after Finn and Cole's dad had passed away, finally drinking himself to death.

Justice was never brought to Finn for all the abuse he endured or the secret he kept in fear of his father. Instead, he was just considered lucky, and the only reason being because his dad died, and the abuse ended.

Finn suffered in silence for years, slowly losing trust in anyone and everyone. He dropped out of school by the time he reached high school and disappeared. Cole expressed to me once that he had not heard from Finn since.

As a child, Finn was a victim in so many ways, even at the hands of the school. I remember hearing stories through the grapevine of the district during my student teaching and first-year at the middle school. People said that it was obvious that his teachers and the counselor missed all the vital signs of abuse and neglect. Some even say the adults that were supposed to protect him and report what they were seeing turned a blind eye to what was obviously happening.

Cole was so much younger when their mother died, so the tragedy of losing her didn't seem to hit him as hard as it hit Finn. I don't think Cole learned the truth about how his mother died until he was older. Likewise, Cole never suffered the same abuse from their father as Finn. It is rumored this was because they were half-brothers, only sharing the same mother, but no one knows for certain.

Over these past few years, I had the opportunity to watch Cole grow, and I looked forward to the year he would be in my classroom.

His fourth grade teacher always said, "Cole showing up every day is a miracle in itself."

I never understood that until I had him on my own roster.

———

I feel Emmett's eyes on me as I read through the articles about Finn. My mind is moving at a rate where I can barely finish a thought before being overwhelmed by ten more. My mind went from Cole to his family to Finn to the lives Finn took.

My feelings about the shooting and everything that has happened since were already so complicated, but this took things to a whole other level.

The latest articles released about Finn had interviews from his grandparents *and Cole.* His grandparents were quoted from their narrative that they haven't seen or heard from Finn in years, and this makes my heart ache for this boy, barely an adult, and how sick he must be to do something like this. But, also making my stomach burn with hatred for him and what he has done.

Cole explains in his interview that his brother had been through so much and how Finn's reality was warped because no sane person would have done what he did. Cole, even in a time like this, showing empathy and kindness for someone who doesn't deserve it, but that same someone who is his brother.

Tears fall down my face, one after another, as I think about Cole and how scared, hurt, and angry he must be, and I'm surprised there are still tears left to fall.

Another article explains how investigators have reason to believe that Finn had been planning the attack for a while, wanting to go and do the most damage as possible for his own vindictive, twisted reasoning. No rhyme or reason to who he was going after, just wanting to pour his hatred into a place he felt he was wronged in.

I can tell that Emmett is worried about me, unsure of exactly how to help me, especially because of the wall I had to put up between us. I'm still unsure if continuing whatever is between us is a good idea, but there are more important things on the forefront of my mind right now.

I close my computer, telling myself that I have had more than enough. I feel a sense of pride that I was able to do this, but it is overshadowed with guilt.

I am okay.

I am fine.

I am lucky.

I came out of there alive, and I owe it to those who didn't.

I owe it to the lives lost and those impacted by this tragedy to ensure that no child ever feels like they were left behind by the adults who are there to take care of them, to teach them, to make them feel valued and part of a community where they can grow and flourish no matter who they are or what they've been through.

My head falls into my hands as I try to make the tears stop, and Emmett's arms wrap around me, pulling me into his chest. I let him even though I'm conflicted because I know I am strong enough to handle this, but is it okay to accept his support and comfort?

I slowly feel myself calm down, and I lift my head from his chest, finding his eyes.

We don't say anything, understanding that this moment may or not be the start of something, but that doesn't matter right now.

———

I wake up the next morning in a bit of a daze. After Emmett went home last night, I went to bed, completely exhausted from the events of the day. It was about eleven o'clock by the time my head hit my pillow, and I was asleep within minutes.

I reach for my phone on my bedside table and find myself smiling at the message waiting for me.

The text reads, *Morning. Did you sleep well? Let me know if you need anything. Vodka clubs with limes are my specialty these days :)*

My heart swoons, and I feel my cheeks heat.

Damn it.

I have to get my body's reactions to Emmett in check because there he goes again, making my belly overflow with fluttering wings.

Emmett has a way of always knowing the right thing to say and the right time to say it to get a reaction out of me. And these days, the reactions go far more deeper than they did before.

I've learned through the reading I've done about trauma and recovering that what is most helpful during a time like this is someone who is there for you, reminding you that they are there whenever you may need it. And, that is exactly what Emmett does.

I "heart" the message and respond with a flirty sentiment: *How neighborly of you :) Maybe see you later.* I see the three dots appear seconds after my message is marked as delivered. I anxiously wait for his reply, hoping my "neighborly" comment keeps both of us in check.

You're more than a neighbor, Drew. I hope I see you tonight.

Well, that didn't work.

It's around 9 a.m., and I have no plans for the day except for the possibility of visiting a bar owner who is somehow always so heavy on my mind.

I have a few days before an email is supposed to be sent out about how the transition back to school for staff and students is going to go. There have been meetings taking place at the district office this week, and they extended the schools' closure another week. I haven't received anything explaining the plans being discussed, but with it being the Wednesday of the second extra week we have off following

Winter Break, I'm sure we'll be getting an email early next week.

I spent the day reading the next book of the Hades and Persephone series, thanks to Emmett's thoughtful gift. I, once again, dive into the beautiful yet catastrophic love story, one built on a connection that neither quite understands.

This book is longer than the first one, so it takes me most of the day, also due to a couple breaks for some snacks and a quick text or two to Lacey about calling her later this week, before finishing just in time for happy hour.

Still in my t-shirt and leggings from last night, I peel myself up from the couch to actually get myself ready to leave my apartment and head over to Lenny's.

I slip on my favorite pair of black jeans and a beige crop top. I let my hair down from the clip it's been in since I woke up this morning, letting my red waves roam free, noticing I need to make an appointment to get the color freshened. I add some concealer and mascara to my face before throwing a black-knit cardigan on and slipping into my winter coat.

I step into my shoes, grab my keys, and head out the door.

THE BAR IS PACKED with regulars for happy hour on this cold Wednesday. Both Annie and I have been swamped all afternoon and into the evening. I was so relieved when five o'clock rolled around and Eddie and Luke got here. The four of us were working like a well-oiled machine, until things died down a little around 5:30 p.m.

The seats at the bar clear out, most of the customers at the high top tables and squeezed into the booths. I wipe down the bar as the rush of the past few hours settles. I feel a gust of wind rush in as the door opens. Looking up to greet whoever walked in, I am met with the most gorgeous view.

Drew waves, smiling at me, showing me she's as happy to see me as I am to see her, and I'm relieved. I wasn't sure if I was pushing too hard with my text this morning, especially after the distance she put between us last night after I apologized for asking her to leave when Riley came over.

For Drew, I'll play the long game.

"Hey," I say as she hops into the seat in front of me. "It's good to see you." Her cheeks blush to match her hair. She is wearing it down, which I haven't seen much before. It is almost always clipped back. The red locks, framing her face, contrasts with the green in her hazel eyes, making my heart skip a beat. Something moves around in my stomach.

Is she giving me butterflies?

"Likewise," she says as I set a coaster down in front of her.

"How was your day?" I ask.

"It was good. Finished the second book of that series I started a few weeks ago, thanks to you." Her arms crossed on the bar in front of her, leaning in towards me.

"My pleasure. How was it?" I grab a glass and fill it with ice.

"Super good. I'm excited to start the next one."

I bend down to the cooler below where I'm standing, grabbing our new seltzer option, "Can I get you the usual? Or…" I pull out a lime White Claw, her preferred hard seltzer brand, "Someone told me Truly sucks, so we switched to White Claw." I hold the white can up to show her.

Her eyes widen and her mouth gapes open. She stands up on the footrest on the bar stool reaching to grab the can from me.

"That *someone* sounds pretty smart." She sets the can down on her coaster. I crack it open from her and watch her take a sip.

"Ahh. It really is the best."

I laugh because she is the most intriguing person I ever met, always keeping me on my toes, always having me begging for more, and I'm feeling like a high schooler with a crush out of my league because I can't believe she is giving me another chance.

Drew sits at the bar with me while I dry glasses, refill drinks, and wipe down the areas where people have come and gone in the hour she has been here. She sips on her second White Claw, watching me as I work.

"When are you done for the night?" she asks, right as Eddie passes by behind her on his way to clear one of the high top tables.

"Yeah, boss. Why are you still here?" Drew turns to face the voice from behind her. "Hi. I don't think we've officially met. I'm Eddie Ramirez, Emmett's best friend and favorite employee." He holds his hand out to shake hers, smiling from ear to ear. The slightest ounce of jealousy runs through me, wanting to be the only one her hand ever touches.

I'm not quite sure where this possessiveness is coming from, so I shake it away knowing that I should really get it under control. Plus, this is Eddie. he is probably using all his willpower not to say what he is thinking: that Drew is the only girl I've talked to since Riley left.

Drew's looking at him, matching his smile, taking his hand in hers. "Hi. I'm Drew Thomas, Emmett's—" she pauses, not sure what to call herself.

Date? Too casual.

Girlfriend? Don't want to push my luck.

Friend? I guess we'll settle on that.

"Neighbor," I hear her say, and I'm starting to hate the word. She must be able to tell when she turns back to me, a playful yet wondering glance. "Friend?" She corrects herself, but there's still a question to it.

Eddie meets my eyes over her shoulder, then glances back towards her. "It's nice to meet you, Drew."

He walks away, back to doing his job.

I grab Drew's can to see if it's empty. I lift it and give it a little shake, glad to not feel any more liquid left. "Let's get out of here."

She smiles in return, hopping off the chair. She waits for me as I round the bar and meet her by the exit. As she goes to push the door open, I grab her hand. She looks down at our intertwined fingers and whispers to me as we walk out together. "I don't think friends do this."

"Sweetheart," I say as we start our walk to our complex, "I'd argue we're a little more than friends."

"Oh? Is that so?" Her voice is flirty as the words leave her lips. "Who are you and what have you done with my grumpy neighbor?"

I laugh out loud at this. "You're lucky you're cute, otherwise I would have been hitting my ceiling with a broomstick telling you to be quiet for the past seven months."

"Have we really known each other that long?" she asks. I squeeze her hand a little tighter as we walk because I don't know what to say. I can't believe that it took me so many months to convince her to give me the chance I wanted when I first met her, but was too stubborn to admit it.

"So, we're more than neighbors?" There's a hopefulness in her voice that gives me the confidence to continue this conversation.

"Wouldn't you agree?"

She looks away, eyes facing forward as she smiles, thinking of what to say. "We haven't even been on an official date."

"Who said dates need to be official?" I challenge her. "Plus, I'd argue that our encounters have meant more to me than any 'official date' I've ever been on."

Still walking hand-in-hand, she looks up at me, cheeks flushed, telling me she agrees, then looking away not being able to contain the smile on her face.

"Drew." We're the only ones on the sidewalk, so I slow our walking to a stop and grab her other hand so she's facing me. "I don't know exactly what we are or what you want us to be, but I know that my feelings for you are unmatched compared to anything I've felt for anyone else.

"You have been through so much, and I think you are absolutely incredible. I cherish every moment I get to spend with you because I feel like I can be myself around you, and I want to be that person for you too."

Her eyes glisten at my sentiment, and I feel my own voice beginning to get caught. I clear my throat and continue, "We don't have to decide anything now, but, just know, I'm not going anywhere. Not unless you want me to." I let go of her hands to find the sides of her face, leaning down and pulling her in. Not being able to fight the urge to kiss her with all I have, wanting to show her the truth behind my words.

It's been thirteen days since I last had her lips on mine, and I never want to go that long again.

I'm not going anywhere, unless you want me to.

CHAPTER 35

DREW

MY MIND IS RACING the rest of the walk home and until we are outside my apartment. I don't want this night with Emmett to end, so I ask, "Do you want to come in?"

His eyes light up as his beautiful smile appears, the one that shows his teeth. "I would want nothing more."

I haven't said much since his declaration outside, but there's so much I want to say and not sure how to say it.

We sit down on the couch, and I still can't find the right words to say. I feel Emmett's hand rest just above my knee. "What is it, Drew? You haven't said much." He squeezes my thigh. "Are you okay?"

"Yes. Yes, I'm fine. I'm great actually. Just trying to find my own words."

I see his face twist with concern, and he grabs my hands in his. "You don't have to say anything. I just wanted to tell you how I feel. I always feel like I can be my realest with you, and express whatever is on my mind. But I don't expect you to feel the same."

"No, I do. Because—" I close my eyes and take a breath, wanting to tell him my doubts but also wanting to tell him that I feel the same. With his hands on mine, feeling his warmth run through me, I let the words pour out of me. "Because, being with you, getting to know you, *feeling* like we connect on this deeper level because you understand me without me having to say a word." The words feel like they've been on the tip of my tongue. It feels good to tell Emmett how I feel, but I instantly feel like I've said too much.

He doesn't respond right away, but his expression is soft and gentle as if my words settled a fear he had. As soft and gentle as when he held me in the elevator or when he pulled me in for our first kiss.

A cloud of doubt grows in my brain, but then Emmett grabs both my hands, one hand of mine in each of his. He pulls one hand to his lips before he kisses each of my knuckles, then does the same with the other. Quick little kisses, each one sending a shock through my system, doubt slowly dissipating. Sparks and butterflies fly, and I feel all of the tension in my body release. His effect on me is debilitating in the best way possible.

His eyes hook into mine, and I feel like I'm being looked at for the first time.

"Drew, I want nothing more than to get to know each and every part of you."

His hands find each side of my face, touching his forehead to mine. "I've been thinking about you since that first day I bumped into you when you were getting out of the elevator." I grab his wrists, wanting to pull him as close to me as possible as he helps relieve any doubt I ever had about him.

He continues, "You with your blushing cheeks, black skin-tight jeans, and stunning smile, I couldn't get you out of my head." He laughs before adding, "It also didn't help that your butterfingers and lead feet reminded me who was above me every single day." I let out a laugh too, more and more doubt subsiding as I listen to his words.

"And then, when I saw your school on the news, I felt this uncontrollable fear that your smile would be gone forever, and I didn't want the world to be without your smile. The smile that met me so many times when I was at my lowest, in my worst moments, and I'm sorry if I ever left you feeling like you should do anything other than smile." His thoughts pour out from his mouth, and I don't want to miss a single word.

"Drew, you fascinate and challenge me, and every time I saw you in that elevator was the best part of my day."

And with that, his lips crash into mine, and I never want it to stop. His kiss is enough to set my entire body on fire making it hard to think straight. With every move of his lips, his tongue, I feel all the doubt I had about us fade, and I fall deeper and deeper into feelings I haven't had in years. Feelings of passion and intensity that I thought were gone for good. Feelings I want to throw myself into rather than run away from. Feelings that make me feel alive and ready to take on the world. My hands find Emmett's chest and snake up his broad shoulders and up his neck, feeling his skin warm under my touch.

I feel his hands move from my cheeks, my neck, and down my arms until he finds my hips, leaving a trail of goosebumps along the way even though his hands are still over my clothes. He squeezes my hips before slowly moving his hands down the sides of my legs to the back of my thighs. He pulls me on top of him, and I begin to feel an intense pressure bud in my lower stomach as I straddle him. This pressure is telling me I don't just want more, I *need* it, and I'm alarmed how quickly my body is reacting.

I can feel him taking control, and I let him.

His hands move up from my thighs, back to my hips, and around to grab my ass, pulling me close to him. He presses me into him, and I can feel him, hard and as turned on as me, the fabric of our jeans being the only thing between us, the words he said moments ago still lingering in the air around us.

There's an edge and an eagerness to Emmett. I feel it in his kiss, in the way he is grabbing on to me so tightly, and I want more of it. Seeing him go from being so gentle, so tender to *this* is enticing, and I no longer want to wait for what is going to come next.

His hands move from my backside, up past my ribcage, peeling my cardigan off me. With my arms bare, he runs his hands down my skin, his touch leaving tingles. His hands find their way back at my sides, pulling my top up with him, as he grazes the sides of my breasts, sending a shiver down my spine. His tongue licking against mine, and then stopping for a moment to pull my top off over my head and throwing it to the side of the couch, never taking his eyes off me.

I feel his eyes scan over me, taking in what he sees, letting out a groan from the back of his throat.

I start to feel a little nervous, being that the only other person to ever see me like this was Reed. My breast size lets me get away without a bra most of the time, and it's something I've been self-conscious about, but I've never had to worry about someone new seeing me. I move my arms to cover myself.

Emmett senses my hesitation, and his hands find my face.

"You are breathtaking," he breathes, pulling my face to his, our foreheads touching.

My voice has a breathiness I barely recognize. "I've only ever been with one other person and—"

I feel his finger touch my lips, causing me to gasp. "Please do not talk about anyone else while you're in my lap." His hungry eyes, peeking out through his dark lashes, showing me that, while he said please, he is feeling anything but polite. "We'll take it as slow as you want. I'm in no rush."

And with that, he knows what I need without even needing to hear me say it. I melt into his hands, his lips finding mine again.

His mouth over mine, I want to feel my skin against his. I

reach down to the bottom of his shirt and slowly pull it up and over his head, seeing that his tattoos don't stop at his arms. I sit back and run my fingertips across the designs on his shoulders stopping just below his neck that I haven't seen before, mesmerized by them and the muscles beneath them. I knew Emmett was built, but I wasn't expecting this.

"Like what you see?" he asks, staring up at me, a dangerous smirk on his face.

I nod as I give him a slight push, so his back is up against the couch. I lean towards him, finding his lips again with no intention of pulling away anytime soon.

His palms pressed down on my hips, and I rub against him. He groans against my lips, and I love the sounds I'm pulling from him. His hands find my breasts, and he takes one in each hand. Kissing me hard as he teases me, slowly rubbing and massaging then taking my nipples between his fingers, making me moan at the sensation it gives me, feeling wet between my thighs.

He sits up, and his lips make their way from mine, down my neck, finding a tender spot below my ear that I didn't know was there. He grazes his teeth against me, biting the sensitive skin softly then licking across the same spot. I can't help the noises I'm making.

"You like that?" he says into my ear. The warmth of his breath is invigorating.

I nod, not sure I'm able to talk but loving that he is. I feel him kissing me down my neck to my chest making my skin pebble.

His mouth finds one of my breasts while his hand continues massaging the other. His other palm pressed against just below my shoulder blade, causing me to arch my back, giving his mouth more access.

I feel his tongue swirl around my nipple, tight and raw. His teeth and tongue create a delicious sensation I feel down to my core. He grazes his tongue across my chest, switching his hands to the opposite spaces, doing the same to my other breast. The sounds I'm making are growing louder.

"Shh." His lips vibrate against me, a whole other sensation, creating an intense pressure between my legs. "You can't be too loud, sweetheart. I can't have others hearing these magical noises you're making. They are for me and me only."

As he says the words, I feel his fingers lightly dig into my skin, staking his claim in me as *his*.

Before I can even so much as nod my head, his lips find mine again, his hands moving to below my thighs. He stands up as if my extra weight is nothing to him. My legs wrap around him as he stands and walks us to my bedroom, gently laying me down on my bed.

His hands move up to the top of my leggings, slowly pulling them down, leaving me in just my panties, red with little black hearts. He stands at the edge of the bed, feeling so far away. As he looks down at me in the darkness, he's a starving man staring at his first meal in days. "I think red is my new favorite color."

"I'll keep that in mind." I breathe, a confidence I've never felt before beginning to bloom inside me.

His fingers line the elastic below my stomach, and I let out an exhale, my way of telling him I like what he's doing. He hooks his fingers under the cotton, his eyes burning into me. "As much as I love these on you, I think I'll like them a little more off of you."

"Nice line." My voice, playful, but my cheeks blush as I watch his eyes. He is gazing hard at what he is doing.

"It's the truth." He pulls me out of my panties, discarding them on the floor.

I'm on display in front of him, glistening and swollen with anticipation. I feel a little embarrassed how eager I am, but Emmett doesn't seem to mind.

"What about you?" I ask.

He meets my eyes. "What about me?"

I sit up on my elbows. "Don't I get to see you?"

He gives me a smirk and slithers out of his jeans, throwing them to the side. His black boxer briefs hugging his thighs and his erection begging to be free from the fabric.

"I guess black is still my favorite color," I tease.

Instead of saying anything in return, he crawls on to me, making me lean back into the bed, teasing me with what his tongue can do. He is holding himself up with his arms, but I want to feel him closer. I wrap my arms around his back, lightly dragging my fingernails against his smooth skin. I hear him groan in response, wrapping my legs around his waist to pull him closer, begging to release this pressure.

As if sensing what I need, he lines me with kisses down the front of my body, crawling down me, settling back at the edge of the bed, kneeling between my open legs. I arch my back, closing my eyes, as I feel his fingers part me, so easily. Feeling his fingers gliding back and forth makes me moan, pleasure beginning to hum through me.

"Are you loving this as much as me, sweetheart?" He breathes—his warm breath just inches away from me

I move my head up and down, not being able to find my words as I feel his fingers part my lips, moving in mesmerizing circles, finally finding my most sensitive spot.

"May I?" After a few breaths, I wield my eyes open to find him staring up at me, he taps his middle finger at my entrance applying the lightest, most perfect, pressure.

"Yes," I moan. "Please."

I see his grin before my eyes roll back as he pushes his middle finger in, steadily and mind-blowingly, letting out a husky, "Fuck."

He starts off so slow, I can feel the length of his finger move in and out before he slowly adds another. My opening, almost dripping, from the intensity of his touch. It glides in easily and so nicely. "Fuck, Drew. You're so wet."

His pace begins to quicken. His fingers pumping into me

while his thumb finds my clit, hypnotically circling, causing me to let out whimpers of pleasure.

"Yes," I moan. The pressure is building. I've never felt the sensations I'm feeling now, finding that there is more to intimacy than I ever thought possible.

I feel his fingers slow, opening my eyes to find him watching me. "I need to taste you." I suck in a breath at his words.

"What?" I hear myself say. His thumb is still making mesmerizing circles, so it is hard to keep my thoughts coherent.

This is all so different than anything I've experienced before, and I don't know what I'm supposed to say.

"Please?" He pleads.

I bring my hands to cover my face, suddenly feeling shy.

And then feel his body hover over mine.

"Look at me," Emmett whispers. I peek at him from under my hands. "I won't do anything you don't want me to do," he kisses my lips as he pushes two fingers into me, and I let out a moan bringing my arms to my sides. "If you say stop, I'll stop." He slowly retreats his fingers before pushing in again. "Just a taste, okay?"

"Yes. Yes," I moan before even thinking about the words. I lean my head back, closing my eyes.

His fingers slide out of me, and he returns to his spot between my legs, his hands finding the inside of my thighs, keeping me open. My eyes still closed, making the sensations of his touch even deeper, I feel his tongue part me agonizingly slow before lapping, sucking, and kissing me, making me squirm beneath his hands. He pauses before pressing down on my clit with the most perfect force, and I can't control the volume of the moan that leaves my throat.

"Shh." His breath warming the parts of me he just licked. "You heard what I said about those noises. Loud enough for only me to hear." I nod in agreement, accepting any terms if it means he never stops.

His tongue finds me again, making me clench the comforter beneath me between my fists, letting out an exhale. My body is beginning to take over.

Emmett continues to lick and nip at the sensitive skin, moving his hands up my body to find my breasts. The sensations in all the right places, bringing me closer and closer to the edge. I open my eyes and watch him work, the sight of him between my legs, meeting my eyes, pushes me to my release.

As all the energy centers of my body activate at once, my muscles contract and the most sensual ecstasy washes over me. Emmett has made me feel things I've never felt before, and I can't believe what I've been missing out on all this time.

As my body begins to descend, I blink my eyes open, feeling a little embarrassed and exposed, not sure if Emmett is enjoying this as much as me.

"I'm sorry," I say because I don't know what else to say with him watching me, staring up at me, looking a little dazed.

He crawls up my body. "Why the hell are you apologizing?" He whispers as he pauses between my breasts, sending shivers down my spine. He kisses his way back up my chest and neck until his eyes are just before mine.

"Did I take too long?"

He freezes on top of me, jaw tightening at my question.

"Why would you even think that?"

"I don't know." I turn my head away from him

"Sweetheart, I'm loving every second of this." He kisses up my neck until he is one kiss away from my lips. I turn my head back to meet his lips with mine.

"Really?" I ask against his lips.

"Of course," he says against my lips. "Don't think otherwise."

I've only ever been with someone who, I have just recently realized, was a selfish, impatient lover. One that didn't take my pleasure into consideration the way that Emmett is.

The closer I grow with Emmett, the more I realize that what Reed taught me about love, and sex, is that it is one-sided, and I'm finding that I have a lot of re-learning to do.

"Now," he breathes, "where were we?"

He leans in, kissing me so hard, I wouldn't be surprised if my lips were bruised tomorrow. He grabs onto my waist, pulling me up and over, so now I'm on top.

His erection is just below me, the fabric rubbing against me, being the perfect pressure where I'm already so sensitive, making me wet all over again. I feel this intense *need* to feel the pressure alleviate, wanting to feel him inside me.

"You're in control. What do you want?" he asks. Hands on my hips, rocking me back and forth on his length.

I sit up on my knees, cheeks blushing, not sure where my confidence from earlier disappeared off to. "You," I whisper, placing my hands on his chest to feel his skin.

"Me?" He whispers back, amusement in his voice. "How do you want me?" Even in the dark, I can see the intense starvation in his eyes.

"Inside me." I exhale.

He lets out a gasp, my words having an effect on him.

"Are you on birth control? Otherwise, I can be back in sixty seconds. I'm clean by the way."

I nod. "Yeah, me too, and I'm on the pill."

Crawling off of him, it is my turn to find my place at the bed's edge. Standing between his legs, he begins to slide down his boxers, his erection finally free. I help him the rest of the way, throwing his boxes to the pile of our other clothes. He sits up at the edge of the bed, looking up at me. My eyes widen at the view below me, unsure of how something so full, so big, will feel inside me.

"I love it when your eyes are on me," he playfully says,

"but I'm aching to be inside you." My attention goes back to his face as he grabs me by the waist and pulls me in. As if making a full circle, he pulls me to straddle him, just like he did on the couch. I hold myself up by my knees on each side of him, anxiously wanting to relieve this pressure that has been building for a second time.

I'm so wet with anticipation.

His gaze holding mine, his hands still on my hips, he guides me down. I wince at the stretching feeling as he starts to pull me down his length. He lifts my hips up, and then back down, sinking in a little farther this time. We repeat this a few times until his erection gets slick.

"You're too big."

"You're just a little tight, sweetheart." His lips find mine. "You can take it."

And with that, the last bit of patience he has dissipates, and he lowers me all the way down, feeling his entire length inside me, an insane intensity that causes me to let out a gasp.

He loses all the control he had just a moment ago, tightening his grip on my hips, lifting me up and slamming me down. He sinks into me, filling me to the brim.

"Fuck," he lets out. The sound of his pleasure exciting me to my core. "That's my girl."

His fingers dig into my hips as he helps me slide up and down, my second orgasm quickly building.

"Emmett." Getting closer and closer.

His pace quickens even more, slamming me onto him harder and harder with every bounce. With my knees on either side of him and my hands on his shoulders, I use my position to move with him to the rhythm he created, getting closer to my release.

"Fuck, Drew. You feel so good." He whines out each word, his eyes rolling back, getting closer to his own orgasm.

Seeing his pleasure is enough to send me over the edge. I

moan out his name as he continues pumping into me, reaching his release a few seconds behind me. Our pace slows as we come down from our high until we come to a stop.

Emmett leans back on the bed, bringing me with him. The room is filled with nothing but our heavy breathing, and I have never enjoyed a quiet moment more.

My head on his chest, listening to his hummingbird heartbeat slowly fade back to its normal rate. I sit up, resting my arms across his chest, my chin on my hands, finding his lazy eyes.

His voice, raspy in the sexiest way as he says, "Now that I know what it's like to fuck you, I don't know how I'm ever going to stop."

———

I wake up in the middle of night, naked and dazed. It takes me a second to remember the past few hours and how I ended up like this. Then the memories flood over me, washing me with a feeling of bliss and exhilaration at the thought of Emmett. I turn over to find him asleep and at peace, tired after our evening together.

We spent the hours following our first time with our second before ordering some pizza and having a late dinner, naked and in bed, laughing and sharing more of ourselves with each other before our third time.

Before we fell asleep, under the covers and all wrapped in each other, I asked Emmett about what I said earlier, I asked why he thinks we connect on such a deep level. I told him I felt it, but I didn't understand how he understood me so well.

That is when he told me about the night Lennon died.

As Emmett revisited the night he has tried so hard to never think about again, he shared with me his most vulnerable side, showing me his own pain and suffering that fit so tragically yet beautifully with mine.

He told me he had never shared so much about that night with anyone, but my mind couldn't help but think of how he could be with someone for years, be engaged, yet never share this part of him. I asked why he could never tell Riley, and he said she never asked. On the surface, this sounds silly. He could have told her if he wanted. But, the more I thought about it as he shared pieces of what it felt like being in a relationship with her, I realized that the simple act of *not asking* spoke volumes.

Riley wanted the parts of him that fit with her picture-perfect life. The easy, pretty parts of him. Not the deep, sensitive, disastrously fascinating parts of him. I didn't want to be happy about the years he suffered, not being able to share every part of himself with someone, but I can't help but be selfishly grateful I got to be the one he finally did share with.

Cheeks damp with both tears of grief and tears of happiness, we fell asleep in each other's arms.

Laying here in the dark, I'm in complete fascination over the fact that this is what sex and intimacy is *supposed* to be like. It's not one-sided, and it can be fun, passionate, and *amazing*. I honestly had no idea.

Until tonight, my idea of pleasure and release was that they were few and far between, but I now see that I just never experienced sex with the right person.

Now, I don't know if I'll ever have enough.

The sex between Emmett and I matches the same description of our relationship that has flowered these past weeks.

Intense.

Raw.

Scary.

Beautiful.

I lay on my back, Emmett's labored breathing filling the room, and I smile to myself. I feel my body sink further into my bed, and the silence around us, as it realizes how tired it is after the past couple of hours. I fall back into a deep sleep, a new feeling of hope for what tomorrow will bring.

I wake up the next morning, expecting to be alone, only left with the memory of the amazing night Emmett and I had. To my surprise, I see a tattooed forearm across my stomach.

I turn over meeting the sleepy eyes, naked body, and restless curls of the most beautiful man.

"Hey," he says, pulling me closer to him, giving me a tender kiss on the temple, igniting the passion in me that was set ablaze for the first time last night.

"Hey," I respond, turning to face him, smiling so big. I can't contain the happiness I feel at this moment, with Emmett. Wanting to relive last night over and over again.

"You're cute when you sleep."

My eyes widen at his statement. "You were watching me sleep?"

He laughs. "I woke up a little bit ago, and you were still asleep. I couldn't help but look at you."

I cover my face with my hands. "I've never had a sleepover with a guy where he's here when I wake up! Please don't tell me I snore or talk." I peek at him behind my fingers.

I see him smiling, starting right at me. "No, you don't snore. But you do talk a little."

"Stop!" I give him a playful hit on the shoulder. "No, I don't. That's embarrassing." I feel the blood rush to my cheeks.

"Not at all. I think it's adorable." He kisses me again. "And, I'm honored to be your first sleepover," he says, trying to pull away to look at me, but I don't let him get far. I pull him back, pressing into his lips, deepening our kiss compared to before. I find myself wanting to feel the same fire that engulfed us last night.

Against my lips, he says, "I need to shower. Care to join?"

CHAPTER 36

EMMETT

I NEVER WANT to know what it's like not kissing Drew. I want to spend the rest of this day, and the next day, and the next day, and the one after that, kissing her.

I turn on her shower and grab her by her hips, pulling her into me. She looks up at me, wrapping her arms around my naked waist, looking up at me with her chin on my chest. I lean down to kiss her on the forehead, on the nose, on the lips, wanting to spend the rest of my days kissing her all over.

When my lips meet hers, her hands snake up my body to find my hair. I haven't put it back up since she took it down during our endeavors last night, and I love how her fingers run through it. She deepens the kiss, making my body feel warm on the inside while the steam of the water from the shower makes my body warm on the outside.

Drew keeps her apartment below the temperature I would choose for myself, but I learned to be okay with it last night when her body found mine under the sheets, looking for my warmth.

Her kisses wave through my body, and I ache for her.

I pull her by her waist, never leaving her lips, and we step into the shower. My back facing the water, blocking the water from splashing her too much, I feel a rush of adrenaline sharing this space with her. It feels intimate, being in the shower I've heard run above me so many times.

Our night together last night showed me that Drew hasn't been able to release herself to someone who was ready for her, giving me an exhilarating feeling of possessiveness that I can't help but feel knowing I pulled this side out for her, and I'm the *only* one who gets to.

So much for getting that under control.

As we tangle ourselves in each other under the water, my need for her, to be inside her, takes over, but I tell my body to not move too fast, knowing that she likes things slow. I twist her hips, so her backside is up against my front, feeling her ass against me, her hands find the shower wall as she pushes her back against my chest, exposing her neck for me.

My hands move to feel the smooth skin of her stomach, finding her breasts. I massage each one, taking her nipples between my fingers, as I glide my tongue up her neck to find the spot just under her ear where I suck at the sensitive skin. I taste the water with a mixture of her sweet skin. She lets out a stunning moan, making me even harder.

Her taste is intoxicating.

Lapping my tongue at the drops of water on her skin, my hands move down her front to find her opening, wet and ready for me. I move my finger in circles around her clit before slowly sinking my fingers into her. She gasps, wincing a little—she's probably sore from last night. Slowly, she leans her head back to rest on my shoulder, arching into me, giving me even more access.

I pump my fingers in and out of her, careful not to go too fast, the mixture of the water and her own wetness allowing me to pick up speed little by little before pressing my palm against her back and guiding her forward and her hips back before rocking into her.

This sensation isn't like last night—like our first time—similar but different. It's raw and new, yet familiar and intimate, and I long for her to know all the different ways I plan on taking her because I don't think I can go a *day* without this.

She takes my whole length in one fluid motion, and I let out a groan as I pull out, almost all the way but not quite, before slamming back into her. She moves her hands down the shower wall, bending over more, creating the perfect position for me to slide in and out of her, increasing my speed. The perfect friction is sending ripples through my body, and the sounds she is making tell me she is getting close, further pushing me closer to my edge.

Through blurry eyes, seeing her beautiful body moving back and forth in front of me, I lean my head back, chasing my release, when she slides off me and turns to face me. Stunned by her sudden change, she bends before me, taking me in her mouth. This confidence radiates off her like the water splashing on my back.

I take her wet hair in my hand, helping her find her rhythm.

Has she done this before?

"Fuck," I exhale through my teeth. Watching her lips around me, feeling her tongue swirl around the head of my cock, and I can't take it anymore.

Saving *that* for another day.

I bring her up, crashing my lips into hers, tasting my saltiness on her tongue, before turning off the water behind me, lifting her up and pushing her up against the wall. Her legs wrap around me as I slide into her again. I can tell she's at her edge, so I keep my rhythm as the sounds of her moans and heavy breathing fill the air around us. I stare right at her, watching her as she comes. As she finds her release, she tightens around me, sending me right into my own orgasm.

Still holding her, my head falls into the crook of her neck, feeling her fingers release their grip on my back, leaning her head against mine.

Her legs unwrap from me, and I set her down carefully before reaching behind me to turn the water on again. I block her from the cold water and move her to be under when it gets warm enough, holding her waist as she leans back closing her eyes.

We still haven't said a word, just flushed cheeks, dazed eyes, and lazy smiles on our faces.

When I step out of the shower behind her, taking the towel she hands to me, I finally find my voice.

"What are you doing today?"

Not what I thought was going to come out of my mouth, but it was obviously on the tip of my tongue. I find myself scared to walk out of this bathroom, not wanting to just get dressed to go home, but get dressed to spend the day with her. I'm not expected at the bar until four, and there's no way it's even 10 a.m. yet, meaning I have at least six, uninterrupted hours to put all my focus on her.

"I don't have any plans," she says, as she takes her towel from around her body and wraps her hair up, leaving her naked in front of me, the most amazing sight.

She grabs her robe from behind the bathroom door, leaving just her bare chest and one shoulder exposed, a subtle circle of deep red just under her ear. A flutter in my stomach at the thought of how it got there.

She sees me staring, and cocks her head. "Emmett?"

My eyes find hers, "Sorry," I take a few steps towards her, wrapping my arms around her, "I just can't take my eyes off you. You're so beautiful." I lean down to give her a gentle kiss. "Can I make you breakfast?"

She blushes, and I take it as a yes. "But, only if it's waffles."

"Anything for you, sweetheart."

After we get dressed and pull away from each other long

enough to make breakfast, we spend the morning with her head on my lap, reading the third book of her series, while I watch a movie. She told me how she's watching the Marvel movies in order, but she doesn't pay much attention. She mentioned how she's seen them all many times before, and I've noticed she mostly just has them on in the background.

I think it's cute.

She is on *Avengers: Age of Ultron*, so I watch as she reads and laugh to myself when she occasionally turns to watch the fight scenes. We don't spend much of the time talking, just being in each other's presence.

I notice she's about halfway through her book when I check the time to see it's about one o'clock. I lean down to kiss her on the forehead, and she tears her eyes from the pages in front of her to meet mine.

"Hey."

"Hey." She smiles.

"We always do that," I say, and it makes her laugh. "I like spending time with you," I add as I stroke her hair, my fingers lingering on her cheek.

"I like spending time with you too."

"I have to be at the bar in a few hours. If you're not doing anything, you could meet me there for a drink, and then, I was thinking, we could go to dinner."

Her cheeks crimson. "I'd like that."

CHAPTER 37
DREW

EMMETT LEFT AN HOUR AGO, and I have a little time before I'm supposed to meet him at Lenny's. We decided I would stop by the bar around six o'clock, and then we'd go to dinner. He wanted me to pick the place, but I told him I wanted him to, so we agreed we would decide on a spot when I meet him for a drink.

After I get ready, skipping the black jeans and, instead, going with black sheer tights, a black leather skirt, and an emerald knit-turtleneck, I grab my jacket, slip on my Doc Marten boots, and head out the door. It started snowing a few hours ago, and my Vans are too close to falling apart. Walking around in the snow may push them over the edge.

When I walk into Lenny's, butterflies take flight in my stomach when I see Emmett behind the bar, meeting my eyes with a bottle of vodka in one hand and a can of lime White Claw in the other. I walk over to the bar and hop onto the stool across from him.

"What'll it be today, beautiful?" he asks.

"I'll do a vodka club today, please."

"You got it."

As he prepares my drink, I look around the bar to see that

it is pretty dead tonight, most likely because of the snow, so I feel a buzz of anticipation and excitement that I'm going to get most of Emmett's attention while we're here.

And damn, he looks good.

He went for a half-up, half-down look today, tying part of his hair back in a loose bun, the rest falling down onto his shoulders. He's wearing a black Asking Alexandria t-shirt, the logo I recognize from the poster my brother used to have in his bedroom at our mom's house, under a black denim jacket.

"Here you go," he says as he sets my drink down on the coaster he had waiting for me. He leans in to give me a peck on the lips, the perfect way to say hello.

"How was your day?" I ask, hoping the lightning in the bar is dark enough to hide the pinking of my cheeks.

"Good, not too busy. Mostly regulars that Annie could handle, so I was able to take it easy."

I look over on the other side of the bar seeing Annie, who I have yet to meet, and Eddie chatting while the few customers in front of them sip on their drinks.

"How long has Annie worked here?" I ask.

Emmett thinks for a second before glancing towards her, maybe doing the math in his head. "Few months maybe. Her dad and my dad go way back, so she started working here when she turned eighteen."

"What about Eddie?" Emmett has told me a little about Eddie. I know they've been friends since college. I was able to meet him last time I was here, but I don't know much more about him. Eddie is only an inch or two shorter than Emmett, and just as built, with black hair that peeks out from his beanie. His features are handsome, and his green eyes appear more striking against his tan skin. He also has a scar across his left eyebrow, down to the center of his cheek, but you barely notice it unless you're a few inches away from him.

"Eddie started her as a bartender when I took over for my dad. When he's not playing gigs with his band, he's here."

"What does he play?" Drew asks.

"Drums," I reply. I glance over in Eddie's direction, and as if his ears were ringing, he turns to us and smiles. He finishes stacking the glasses he and Annie were drying and putting away, and he walks over to where Emmett and I are.

"Hey, Drew. Glad to see you here again. Emmett hasn't stopped talking about you since the last time I saw you."

I smile, but before I can say anything, I see long, brown hair, so silky and smooth that it looked like it was shining. Big brown eyes and prominent cheekbones peak behind Eddie, joining the conversation.

"You're Drew? Hi, I'm Annie! I'm so excited to meet the girl Emmett told his regulars is the reason he's so smiley lately." She glances over at Emmett who is seemingly all of a sudden very distracted with drying the perfectly dry bar area next to me.

Annie is young but has a maturity to her that you wouldn't expect from a newly nineteen-year-old. She radiates a confidence and comfort in herself that I wish I had when I was her age.

"That's what he told them?" Eddie turns to Annie who is now next to him. "They must have loved to hear that! I think the three of them thought he slept here. They were probably eating it all up!" Eddie laughs.

I decide to join in on all this fun. "Aw, Emmett, you talk about me?" I give him a playful glance and touch my hands to my heart. "I'm so honored."

His eyes find mine and if looks could kill. He looks like he wants to kiss my mouth to shut me up, but I'm enjoying this way too much.

Eddie chimes in. "You have no idea. He's finally taking time away from this place, thanks to you! I never thought I'd see the day."

Annie adds, "And you should see how he talks you up to the regulars. I'm convinced they think you walk on water by the way he talks about you." She gives me a smile before turning to look at Emmett. "And you were right. Her looks *do* draw you in. It's no wonder you're in so deep." She walks back to where she and Eddie were drying glasses and keeps walking towards the EMPLOYEES ONLY door. "I'll catch you losers later. Luke will be here to pick up where I left off. It was nice meeting you, Drew. Come back soon, alright?"

"Of course. Nice meeting you too!" I send a wave her way, and she gives me a wink before turning to head through the door.

Eddie shoots me a smile before heading back to his side of the bar, rightfully assuming that Emmett doesn't like to be messed with or outnumbered.

Emmett places his forearms down on the bar, leaning in towards me, so I'm the only one who hears. "Glad to see your charm works on everyone, not just me." His whispers tickle the side of my face. He leans in a little more, and a shiver goes down my spine as he whispers, "And, you're supposed to be on my side." I can hear the smirk in his voice, and I almost fall out of my chair.

He can say all he wants that he doesn't like me shooting the shit with his bartenders, but the reaction I am getting from him right now tells me otherwise.

"I'm just glad they like me," I whisper back.

"You're joking. There's nothing to not like," he replies, causing goosebumps to cover my arms, even under my sweater.

"Well, I can't be the *only* girl you've ever brought here, right? I mean you were engaged." I instantly feel like I struck an out of tune chord because he leans back, no longer close enough to whisper in my ear.

"Riley never came here."

He's not mad. There's no edge to his voice. He states this

very matter-of-factly, and I'm relieved to know I didn't ruin our playful atmosphere, but I can't hide my confusion.

"What? How is that possible?"

"She didn't like it here, didn't like that I worked here, didn't like the crowd, or Eddie, so she never came."

I'm having trouble understanding how Riley, a huge part of Emmett's life, just wasn't a part of another big part of his life. This is *his* bar. The bar his father owned and trusted him with. The one he named after his sister and puts all of his time and energy into making a place that people enjoy.

"Why didn't she like it?" I feel more and more questions formulate in my head, but that is the one that comes out first.

He looks past me, at something I don't think is behind me but he is seeing anyway. He exhales before answering, "I spent way too long trying to understand what she wanted and why she didn't want to share this part of my life with me." He looks around the bar, seeing the few regulars finishing their drinks, Eddie pouring them another, the door Annie just went through. "I know it's not much, but it's my job. I have so many memories of this place, with my parents, with Lennon."

"You don't have to explain that, Emmett. I've seen the way you work, both inside and outside, to make this place what it is. It's Riley's loss." I put my hands on his forearms in front of me and lean in to give him a little kiss on the nose. "Her loss and my gain." His smile reappears, but I barely see it before his lips find mine.

Before either of us can lose ourselves in the kiss or can reach the point of no return, he pulls away, finding my eyes again. His face has a shine and his smile shows his teeth. The one that only comes out once in a while, and the one that he has been sharing with me more and more as we spend more time together. The smile that I find myself needing to get as much of as I can.

"So . . . what do you want to do for dinner?"

I'm confused by his question at first, and I then remembered why I came here in the first place, to have a drink and pick a spot for dinner.

I think for a second as I try to figure out what I feel like eating. "I think either Mexican food, or Italian food. Or, burgers." I pause then add, "Or, maybe sushi."

"So, you're basically saying that you're up for anything?"

I roll my eyes, needing to release my eyes from him, to avoid my cheeks heating up too much.

"Yeah, I guess I am." I let out a laugh. "I'm so bad at making decisions, why don't you pick?"

"Okay. One through four?"

"What?"

"Pick a number. One, two, three, or four."

"Two."

"We're going for Italian food."

"Sounds good to me." I take the last few sips of my drink before Emmett grabs my glass, wiping down the space in front of me.

"Let me go to the back quickly to let Eddie know I'm heading out. I think he went back there to grab something just now because I don't see him." He nods towards the door. "I'll meet you over there." He nods towards the front entrance before heading to the back, disappearing behind the EMPLOYEES ONLY sign.

I hop off the stool, making my way over there when the door swings open, and my stomach drops.

CHAPTER 38
DREW

REED'S EYES light up as if he was a child being given a brand new toy. I instantly feel the bubble Emmett and I were in pop, almost causing me to lose my footing before catching myself, using a high-top chair near me. It's hard to fathom how quickly the energy around me changed, going from everything I have ever wanted, to everything I used to think I wanted.

Why can't I catch a fucking break, I think to myself.

"Fancy seeing you here, D." The words sound clouded with alcohol, like this isn't his first stop of the evening. He has a few of his friends behind him. Two guys and a girl I recognize, but couldn't tell you their names.

Reed pulls me in for a hug as if our past three encounters haven't unfolded the way they have. Between him showing up unannounced to my house *twice,* and then the fight we had the last time we saw each other, after he forced himself on me, he has to be clinically insane to think we can hug like old friends.

I tense beneath his touch, but I don't think he notices. Being this close to him, I can see the subtle cuts and bruising on his cheek where Emmett punched him.

"I miss you, D." There's a slight slur to the words. His lips find my ear, and he whispers in my ear, "Did you dump that long-haired douchebag?"

I nudge him away, breaking from his hold. "Reed, his name is Emmett, and no. This place is actu—"

"We're going to go grab a drink." One of his friends chimes in, obviously not caring that I'm in the middle of a sentence. Reed nods at him, then turns his attention back to me. I'm surprised to see him out this way. He usually sticks to the bars around our hometown.

"Drew, I don't care what his name is, especially after he interrupted us that night."

Reed steps closer to me. I've been inching away from him, but he is just a foot away from me now. My stomach is in knots, and my chest tightens at the reminder of feeling him on me after he wouldn't listen to the word "no." The fact that he sees nothing wrong with how that night went speaks volumes.

As a couple goes to leave, we have to move out of the doorway. I'm forced to step towards him as he backs up against the back of an empty booth just inside the door. He puts his hand on my shoulder and snakes his hand down my arm, trying to grab my hand. I pull away. "I have to go. I'm waiting for someone."

His jaw locks, and he says through his teeth, grabbing me by the wrist as I go to walk away. "Waiting for someone? I don't think so." He closes the space between us, his eyes burning with anger but his mouth is turned up in a smile. "Why don't we get out of here?"

I want to throw up.

"We can pick up where we left off the other day." His other hand finds my cheek, a gesture that fills me with warmth when Emmett does it, but I freeze under Reed's touch.

"Reed, no. This. Us." I step back and use my hands to

gesture between us. "This doesn't work, and whatever it was, it's over."

He has the audacity to smirk, as if this whole conversation is fun for him.

"No, D. It's not over. It's not over until I say. So you can let what's-his-nuts know that you have other plans tonight."

Before I can say anything, I feel a familiar presence behind me.

"Excuse me?" I hear from behind me, and it's not said in a polite way. Reed looks over my shoulder and up at the person I now feel is just a few inches behind me.

Emmett.

Reed's drinks he had before this must have slowed his reaction time, or maybe that is just how fast Emmett moves.

Before Reed can even react, Emmett has him by the collar of his shirt and pushes him up against the booth behind him.

"What did I say about touching her?" Emmett spits. He is fuming, fury radiating off him. "If you ever come near *my* girlfriend again, you're dead."

I look around to see all the eyes in the bar are on us. Eddie is now behind the bar, ready to intervene at any moment, standing next to Luke who must have gotten here in the last few minutes. Reed's friends have their eyes glued to what's happening from where they are standing at the bar, but they don't look like they have any intention of trying to help Reed.

"Get the fuck out of here before I throw you out on your ass myself."

Reed has the audacity, or maybe the stupidity, to laugh in Emmett's face. "You don't get to tell me to leave." Emmett's hold on Reed tightens, his knuckles turning white, his other arm ready to swing.

Before Reed can say another word, Emmett brings him closer just to shove him back, Reed's head hitting the wooden back of the booth behind him, pissing him off.

"Ow! What the hell? Get off me!" Reed tries to push Emmett away, but Emmett doesn't even flinch.

"This is *my* bar, asshole." And that's when Emmett drops his hold on Reed's shirt, swinging his other arm around in a fist. A massive, overpowering shock to Reed's cheek, the sound of the direct fist-to-face contact echoing in the quiet bar. As Reed falls to the ground, I realize that Emmett held back last time in my apartment, almost like last time was a warning. Now, in this moment, there's no ounce of him that is not emitting intense hatred, causing him to release his full strength onto Reed.

Reed is clutching his face, blood seeping out his nose. That's when Eddie and Luke run over and grab Emmett, bringing his arms behind his back and taking some steps back. Good thing too, because I'm positive Emmett wasn't going to stop there.

Reed's friends rush over and help him up. They don't have to hold him back because he isn't *that* stupid. The four of them stumble out of the place, the murmuring of the audience behind us being the only noise once the door closes behind them.

Emmett pulls out of Eddie's grip and comes right up to me, wrapping me in his arms, his lips in my hair, whispering, "Are you okay? I swear, he will never come near you again. I'll make sure of it."

I breathe him in. "I'm totally fine." I exhale. "I just wasn't expecting to see him here."

"Let's go." Emmett wraps his strong arm around my shoulder, protective and possessive, and ushers me out. "I'll see you guys tomorrow." He doesn't even turn to say it, just says it loud enough for Eddie and Luke to hear. Then, we head back to the parking garage of our complex, getting into his Jeep.

As Emmett drives to the restaurant, I can tell that he still hasn't come down from the heightened state of anger he was in just a few minutes ago. His hand is in my lap, resting on my thigh, wrapped in both of my hands, but I can see his grip on the steering wheel is enough to snap the steel below the rubber casing.

"Emmett." His eyes on the road, while mine are burning into the side of his strained face.

"Emmett," I say again. "Are you okay?" We approach a red light, and he turns to me. I see his expression soften.

"Why are *you* asking me that? I should be asking you. Are you okay?"

"Yes, I'm perfectly okay, but I'm worried about you."

He glances to see the light is still red and then back at me. "Seeing his hands on you makes me want to beat the living shit out of him. The way that his smug face was looking at you, his hand around your wrist—" he shakes his head at the thought. "I was ready to kill him."

I take one of my hands from my lap and put it to his cheek. I want him to relax, to stop wasting his thoughts on Reed. So I smile and say, "You called me your girlfriend." And with that, his cheek melts into my hand, one side of his mouth curls upward.

"Yeah." His eyes burn into mine. "Because that's exactly what you are." I see the red light turn to green, but he doesn't move. The car behind us honks and goes around. I feel him wanting to say more, but he doesn't, bringing his lips to mine instead, giving me a gentle kiss.

I pull away, my stomach growling and ruining the moment. "So, about dinner?"

He returns his focus to the road, a soft smile on his face, and we drive to the restaurant where we have the most wonderful dinner. We eat and talk and laugh and then drive home with full bellies and full hearts. We make our way up the stairs, my trust issues with the elevator still apparent, pausing at the top of each flight to steal eager kisses and touches.

That night, we spend the night at his place, falling apart together to put ourselves back to just fall apart again.

CHAPTER 39
DREW

"HE DID WHAT?!" Lacey's shrill voice is filled with anger as I relay to her my past few encounters with Reed. I've been holding on to the promise I made to her—but mostly myself—to text and call her throughout the week to avoid going weeks with just a few *"Let's get together"* texts from her being left on read. It's been three days since the whole Reed fiasco at Lenny's, and Emmett had to go into the bar earlier than expected today, so I'm home on my couch giving Lacey all the details of the past week.

"That's not even the worst part, Lace. Let me start from the beginning."

"Okay, I'll try to keep my commentary to myself until the end." She's such a smartass, but I love her.

I start by telling her what I should've told her weeks ago, but I know now that there's no point to dwell on the past. I can only change the trajectory of now, or at least that's what my therapist always says.

"Remember when we went to lunch, and I told you how Reed stopped over, and it felt weird."

"Yes." That is all she says because she has learned Reed

can be a sore subject for us, but I'm not going to ever let that happen again.

"Well, you were right. I shouldn't have felt bad about not being happy he came over, and I shouldn't have sent that apology text to him."

"YOU WHAT?"

Oops. I forgot to tell her that part.

"Ugh. Forget about that. Anyway, he never texted me back, so we didn't talk for a few days. Not until—"

"No, Drew. Don't tell me you texted him again."

"Well, it was a momentary lapse of judgment, and Emmett and I had a misunderstanding, and—"

"WAIT. There's a *you and Emmett* now?" She doesn't even pretend to hide the excitement in her voice. "I could tell by the way you talked about him when I saw you last that there was something there."

"Lace, if you keep interrupting, I won't be able to get to that part."

"You're right, sorry. I just didn't think there would be so much for you to update me on. It's only been like two weeks since I've seen you!"

And yet, I feel like I've lived a lifetime in these two weeks, I think to myself before continuing with the Reed part of this update.

"Anyway, like I was saying, I was having a momentary lapse in judgment, and I needed help with something." I just know her mouth opens ready to say something, but I beat her to it. "And before you can say I should've called you, I know that now and hindsight is twenty-twenty, so please don't say I told you so."

She says nothing, but I just know she is biting her lip, holding back what I already know.

"So, I texted Reed. He came over, and he thought I was asking him to come over for sex."

"What a fucking prick."

"I know! So, I said no, but he wouldn't stop trying to kiss me and touch me and stuff, and I just wasn't into it. I just wanted him to be there for me like he was in high school." I pause, knowing that I'm about to admit something my gut has always known, but I never wanted to admit to myself. "But, he was never good for me, and I know that now."

"I'm sorry, Drew. That couldn't have been an easy conclusion to come to." I feel tears sting my eyes, threatening to fall, but I blink them back.

"Thank you for not saying 'I told you so'."

"Never. I knew you just needed time to figure it out. I'm just so pissed that it had to happen like this. He really forced himself on you like that?"

"I never thought he'd be someone to do that, and I just kept screaming at him to get off me, and he was getting pissed. I didn't know what to do."

"So, then what? You didn't let him, did you?"

"No, Lace! Of course not. But I don't know what would have happened if Emmett didn't hear us. Reed and I were screaming at each other. He could probably tell something was wrong."

"Did he come up?"

"Yep. He banged on the door until Reed opened it."

"Wait, you *both* were screaming? Not that I don't know you can handle yourself, but I don't think I can think of a time you, you know, fought back."

Lacey was right.

Reed and I never fought, and things never escalated. But it was because I always gave in. I never pushed when I really should have.

I let out a sigh. "I just couldn't hold it in anymore. It was like a total fight or flight response, and I guess my gut told me to fight."

Lacey doesn't say anything at first. Maybe processing the same thing I am. How that kind of trauma-response has never come out of me, not since that day in my classroom when I told my students we had to barricade the door.

"Good for you," she finally says, and I feel how proud she is of me over the phone, my heart growing a little in size because of how full it has felt lately.

"So, long story short, Reed got what he deserved. Emmett helped me get him to leave.""

"I'm really liking this Emmett guy. You guys a thing?"

"Well, we were just neighbors up until that night." I can't hide the smile in my voice, and even though we're on the phone, I'm positive Lacey knows the look that's on my face right now. "But we've been spending time getting to know each other—no longer as neighbors."

"Oh, Drew. You think you can hide that you're getting laid. Don't even try, honey. Spill it."

"Hold on! I'm not done with the Reed part of the story."

"There's more?!"

I take the next few minutes to dive into what happened at the bar, and how I don't think Reed will be bothering me anymore. I add that I also don't plan on searching my memory for his number ever again.

After answering all of Lacey's questions and giving her a play-by-play of the punch, I know it is time to tell her about Emmett.

I decide to start at the beginning.

"So, you've known each other for seven months now, have been thinking about each other all this time, and you're just now acting on it?"

"Well, when you put it that way, yeah. But, there's so much more." I give her the details of all the times he seemed to be there when no one else was, and the more I tell her, the more she seems to understand that while it was tragic what brought us together, something beautiful came out of it.

"I'm glad to know Emmett is there to protect you. Not that you need it, but I'm happy to know you're not all by yourself anymore." Her words are heavy with love, and I'm further reminded that, while I was alone by choice, it doesn't mean I have to continue making that choice. "Let's double-date soon! I'm dying to meet him now that I know for sure he treats you how you deserve to be treated."

"For sure. I'll call you this week, and we can find a time. I love you, Lacey."

"I love you more. And, yes. Please do. Plus, I want to hear about how going back to school goes. Call me if you need anything, okay?

"Okay. I promise. This is the last week off before we're supposed to go back, so I think I'll send an email in a few days about the plan for going back. I'll keep you updated."

"Perfect. Alright, honey, talk soon!"

When I hang up the phone, my heart feels like it's over-flowing with love, gratitude, and hope. Not only because I had an hour long, uninterrupted conversation with my best friend about things we haven't been able to talk about in years but because so many of those things have been weighing on me, and I feel like they have disappeared.

For some reason, telling Lacey about my realizations about Reed and my relationship with Emmett, makes them both feel real and within my realm of control. Even talking about going back to school is something I never thought I'd be able to do so casually. It still brings some feelings of anxiety and uneasiness, but I'm still in control.

Something I never thought would happen again.

CHAPTER 40
EMMETT

THE NEXT WEEK IS A DREAM.

Alternating between nights at Drew's place and nights at mine, I feel myself falling so hard for this girl. I don't know if I'll ever be able to spend a day without her.

Last Sunday night, I was working at the bar, and I came home to a Drew that I don't think I could ever get enough of. She had just talked with her best friend, Lacey, and she was so smiley for the rest of the night.

I asked her what they talked about to put her in such a good mood, but she wouldn't tell me. I was selfishly hoping *I* was part of the secret she was keeping.

At the beginning of the week, Drew's school district sent the email with the plan to return to school. It said that the staff's first day back will be the following Monday, January 22nd—a full month following the shooting. The students will return the Monday after that, if all goes according to plan.

We were at Lenny's when Drew got the email, and I could tell she wasn't expecting the communication when her phone pinged.

I watched her soft grin twist into worry, and she reached for my hand as she read the email. When she went to show me, I could hear that her breathing was getting a little heavy, but her breaths were even and deep.

She was in complete control.

Now it's Friday, and we have plans to stay in and order pizza. I thought I ate a lot of pizza before Drew, but this girl takes the term "favorite food" to a whole other level. I got a text from her right as I walked into Lenny's this morning, after I had just pulled myself away from her to get to the bar for a meeting with my bartenders about some new specials as February approaches. Her text said she wanted to watch her favorite movie tonight, *Scream*, because I told her a few days ago that I have never seen the whole thing, beginning to end.

I check the time and see I only have to get through these next two hours before I can see my girl.

As I ride up in the elevator, I can't help but think to myself, *how did I get so lucky?*

How did I get so lucky as to find someone that fits with me so perfectly?

How did I get so lucky as to find Drew?

This amazing girl who understands me, who wants to know me—all of me. Who gave me a chance I probably didn't deserve. A girl who can't get enough of me, just like I can't get enough of her.

When I get to her door, I knock gently three times, and then let myself in with her spare key. She started keeping her door unlocked when she knew I would be coming over, and that was not okay with me. I didn't like the idea that anyone could walk in, so I told her she had to keep it locked.

"You're a little overprotective, you know that right?" she told me.

"I'm overprotective when it comes to *you.*"

Later that day, before I was heading out, she went over to the junk drawer in her kitchen and gave me her spare key without a word.

I walk through her door to see her reading on the couch.

She finished the third book of the series I got for her, so she started a different romance series about vampires. And according to her, it's almost as good as the *Twilight* series, one of her favorites.

She's in one of my t-shirts I left here, with wet hair, and no pants, and it's my new favorite view. This girl has kicked my sex drive into gear, and I cannot keep my hands to myself.

I kick off my shoes and jog up to her, settling between her legs on the opposite side of the couch, expelling a squeal from her. I dig my fingers under the cotton of her underwear and slide them down her legs.

Her book is still in her hands as she asks, "What do you think you're doing?" I smile to myself because she asks as if she doesn't already know my favorite place to be in between her thighs.

"Keep reading," I whisper against her soft skin. Drew hides behind the book as I part her with my tongue. "I've been thinking about this all day, don't mind me." I grip her thighs, keeping her open, as I suck, nibble, and kiss the sensitive pink skin.

"I can't focus when you do that," she breathes, dropping the book off to the side.

I keep lapping her up, loving the taste, and loving the view. Her eyes fall back in her head, her arms gripping the couch. "Then focus on me, sweetheart." My words are always exactly what she needs because I watch as she gets closer and closer before falling apart before my eyes.

I leave her with a few last kisses on her most sensitive spot before standing up, unbuttoning my jeans. I kneel back down, one knee down, one knee up, and I pull her hips to meet me, the couch being the perfect height for me to bring her to the edge, and then I sink into her, wet and ready for me.

Still coming down from her first orgasm, I pump into her. "Give me another one, baby."

She feels like heaven, if heaven was real.

I tighten my grip on her hips, her back arching in pleasure, I can tell she is right there. "You take me so well, don't you?" I tell her, and she moans at my words.

A few more rocks of my hips, and I'm sending her right into her second orgasm. "Atta girl," I praise her. The tightening around me is the perfect sensation as I pick up speed, slamming into her.

She's my heaven.

"Fuck." I groan, releasing inside of her. She lets me every time, always giving me a flutter in my stomach at the thought of filling her up.

Her hold on me is growing more every second.

We eat our pizza on the couch, laughing at the fake blood and how the nineties style is making a comeback. She tells me how she and Lacey used to fight over who was better looking: Skeet Ulrich or Matthew Lillard, her vote being for Skeet Ulrich.

Just like her, the night is perfect.

Perfect until the movie ends, and we get into bed.

I noticed she has been quiet since I pulled the covers over her, and I need to know what is going through her mind. My arm is around her, her backside flushed to my front.

I kiss her on the shoulder. "Is everything okay?"

She turns to face me, tears welling in her eyes. "What if I can't go back?"

My heart breaks, because I know she is talking about school—about her classroom.

"One day at a time, " I remind her. Just like she told me her therapist tells her. She has been going to therapy every Tuesday, adding an extra session this past Thursday with the return to school being in just a few days. Drew says hearing the phrase helps when she feels herself getting anxious or nervous or when the thoughts of the shooting flood in.

I wipe away a tear that runs loose from her eye with my thumb, bringing her in closer to me, just to hold her. "I know it doesn't feel like it now, but you can do this." I rest my chin on the top of her head, feeling her breath against my chest.

"But, what if I don't want to?"

"What do you mean, sweetheart? You love teaching. You love your kids."

I think of all the stories she has told me about her kids and the wonderful chaos that takes place in her classroom. She once told me that she loved her students so much, and it gave her a glimpse of the love a mother has for her children. I remember my stomach flickering at the comment of her being a mother, a foreign scene of us with a mini-Drew playing through my head for a brief moment when she explained this to me.

Drew has taught me so much about the education world and the work that teachers do, and it has made me fall for her even harder, seeing the passion in her eyes as she talks about it, the love in her voice when she tells me the stories, even the ones about the amount of penises she finds drawn in all the nooks and corners of her classroom.

I thought I had an idea about teaching before I knew Drew, remembering the stories my grandma would tell me, but I truly didn't understand how people could do it until I watched Drew light up when she talked about her students.

"I know," she says, her voice breaking, "but—"

"But what?"

"But, I'm scared." It's all she says, but I know the statement holds more. Of course she's scared. Scared to go back to somewhere she used to call her "happy place," but it now reminds her of the most horrific day of her life.

"It's okay to be scared. You went through something terrible—horrible. These feelings are perfectly okay."

"I know." She sniffles before continuing, and I give her a kiss on the top of her head. "I just keep going back and forth on whether it's worth going back."

"What do you mean?"

"I mean, what if I'm not cut out for this. I can't imagine going back and telling the kids we can go back to normal when I don't even think I believe it myself."

She's right.

What is normal after experiencing what she and her students experienced that day?

I pull her into me even closer, wishing I could take all the doubt she is having away. "Let me take you to school on Monday." She pulls back from my hold, just a little, to meet my eyes.

"I don't think we can have visitors in the building. Not after what happened."

"I'll wait for you outside. I'll be there whenever you need a break or fresh air. Or this." I kiss her, feeling her smile against my lips.

"I have an eight hour day with only an hour for lunch. The students won't be there, but I'll be in meetings all day, and—" I stop her with another kiss.

"I have nowhere else I need to be. I'll be there, just in case you need me."

"I don't want you to feel like you have to do that."

I pull her into me. "Sweetheart, I wouldn't offer unless it was something I was willing to do. Plus, you'll be the one doing the hard work. I'm just there to cheer you on."

Her head nuzzles more into my chest, and I rest my chin on the top of her head. "Thank you," she whispers.

I kiss the top of her head and draw mindless circles on her back with my fingertips. Her breathing becomes a little more even, and the tears dry.

Against my chest, her breaths become deeper. "Drew?" I whisper, making sure she is asleep. The words flow off my lips easily, knowing she can't hear me. "I think I'm falling in love with you."

CHAPTER 41

DREW

AM I DREAMING, or did Emmett just tell me he thinks he's falling in love with me? I keep my eyes closed, trying to keep my breathing the same, so he doesn't sense I'm still awake.

I was just about to fall asleep when I heard the words, but I'm almost positive he doesn't want me to hear him say them just yet.

I focus on keeping my breathing steady, even as my mind begins to race, and butterflies evade more than just my stomach. I feel flickers of excitement everywhere I feel his body touching me, knowing that these feelings of passion and security will never go away.

I'm no longer tired, but I make myself fall asleep, and I can't help but do so with a smile on my face.

The next morning, Emmett and I get up and go for a walk. It's oddly nice for a Saturday in January, so we take advantage of it. We walk to a breakfast place near our complex, the smell of coffee fills the air as we sit down. There is a subtle hum from the people around us, yet, I feel like we are the only two people here.

I am still buzzing from Emmett's whispered declaration of

potential love last night, but I am trying my best to disguise it.

"What are you going to get?" he asks. I watch the subtle lines appear on his forehead, the ones that come out when he is deep in thought, or deep in a task.

My cheeks heat at the dirty thoughts that evade my brain from the last time I saw those some subtle lines. Only we were not deciding our breakfast options, he was pushing inside me.

I quickly shake the thoughts away, fanning myself with the menu. "Hmm, I can't decide if I want something sweet or something savory," I reply. His eyes look up to meet mine, and he gives me a smirk. "What?" I ask. I can tell something just popped into his head, and I'm hoping it is not the same dirty thoughts currently in mine.

"Remember when I saw you at the grocery store?"

My heart skips a beat as I recall that day, and my cheeks are thankful that I am revisiting a less sexual memory, but I'm sure they are still pink.

That day in the grocery store was the first time I saw Emmett outside of the elevator, let alone the apartment, and it is also a day that plays over in my head quite often. It was the beginning of my recovery, early in my journey of living in the aftermath of a trauma. It was also the beginning of us. "Yes, I remember." I glance towards the menu, as if not looking at him will help my cheeks go back to their natural shade.

"Do you remember what you had in your cart that day?"

"Yes." I look back up at him, my menu hiding my face, so he can just see my eyes. "Why?" I'm starting to get suspicious of these questions.

"You had two containers of ice cream. One was chocolate and the other was sherbet."

I narrow my eyes at him. "I don't know how to respond to that."

My deadpan response gets a chuckle out of him. He tears

his eyes from me and goes back to looking at his menu. "What I'm trying to say is if you can't decide on sweet or savory, why not just get both?"

I don't know how to respond at first, and this is for a multitude of reasons.

One, this man remembers what was in my cart during our first *normal* interaction, and by normal, I mean him not completing being a jerk or me not forgetting how to formulate words in his presence.

Two, he caught on to that teeny, tiny little detail and remembered it.

My silence must cause him some alarm. He sets his menu down and looks at me. "Did I say something wrong?"

"What? No, no. I just . . . I just didn't think you'd remember something so small about me." I put my menu down in front of me and interlace my fingers, resting my hands on the table in front of me.

"I told you. I like learning about you, and a lot of the learning I did, before we started talking, was through observation."

He did tell me that the first time I went to Lenny's.

I didn't think it would come to have so much meaning to me at the time, and I didn't think I was anything of interest to him before that day in the grocery store. He continues, "The first time I ran into you, and all the times to follow, I was a complete dick to you. I regret brushing you off or making you feel like you weren't worth my time." He reaches across the table and wraps his hands around mine "And I'm sorry about that," he adds.

I nod, telling him I accept my apology without saying a word. "I'm sorry, too. I should've taken the hints you weren't so subtle about. It didn't take a rocket scientist to see you weren't in the mood to talk."

He squeezes my hands in his. "Please don't apologize. You were just being neighborly, and I was always getting on you about stupid shit that doesn't even matter. And I . . ." He pauses and looks down at our hands, stealing his eyes away from mine.

"What?"

Without looking up, his voice loses the confidence it usually has and is just loud enough for me to hear over the buzz of the restaurant around us.

"I saw you that morning." I feel the air around us turn to freezing temperature, and suddenly we really are the only ones in the diner. "I saw you in the elevator that morning, and my priority was taking my shitty mood out on you, not caring what kind of day you were walking into."

I open my hands beneath the hold he has on them, and I switch our grip, so I'm the one holding his.

"You couldn't have known what was going to happen that day." My voice has an edge, not one of anger, but one that will help to rewrite the guilt manifesting in there. "Don't you dare think that you had any control over what I went through that day."

"No, I know I couldn't control the shooting. That's not what I'm talking about, I—"

"No." My response finally makes his eyes find mine again. "I'm not talking about the shooting either. I'm talking about how you cannot take any ownership for anything that happened that day, or any other one."

I can see the confusion overwhelming his handsome features, his eyes asking what I mean.

"Yes, you were a grumpy, downstairs neighbor, but it's not like I was the quietest, upstairs one." He lets out a chuckle, telling me he knows that we both can admit we weren't the best neighbors to each other. "But what happened in the past doesn't matter. If there's one thing I could've counted on that morning, it was running into you and forgetting how to speak." I shake my head at the thought of ever thinking I had any control in my happy place. "I didn't know how the day would play out, and I never do—my classroom is the most unpredictable place."

Emmett watches me intently as I continue. I feel my cheeks heat and my stomach drop at the confession I'm about to make.

"For the past six months, while it wasn't the most pleasant, I knew what to expect with you. I knew you were easily pissed off, but you somehow managed to make me never stop thinking about you."

His eyes widen at the admission. At the admission that while I never thought we would end up where we are now, deep down I had hoped to see him beyond the walls of the elevator. The same admission he made to me just a few days ago, just before he came home with me, just before we made love for the first time.

A smile appears on his face, and he leans over, reaching his body across the table, his lips finding mine, until we are interrupted by a clearing of the throat of our waitress.

"I can see you folks still need a minute."

Emmett sits back down as I drop my hand into my hands, my face reflecting, not only my reaction to Emmett's kiss, but also the embarrassment that we are not as alone as we feel.

"Uh, yeah." Emmett coughs into his fist. "That would be great."

The faintest hint of smile crosses her face as she rolls her eyes and walks to another one of her tables.

Emmett grabs one of my hands that is currently shielding my face. "And that right there is what I never got out of my head." His other hand finds the side of my face, feeling so cool against my cheek. "I was selfish because I did everything I could to see you all flustered and bothered, loving the way I could get under your skin."

I laugh, and he smiles at me, bringing his hands back to himself and picking up his menu.

"So, savory or sweet?"

Damn, I've got it bad for this guy.

We end up sharing an order of pancakes and an omelet, and I make a mental note to do this every time Emmett and I go out to eat.

As we eat, we reminisce on our first few encounters when I first moved in, telling the secrets about each other we've kept to ourselves until now. It turns out we both secretly thought of the other more than we led on, and I can't get my butterflies under control at the observations Emmett made about me. "Why didn't you shake my hand the first time we met?"

"You remember that?" He asks, looking as if he hoped my answer was no.

"Of course I remember, and I know you do too. You said you couldn't stop thinking of me after that, yet, I'm pretty sure you hated me before we even met, and it showed."

"One"—he holds up his pointer finger—"I never hated you." I am about to remind him of that first interaction again, but he stops me with, "Two, you caught me completely off guard."

I let out a dry laugh, "What is that supposed to mean?"

"I was getting home from work, pissed with something that happened with Riley, and then you bumped into me, and . . . This is going to sound so stupid." He shakes his head as if shaking off the embarrassment he's feeling.

"Come on, it can't be *that* bad," I say, hoping I sound convincing enough because I need to know what he is about to say.

"You caught me off guard, and I had never seen you before, and I remember instantly having the thought that you had a beauty I never seen before—red hair, green eyes, little black shorts, and your My Chemical Romance hoodie."

"What? There's no way you remember what I was wearing. *I* don't even remember."

"Oh, I remember." He leans back in his chair and chuckles to himself. "And, it's the truth."

"Okay, well then why were you such a dick to me that night and from then on?" I grab the hot sauce to put on my omelet, ready to switch from sweet to savory.

He crosses his arms, tension spreading across his shoulders, not sure how he wants to answer. He lowers his eyes, looking at the table rather than at me. "You made me . . . nervous."

I can't help but let out a laugh so loud, the tables near us turn to see what the commotion is. I'm so caught off-guard by his admission, I can't help but find it funny that this giant of a man, with tattoos and a semi-permanent scowl was nervous around *me.*

Me, who literally could not speak when he was around me.

Me, who turned as red as a freaking firetruck when he looked at me.

Me, who got flustered in every single conversation we had.

"I told you. See, so fucking stupid." He picks his fork back up and starts moving around the food on his plate.

"No, no. Not at all." I finally catch my breath after my mini laugh attack. "I was just surprised. I thought you were a lot of things when we first met, but nervous? That was never one of them."

The tension in him relaxes a little. "When I saw you that night, Riley and I had decided she was going to move out, and I thought it was the world continuing to mess with me by putting you in my path—like it was too good to be true." The atmosphere around us turns serious, the words beginning to pour from him. "You were so beautiful, and you had a smile on your face that could have spread to my lips if I would have let it. You had this positive energy radiating off of you, and I wanted to let it pour over me."

He pauses, and I'm still frozen, not wanting to make any sudden movements or noises that may scare him from continuing. "But instead, I told myself you were too good to be true. Too good for me, and I walked away." He exhales and then continues, "I walked straight to the elevator and was hoping it would close before you decided if you wanted to turn around or not."

"I couldn't help but turn around. I was so confused. I thought I pissed you off."

"No, not at all. You turned, and I was hooked. I'll never forget the first time our eyes met before I told you my name because I don't think another day went by after that where I didn't think about you."

My mind is swirling with all of this information, and I don't know what to say aside from the obvious. "Well, I did make it kind of hard to forget me."

We both laugh and the seriousness of the words floating in the air around us subside.

"So all the encounters after that, you were a dick because . . ."

He smirks. "I told you already. I liked making you mad. Your cheeks would blush, and you couldn't find your words. It was cute."

"You know, I think any other guy in your position would've used our similar music tastes as a conversation starter, but I guess you wanted to play the long game," I say, stealing a strawberry from his plate of pancakes.

"Fuck the other guys. My long game worked, you're mine." I freeze mid-chew, stunned by his ease of saying I'm his. His possessiveness shouldn't give me the amount of butterflies that it does, but I don't care.

After being independent and on my own for so long, the thought of having someone protecting me, especially after everything that happened, is something I never thought I would love, but I do.

Emmett continues eating his half of the omelet like what he just said doesn't hold the weight that it does, looking up from his plate to give me a wink. That's all it takes for me to feel like my body temperature just shot up one hundred degrees.

I can tell he's happy with my reaction, and I let him have his fun. I know he has the same reaction to me as I do him, it just doesn't show on his cheeks. His flush shows on his chest and creeps up his neck, but I haven't told him yet—wanting to keep the secret for myself.

As we continue eating and talking, my heart grows bigger and bigger as I realize Emmett thought about me way more than I thought about him—another secret I'll keep for myself.

We finish eating, and as we are waiting for the bill, I feel a question blossom in my brain, one that begins to feel like a weed that will grow bigger and bigger if I don't deal with it now.

Emmett takes a sip of his coffee, and he pauses mid-sip, instantly able to tell that there's something on my mind.

"Drew?" He sets his coffee down.

"Emmett?"

"What is it?"

"How did you know?"

"I just did. Now, what is it?"

I take a deep breath and decide to deal with it now. "Do you think we would've ever gotten here without what happened?" I take another deep breath, inhaling and exhaling before correcting myself. "Without the shooting?"

"Yes."

I'm a little taken aback by how fast he responded, but before I can say anything, our waitress drops off our check.

"Whenever you two are ready," she says with a smile.

"Here, you can go ahead and take it—keep the change." Emmett hands it back to her with some cash.

She gives us a smile before telling us to have a good day.

Emmett turns back to me, probably already knowing his answer requires more of an explanation.

"Come on, let's head home."

I guess not.

We walk back to our complex, hand in hand, feeling the sunshine mixed with the cool air as we match each other's strides.

"So," he starts, "I'm assuming you're trying to make sense of my answer from before."

Our fingers interlocked, arms swinging between us with each step, we pause at a stop light to wait for our turn to cross the street. Emmett turns to face me.

"Is my assumption correct?" he says as he takes his other hand to lift my chin, so my eyes can't look anywhere but up at his.

"Yes," I respond, repeating it the same way he said to me just a little while ago.

"Do you think otherwise?"

"Yes. Wait, no." I exhale. I try to look down, but he doesn't let me pull my gaze. "I don't know," I say.

"Well, I do." The look in his eyes holds nothing but sincerity. "No one shines as bright as you, Drew, and while it might've taken six more months for me to come to my senses, I would've realized that you were someone worth getting to know."

I feel a smile overtake my lips, "I probably wouldn't have given you the time of day," I respond, a playfulness in my voice.

Emmett leans down to kiss me before saying against my lips, "Then it's a good thing our paths found a way to cross."

I'm not sure if he meant it as *literally* crossing paths in the elevator, or if he was just hopeful our paths would have figuratively crossed another way.

What I do know is, holding this man's hand, kissing his lips, being in his bed…

That is where I *want* to be.

The rest of our weekend together flies by, spending time in each other's apartments, Lenny's, and enjoying the frigid sunshine.

I lay still, awake, feeling Emmett's breath on the back of my neck. He likes to stay awake until I fall asleep, but he was tired after our day.

We went for another walk this morning and then went back to his place to watch *his* favorite movie, *Iron Man*. I told him how I skipped it during my Marvel movie marathon, and he told me that we had to go back and watch it, along with the sequel, before picking back up where we left off with *Thor: Ragnarok*. Then, I stayed at his place when he went to the bar for a few hours.

Eddie had called him saying they were swamped because of the nice weather, and Emmett wasn't planning on going in at all because Sundays are usually pretty dead. After a week of cloudy, dreary skies, the clear blue ones we're getting this weekend are drawing everyone out, so it ended up being packed for only one bartender.

When Emmett got back, we made dinner together, and I could tell he was exhausted when we sat down on the couch to watch TV.

Instead of moving on to the next Marvel movie, I turned on our next episode of *New Girl* because I knew he wouldn't last through the two hour run time. To break up the Marvel movies, we have been watching *New* Girl starting from the beginning because I told Emmett he *had* to watch my favorite/comfort show, and I think he likes it more than he's letting on.

When I noticed he was falling asleep sitting up, I turned off the TV, and we got ready for bed. We decided to stay the night at his place, so I set my alarm for 6 a.m., giving myself enough time to get to my first meeting at 8 a.m. tomorrow.

While Emmett was in the shower, I ran up to my place to grab everything I needed for tomorrow and then joined him in the hot water, feeling lucky that showers didn't feel so lonely anymore.

Emmett's head hit the pillow, his arms around me, and he was out within minutes.

Now, here I am, listening to his breathing and the sound of his heartbeat against my back, and I feel safe and secure enough to let myself think of tomorrow. Emmett has helped me feel strong throughout these weeks together, and things like the toasters popping, microwaves beeping, or silence don't steal my breath from me anymore.

Staff is supposed to report to the school cafeteria at 8 a.m. tomorrow to begin our day of meetings and discussions, talk about how we all are doing and our thoughts on how best to welcome kids back. I got a second email, after the initial one sent from the superintendent on Tuesday, from my school's principal, messaging me and me only, about waiting to go to my classroom until the afternoon.

Not knowing if I'm ready to go back to that specific place just yet and knowing that the room across the hall will never be the same, I emailed her agreeing.

I feel myself getting worked up, and my heart begins to beat a little faster. My breathing starts to pick up, making my inhales and exhales short and hard to manage, but then I focus on the feeling of Emmett's arm around me and level my breathing with his.

I remember that he will be there tomorrow—*be there for me*—just in case I need him. I tried to convince him I would be fine, but he refused to agree to drop me off and pick me up. He tried to make me feel better by saying he was going to use the time to get ahead of some phone calls and paperwork for this week's deliveries and other miscellaneous behind-the-scenes things he does for Lenny's, and I was relieved to hear him say he would be there regardless. Just knowing he'll be there, in case I need him, is more than enough.

I feel my heartbeat steady, aligning with his, and thank whatever power is out there for bringing him into my life. Not only has he been there for me, but he has made me feel strong and capable, and I can—

No, I will.

Get through whatever comes my way tomorrow.

Emmett and I have known each other for months, but we have just finally let ourselves *know* each other. Those months we spent arguing, ignoring, or giving each other a hard time could be seen as wasted, but I think those interactions planted the roots that allowed our current relationship to flourish. It allowed our own experiences and traumas to guide our unspoken bond that blossomed into something beautiful.

"I think I'm falling in love with you too," I whisper, thinking he can't hear me, then close my eyes to try to get some rest.

I hear a whisper against my ear. "You are?"

I turn around, seeing that his eyes are open.

"Yes," I breathe, feeling ready to give all of myself to him.

CHAPTER 42
DREW

I DRIFT OFF INTO A SLEEP, but it's not heavy enough to ignore the voice creeping into my head. It's a voice that I don't recognize but reeks with doubt I have tried to ignore. A voice that is whispering into my ear when things seem to be going well but is there to remind me of truths I don't want to see.

What if I can't do this without Emmett?

The sickening, familiar thought instantly makes my stomach turn as my eyes pop open. I feel my heart beating too quickly, quicker than before when I was thinking about going back to work. I try again to match my breathing to Emmett's, hoping my heartbeat will match his rhythm, but it doesn't work.

I have to calm myself down without waking him up.

Five things I can see…

The fan above us, spinning, the TV's black screen, the bedroom door, slightly ajar, Emmett's dark hair, spread on the white pillow—his black ink swirling along his arms.

Four things I can touch…

My sheets, Emmett, the bedside table, and the glass of water that is there.

I feel my heartbeat begin to steady, and I take in a deep breath, so I can focus on what is making my body go into overload.

And not in a good way.

Slowly being able to think straight, the voice in my head becomes a little louder and a little clearer.

You won't be able to do this without him.

You're not strong enough on your own.

You need him.

Is this voice saying those things about Emmett?

All those months I let Reed make me believe that I was nothing without him, make me believe I was completely incapable of being loved unless it was by him, come back to me all at once. He used what I told him about my parents to skew my idea of what it meant to be loved, and I became so small that I was lost within the palm of his hand.

And I let myself fall into this all over again.

No.

Emmett isn't Reed.

And I'm not seventeen anymore.

Reed doesn't have any power over me, and I'm not going to let him impact any more decisions I make, or impact how I feel about myself.

Emmett has been there for me, and—

What would I have done if he wasn't at the grocery store?

What would I have done if he wasn't there after my toaster popped?

What would I have done if he wasn't in the elevator with me?

What would I have done if he didn't help me get Reed to leave?

These overwhelming feelings of doubt engulf me, and I feel myself rethinking all these moments over the past four weeks where I thought I was strong and regaining control.

Have I ever been in control?

Can I even consider myself strong?

My thoughts spiral over and over in my head, getting louder and more powerful with each shallow breath I take.

What if I can't go into tomorrow without him?

What kind of scared, fragile girl needs her boyfriend waiting for the moment she crumbles?

I refuse to be that girl, but here I am anyway.

I'm stuck—paralyzed.

Three things I can hear …

My heartbeat in my ears, this voice getting louder and louder in my head, and… I can't think of another.

Two things I can smell…

Nothing. There's nothing.

One thing I can taste…

Again, nothing.

It's not working.

During one of my first sessions with my therapist, I told her how my thoughts sometimes feel most powerful at night when it is time to go to sleep.

Maybe that's why the 5-4-3-2-1 Method isn't working right now.

I feel like I'm being weighed down to the bed, unable to send thoughts to my body to let it know that the pressure holding me down is not actually there.

No.

I am no longer someone who freezes.

I am someone who fights.

These thoughts are just thoughts.

I need to get them straight.

I need to be in control.

Dr. James suggested that finding the will to just sit up, no matter how hard it may seem in the moment, will help me jump out of the spiral, so I desperately peel myself out of Emmett's arms, instantly feeling less secure when his arms are no longer around me, but the pressure in my chest instantly releases.

The thoughts shrink back to their normal size.

Fuck.

This is happening again.

I'm relying too heavily on someone rather than relying on myself.

I put in the work.

I am recovering.

And I don't need someone holding my hand.

But I'll crumble if he's not there with me tomorrow.

I can't let myself fall into the same trap I did with Reed.

I can't allow someone else's affection to give me worth.

I can't rely on someone else's strength to keep me standing.

That is how you get taken advantage of.

I won't let that happen again.

I tip toe to Emmett's side of the bed where our phones are charging at the bedside. I check the time to see it's five-fifteen in the morning. A good forty-five minutes before my alarm was going to go off.

I turn off the alarm, deciding to start my day now. It may not go as Emmett and I planned, but it is what I need to do. Luckily, he is currently comatose, so tired from yesterday and our endeavors after he heard me admit I was falling in love with him too.

He is currently blissfully unaware that last night was the last time I would let myself into his bed.

I take my phone, leaving Emmett's plugged in, and head to his bathroom that is slightly overtaken with things of my own. Over the past week, both of our apartments have remnants of the other's—clothes sharing drawers, toiletries sitting next to each other.

I grab the bag with the outfit I picked out for my first day back: black joggers and a black long-sleeve, casual and comfy for a full day of meetings. I brush my teeth, wash my face, and clip my hair back in a claw clip. I pull down two pieces to frame my face, and I have a sense of déjà vu as I remember the last time I got ready for work.

I skip the makeup and quickly grab my toothbrush, face-wash, deodorant, and anything else of mine and throw it all in my bag.

I left my backpack with my work things by the door, and I grab that too before putting on my Vans and quietly opening Emmett's front door. I allow myself to glance back at his place before leaving, coming to the realization that this is the last time.

As I look back, I see his keys with the spare key to my apartment dangling next to his. I set my stuff down in the doorway, and I grab the keys from the hook. I feel tears forming in my eyes as I unhook my spare from his key chain, putting it in my pocket to put back in my junk drawer.

This is the last time.

It has to be.

I can't let myself fall back into the place I was with Reed, allowing someone else to have such a hold on me, making me think I'm in control when it was never even in my grasp.

I feel a crack in my heart, as I turn back towards the door, and my heart breaks into two as I shut the door behind me.

As I walk towards the school, I remind myself why I'm here, why I'm doing this: for me *and* for my students.

I'm doing this because our sense of normalcy—our safe space—was taken from us, and I am going to do everything in my power to rebuild what Finn destroyed.

When I walk into this building, I remember that I am no longer the girl who is hung up on her ex-boyfriend.

I am no longer the daughter who isn't good enough for her parents, or the inconsistent best friend.

I am no longer afraid of the toaster, or falling asleep without the TV on.

I am no longer the person who drowns in the silence or allows being scared to take my breath and hold it hostage.

I am someone who will walk through the door no matter how afraid I am.

I am someone who will never let anyone take any more pieces of me without my permission.

I am someone who will never let anyone make me feel weak or powerless ever again.

I am strong enough to stand on my own two feet.

The hallways are empty as I walk towards the cafeteria, and I am nervous but ready for whatever is coming my way. As I approach the cafeteria doors, I hear the faint buzzing of staff who are already there.

I hold my shoulders up high and remind myself that, no matter what, I am meant to be here. I will pick up the pieces of what we thought we know and rebuild from the ground up.

That Friday morning in December will always be a part of this place, the students and staff, the community, and me. It has changed the way we feel about what was once our happy place, but I am here to put in that work because I know I am capable, and I know I am strong enough.

Now that I'm here, I'm no longer just Drew.

I'm Ms. Thomas.

CHAPTER 43
EMMETT

WITH MY EYES STILL CLOSED, I notice that there is no bare back pressed to my chest, and my arm isn't draped over the delicious curve of Drew's hips. My eyes slowly open as I reach my arm further, hoping she is just a few inches out of my reach, but I feel my palm meet the edge of the mattress. No Drew to be found.

I spring up, instantly feeling like something is wrong.

We were supposed to wake up to her alarm and get ready.

I was supposed to drive her to the middle school, and I was going to wait for her there.

Our backpacks are both currently sitting side by side in my entryway with our work stuff ready to go . . . *Right?*

I was dreaming about rubbing her lemony body wash all over her in the shower before having to officially start the day.

Something is wrong.

I grab my phone and notice hers isn't next to mine, so I jump out of bed and head to the bathroom. Her toothbrush isn't next to mine, her face wash isn't there for me to steal, her cucumber deodorant isn't where she set it down before bed last night.

No.

This is wrong.

Where is she?

My phone is still in my hand, but I have yet to check it. I tap the screen to see the time: 7:58 a.m.

Fuck!

I overslept.

She probably tried to wake me up, but I was too tired from my shift yesterday. Because I've been spending so much time with her, and she's been keeping me up at night in ways I have only dreamed of, the shifts at the bar have been taking it out of me way more than I'm used to.

I feel like the biggest asshole after convincing her to let me take her and then fucking it all up.

She had to go alone.

I quickly go to call her, and I'm sent straight to voicemail.

Her first meeting starts at eight o'clock this morning, and she probably can't take my call right now.

I hope she's not mad at me.

I send her a text, hoping to hear from her in some way.

> I'm so sorry I overslept

> Call me when you can

I don't want to freak her out, but I am freaking out.

How could I have been such an idiot?

Why didn't I think to set my own alarm?

I knew how nervous she was for today, and I'm supposed to be there for her.

She shouldn't have had to go alone.

Getting showered, ready, and out the door is a complete blur. I don't know what my plan is when I shut my front door behind me, but I let my body take over for me because my mind is incapable of stringing together coherent thoughts.

I don't have time to wait for the elevator, so I just book it down the stairs. Feeling like I fully deserve the strain and slight pain in my quads as I race down the flights separating me from the parking garage.

The spot that houses Drew's car is currently unoccupied, further pushing the dagger into my gut that she had to face today alone.

Is she going to be okay?

I jog to my Jeep and hop into the driver's side. I grab my car key to stick in the ignition.

I throw the car into reverse, closing the distance between me and my girl.

I'm cruising on the highway, driving safely but with a sense of urgency that other drivers on the road don't seem to have at 8:15 a.m. on this Monday morning.

When I was thinking about this drive yesterday, I pictured it much differently. I pictured holding on to Drew's hand as I drove, asking her about the agenda for the day because I knew there would be no point in trying to get her mind off what the day held for her. I knew she would be too anxious to let herself forget so asking her about it felt like the right thing to do.

Right thing to do.

Do I even know what that is for her?

I planned on listening to her explain the day full of meetings and what they were going to be about. I was so excited to hear the passion and love in her voice as she talked about anything having to do with her students and helping them recover.

I was going to ask her what breaks she had and remind her to eat lunch because I knew she would be too nervous to remember to eat.

I was going to ask her if she was going to go to her classroom and see how she felt about that, and I was going to squeeze her thigh and give her kisses on her knuckles.

Kisses of reassurance that I was there if she needed me or not.

As I'm getting off the highway, shaking away what may have happened this morning if I didn't fuck it up, I can't help but wonder if maybe she didn't want me there. Maybe this was something she needed to do on her own, and I was getting in the way of that.

But why wouldn't she have told me?

I thought we told each other the truth because we knew the other could handle it. I thought we both knew she was strong and capable, but I still wanted to be there for comfort and support. I thought we were the beauty that came out of a tragedy.

I pull into the staff parking lot twenty minutes after her first meeting started. I see her car parked in a spot near the exit of the lot, and luckily there is an empty spot next to her. It takes everything in me not to rush into the school and find her, but I know the policies and would not want to do anything to upset anyone, especially Drew.

I'm not sure if she will be coming out to her car for anything, but if she does, I'm going to be here.

Just in case.

I make the time pass by scrolling on my phone after trying to do the paperwork I had planned on completing, but gave up on after I accepted that I'm not in the right mindset. I couldn't focus on anything for more than a few seconds, so scrolling through Reddit and Twitter—endless amounts of distractions—was all I could manage.

At about noon, I hear the voices of a few staff members walking together to their cars. I assumed the staff had a break for lunch, and it was probably a much-needed opportunity to leave the space for a bit. I watch the small crowd of teachers and other staff members file out the exit leading to the lot, but I don't see the one face I'm looking for. The door shuts behind a small group of men and women chatting, and my heart sinks.

I'll just have to wait longer.

Right as I'm about to look back down at my phone, the door opens again and the most beautiful woman appears. The red of her hair contrasts with the snow around her, brightened by the sunny January afternoon. She is alone, holding her backpack in front of her as she walks, presumably looking for her keys.

She doesn't see me yet, so I take this moment to notice every part of her. She is wearing black joggers that accentuate her legs, and her black long sleeve is tucked in, hugging her frame enough for me to notice the curves of her upper body and her slender arms that I love having wrapped around my neck.

Drew looks up to unlock her car, and our eyes meet through my front windshield, having backed into the spot to keep an eye on the door. The green in her eyes is overtaken by the strokes of gold that sparkle bright enough to light my darkest days.

She stops in the middle of the parking lot, and my protectiveness takes over as I can't have her standing in the way of possible cars coming through.

I open my door and begin walking towards her, but as I approach, she takes a step back and holds a palm out, making me stop a foot further than where I would like to be.

"Drew, sweetheart," I begin, and she slowly drops her hand to her side and swings her backpack on her shoulder. "I'm so sorry about this morning. I overslept. Did you see my text?"

She steals her eyes away from me, looking at the concrete to the left of my Vans. "Yeah, I saw it."

Why won't she look at me?

"I promised I would take you and didn't, and I know it

was shitty." I'm expecting her to tell me she is mad at me, yell at me, or react in some way, but there is a coldness to her. The warmth I have always felt around her is nowhere to be found.

"I needed to do this myself," she finally says. "I don't want to have to rely on someone else."

This is not the conversation I thought we were going to have.

"No, of course not. You're strong, you can do this, but I want to help—"

"No," she cuts me off. "I don't need your help." Her words are sharp enough to break skin, and I see her eyes grow foggy behind tears she doesn't want to let fall. "All my life, I thought I wasn't worth the love you didn't have to work for, and I became weak. Weak enough to let a guy determine if I was happy or sad, alone or worth company, empty or fulfilled, and I didn't even realize it was happening. I let Reed convince me I wasn't capable of love that didn't come with strings attached.

"These past three weeks have reminded me how weak I am and how, if I want to get stronger, I can't rely on someone else's strength. I have to find it myself. And I'm getting there. I know I am, but I can't let you get in the way of something I need to do myself. I have to put myself first." She wipes the one stray tear that escaped the corner of her eye and sighs. "I have to give love to myself first, Emmett."

The world is closing in on me, and I don't know what to say to convince her that she is right, but also that she is stronger than she even realizes. Yes, it is not my job to do it for her, but I want it to be my job to support her.

"Drew," I manage to say her name before she's walking right past me to her car. She goes to the passenger side door and grabs a bagged lunch she must have packed at her place this morning.

"There's nothing left to say. It was nice of you to come here, but you should go. I'll see you around."

And with that, she's walking back towards the school, not saying another word or looking back to see me watching her walk away.

She leaves me with my heart in pieces, broken but still all hers.

CHAPTER 44
DREW

IT TOOK everything in me to say those words to Emmett, but I knew they had to be said. I had to end things now, before I fell into the same trap I fell in with Reed. This morning was tough, and there were moments I wanted to forget what I told myself when I got up this morning, but I knew I had to power through.

It was bittersweet to be among the staff again, especially because there are members who are missing. There are also a handful who decided they didn't want to come back, and no one blames them.

The trauma-informed care presentation, and the presentation about how to address questions and concerns from students and families was tolerable, and I kept trying to remind myself that I was here for my students. To right the wrongs of what happened to us. To get stronger and show them how it is possible, even when it doesn't feel like it.

After grabbing my lunch from my car, I head back into the building, trying to leave what happened in the parking lot out there, knowing I have other priorities to deal with inside these walls. Because my principal wants me to wait to go to my classroom, I head to the staff lounge.

I feel a sense of relief when I get there to see that it is empty. I sit down at one of the tables to eat the lunch I packed, but I can't find my appetite.

I pull my phone out of my backpack and do some scrolling to pass the time before it's time to be back in the cafeteria for the afternoon meetings. Those being the ones I'm dreading the most because part of my team was lost on that Friday, and it's time to face that head-on in about forty minutes.

I stick to my habit of skipping Instagram and Snapchat, not wanting to be reminded of the highlight reels of everyone else's lives, and open my messages to text Lacey. I haven't called her since I gave her all the details about Reed, and Emmett last week.

Emmett.

It would be so easy to send him a text, telling him we could talk more tonight.

No.

I had to stand my ground.

I never did that with Reed, not until recently.

I'm strong enough now.

Maybe Lacey can talk.

I send her a quick text asking if she has some time. I know she is at work, but I'm hoping she has a few minutes to spare. She texts me back a few seconds later saying she is swamped with back-to-back meetings but will call me tonight. She asks how my first day back is going and says she's sending me all the good vibes.

I respond telling her it's going, and that I'll tell her all about it tonight.

My heart has been hurting since I left Emmett's apartment this morning, and I think those individual pieces shattered after seeing his face in the parking lot.

Because Lacey can't talk until tonight, and I decide to do what I do best and distract myself with work. I pack back up my untouched lunch and head back to the cafeteria where a few other staff members are discussing aspects of this morning's presentations. I join them and talk about work, worrying about the after-effects of ending things with Emmett will have to wait until later.

———

"Drew! How was your first day back? I want to hear all about it!"

As promised, Lacey called me this evening. I got home around 3 p.m., leaving an hour early because the last hour of the day was planned as classroom time, and I didn't have a classroom to return to just yet. My principal said I could just do the work I was going to do there at home. "Did you end up letting Emmett drive you?"

"No. I decided to drive myself," I respond. "I actually decided that I wanted to do things all by myself from now on."

Lacey laughs as if I'm joking. "What do you mean 'by yourself'? That's all you've ever done, Drew."

"Not really," I throw back.

"Yes, really." Lacey's voice is suddenly more stern than before. "You moved out at eighteen, *by yourself.* You went to college and paid for it, *by yourself.* You live in a nice apartment and pay for it with a steady job you got, *by yourself.* Must I go on?"

"No, I didn't do those things by myself, Lace. I had you, and I had Reed, sort of." I sigh at the thought of how intertwined Reed is in my life up until now. "I was constantly leaning on you two to get me through the shit I couldn't handle myself. I couldn't even live alone without calling Reed to keep me company. I could barely make it through college without calling you about shit my parents never taught me."

Thoughts of having to learn about things like sex and love

from my high school boyfriend or birth control and STIs from my best friend surface as I recall how my parents never felt the need to talk to me about anything of substance.

"I rely too heavily on the people around me to be my strength rather than just being strong enough myself." I feel the tears I tried not to let fall when I was talking to Emmett roll down my cheeks now.

"Someone else's strength doesn't cancel out yours, Drew. When someone you love lends you their strength, it makes you stronger."

Her words are somehow beginning to stitch my heart back together, but the doubt still overwhelms me.

"But that's not what it felt like with Reed. I feel like I don't even know who I am without him, and I don't even want him in my life. Lacey, I can't continue being this person who needs to depend on someone to keep them from crumbling, yet that's all I feel like I'm capable of being."

"Honey, leaning on someone who is there to support you doesn't make you any less strong. And I'm not talking about Reed. Fuck him and make sure you talk about him in thera-py." I let out a laugh through the tears because she is abso-lutely right, and if I don't laugh right now, I'm going to cry more. "You don't have to be alone to be strong, Drew. You deserve to surround yourself with people who want to support you. Like me. Like Emmett."

I sniffle, trying to make sense of everything she is saying. It makes sense, but it goes against everything I have ever believed. "I already pushed Emmett away. Just like I do to everyone else—my parents, Cal, you,"

"Me?! Honey, I'm not going anywhere."

"But I've been such a shitty friend. Not making an effort. If it wasn't for the shooting . . ."

"Hey, don't you dare think that. We made a promise in Kindergarten to be best friends forever, and I am keeping that promise." I let out another laugh, my heart slowly becoming less and less separate pieces. "And pushing away your parents was something you needed to do, and Cal . . . well, you should reach out. It's never too late for your two. You guys have a lot of shared experiences growing up. Even if you didn't support each other then, maybe you could now." Her words are reassuring to hear, and I'm slowly seeing that I have a lot of re-learning to do about my relationships and how strength and support are not mutually exclusive.

"Maybe I'll call Calvin tonight."

"I think that's a great start. What about Emmett?"

"I don't know, Lace. You should've seen his face. I doubt he wants to hear from me after my complete one-eighty."

"What do you mean? Last we talked, you both seemed head over heels, you were talking about butterflies again, Drew! I haven't heard you talk like that since junior year of high school!"

"Exactly! These past three weeks showed us that something beautiful can come out of something tragic, and then I woke up this morning feeling like I was losing myself again. And I just got myself back."

"Butterflies don't just symbolize falling in love, honey. They also symbolize change. You're not the same girl you were at seventeen, and Emmett is not Reed."

"Lacey, you didn't see him, it was like I caught him by surprise. Then kicked him when he was down," I deadpan. "Then ran him over with my car."

She laughs even though I'm completely serious.

"Don't let your mind trick you into thinking you know what Emmett is feeling. Let him be the one to tell you."

CHAPTER 45
EMMETT

THE WEEKS HAVE FELT dull despite the sun shining and the brisk air refusing to subside. January has come and gone, fading into February, and my life has gone back to the days blending together because they look almost identical. My demeanor is at a constant level of just above pissed off, the slightest shift making me want to throw something at a wall just to feel an ounce of relief.

I haven't heard from Drew since that day in the parking lot of her school, giving her the space she needed to grow on her own, even if letting her go was one of the hardest things I've had to do.

I have realized over these few weeks apart that I knew she was strong, but I didn't do a good job of letting her know. Instead, I let my possessiveness take over, and all I wanted to do was protect her rather than support her. I don't regret being there for her in her moments of need, but I do regret not helping her see how strong she truly is and reminding her of it every day.

The temptation to reach out has been heavy on my mind, along with waiting out in the elevator for the chance to run into her, just to see how she's doing.

It's been almost two weeks since students came back to school, and I'm sure it has not been easy for her.

Our schedules no longer align, and that is something I made sure of. Over Drew's Winter Break and those months leading up to it, I learned when I could expect to run into her in the elevator either leaving or coming home. After she ended things, I decided that that wasn't fair, for either of us. So, I have been taking all the closing shifts at the bar, leaving before she is even due to arrive home, and not coming home until she's fast asleep. The late nights, and getting back into going to the gym, allow me to come home tired enough to sleep through her lead feet and butterfingers. Coming home so tired also helps my sleep deep enough to not have to worry about seeing her in my dreams, remembering what it is like to feel her in my arms.

As the first few days after we broke up went by, her smell lingered in my bed. That was when the dreams were most prominent. It was like I couldn't escape them. It was similar to what I felt when Lennon died, but this pain was much more tolerable. It was less of a sharp sting and more of a dull ache but still hard to ignore.

"Hey, boss!" Eddie pulls me from my thoughts. I focus on what my eyes were looking at for the past few minutes to notice I had been drying a glass that was never wet.

"What's up?"

"Why don't you head out?"

"Nah, I'm good. Just tired."

"Yeah, I know. You've been tired for almost a month now."

And it's true.

It's been my excuse since my first shift after the last time I saw Drew. I knew both Eddie and Annie could see right through me, and Luke didn't know me enough, but was still able to tell a difference in my demeanor.

But it's easier to say I am tired rather than dive into how I feel like my heart is no longer beating in my chest.

I've been on autopilot the past three and a half—almost four—weeks. I'm here but not really here. I'm doing my job, but don't have the bloom of anticipation in my stomach at the thought of seeing Drew walk through the door, or sitting at the bar, or lying naked in my bed, waiting for me to come home.

"It hasn't been a month, it's only been a few weeks," I reply.

"Same fucking difference. You're miserable."

"Seriously, man. I'm fine."

"No. You're not fine."

I throw the towel I was holding onto the bar. "Damn it, Eddie! What do you want me to say? You're right, I'm not. The girl I want doesn't want me anymore, and there's nothing I can do about it." I lean onto my elbows, my head falling into my hands.

Eddie lets out a sigh. The place is empty aside from a few couples seated at the high tops, so he takes this moment to say what I'm sure he has been holding in.

"I've never seen you like this, Emmett, not even when Riley left."

"You didn't even like Riley," I mumble, my face still in my hands.

"You're right, but I like Drew."

"Yeah?" I let out a humorless laugh. "Well, I love her." Eddie's eyes widen at my admission, but I continue, "And she wants nothing to do with me."

"Then you have a choice to make."

"A choice?" He lost me.

"You can either move on," he says, and the thought of that makes me literally sick to my stomach. "Or, you can fight like hell to get her back."

I shake my head, knowing exactly what choice I would make but knowing it wouldn't change anything.

"It's not that simple, Eddie. I think she loves me too, but there's something in her own way, and I don't think there's anything I can do about it."

I can see he is trying to think of the right thing to say, not to make me feel better, but to help me figure out what the fuck to do.

"Why don't you head home for the night? It's Valentine's Day weekend, and I'm sure couples aren't coming here to celebrate." He places his hand on my shoulder.

The actual day, the fourteenth, fell on a Wednesday this year, but most of the celebrations waited for tonight and the rest of the weekend. "I can handle it while you take some time off."

"What? That's not what we were talking about."

"I know, but I think there's nothing for you to do but wait, and if you wait here, you'll scare off the pretty single girls coming here to flirt with their handsome bartender tomorrow night."

I push his hand off my shoulder and give him a push to his. It's the first time I laugh because something is funny rather than to let out a sound that resembles laughter.

"Seriously," he laughs, walking back to his side of the bar. "I can handle things here for the rest of the night—Saturday and Sunday too." I let out a sigh, but I'm getting closer and closer to being convinced. "I'll make sure Annie and Luke stay on top of their shit, and that they stay on opposite sides of the bar." This gives me another laugh at the thought of the hard time we keep giving Annie for Luke's crush on her.

"I got this," Eddie says, and he gives me a look that reinforces that I can take a few days off and trust he has things under control.

Finally, I give him a nod before heading to the back office to grab my things before heading home.

It's about seven o'clock in the evening by the time I get to the parking garage's elevator, and this is the first time I've been out of the bar, while most people are still awake, in almost a month. I push the button and wait in the frigid garage, looking down at my shoes and thinking how I need to get another pair of Vans before these disintegrate off my feet.

I hear the bell ring, and the doors open. I take a step forward before looking up and seeing a view I haven't seen in weeks, but one that has been heavy on my brain.

My eyes start at the bottom and work their way up, starting with her shoes which are the same as mine, just a few sizes smaller. My eyes scan up Drew's legs, and I see she is wearing my favorite pair of black jeans, the ones that wrap around her thighs and accentuate the curve of her ass in a way that makes my legs give out. She is bundled up in her black winter coat, but my eyes stop at the arm of her coat wrapped around someone else's arm.

And that is when I finally see her face. Her hair is shorter and brighter, the red being less of a burgundy and more of crimson. It's down, framing her face that is surprised, as if I caught her when she was least expecting. One of my favorite views.

She was in the middle of a laugh with the stranger by her side when our eyes met. The widened look of hers makes them even more striking, like a meadow stretching wide, asking me to get lost in them.

And I do, just like the first time.

Only this time, I don't think the flush in her cheeks is my doing.

It was the doing of the man standing beside her.

CHAPTER 46
DREW

"EMMETT," I breathe, not believing the sight in front of me. We haven't crossed paths in almost four weeks, and I had a feeling it was because he was avoiding me.

At first, I thought running into each other, in this very elevator, would be a sign. A sign telling me that Lacey was right when I called her that day after Emmett and my breakup in the parking lot. I told myself that if I ran into him, it was a sign that I needed to talk to him and let him tell me he didn't want to let go of what we had.

But, when I never saw him, I let the thoughts in my head win.

Cal looks between Emmett and me, and I think he puts the puzzle pieces together. After Lacey and I got off the phone that day, I texted Cal. Turns out, it only took a few texts back and forth to realize that we were both missing the other, wishing we had family in our lives, both hesitating to make the first step of reaching out. He expressed how glad he was to hear from me which contradicted what my mind was trying to convince me. I was sure he would tell me to fuck off or say it was too late, but my thoughts were wrong.

The texts between Cal and I turned to phone calls, which

turned to FaceTiming, and then we decided it was time to make plans to visit each other—show each other our spaces and lives, so we could become a part of each other's. Cal drove up from Northwestern for the weekend, getting here just two hours ago. I showed him around my place, and now we were on our way to get dinner.

His partner, Emma, had plans with her girlfriends for this weekend, so the two of them celebrated Valentine's Day the prior weekend.

Throughout the exchanges Cal and I had, we both apologized for not being there for one another, resulting in both of us feeling like we were alone. He learned, much earlier, that family doesn't have to be blood, and he found a group of friends who showed him what it meant to be part of a family that loved you unconditionally.

Cal was also lucky to find Emma, who helped him re-learn the idea of love, working hard to unlearn what our parents taught him.

This made me realize that it was possible to put the work into yourself and come out stronger, but that it's still okay to lean on the ones you love for support.

It is safe to say that the last two hours, as well as our phone calls and FaceTimes over the past month, have been a substantial amount of trauma-dumping, but it helped Cal and I rebuild what seemed so broken beyond repair all those years ago.

We also had a lot of making up for lost time.

Between Cal and Lacey, I feel stronger. Not because I am relying on them, but because they love me enough to lend me their strength, the same way I would do for them.

"Hi, I'm Calvin." Cal reaches his hand out towards Emmett who just continues to stare at me. His hair is down, but tucked under a dark purple beanie, leaving his curls resting at his shoulder and down his neck. His warm, chocolate eyes are impenetrable to what he is thinking, but the butterflies that lay dormant in my stomach for so long quickly awakened when the familiar warmth of his gaze covers me.

He is wearing his usual bartending attire: washed out black jeans, his high-top Vans, and a black hoodie, telling me he just came from work. His cheeks are as red as mine probably are, most likely from not wearing a jacket on his short walk from Lenny's in this cold. I see a similar redness creeping up his neck the longer we hold each other's gaze.

Cal takes his extended arm back and coughs into his fist, breaking Emmett away from my eyes.

"Emmett," he says. Not making a move to take his hands out of his pockets.

I've seen that before.

Emmett meets my eyes again for a moment before turning towards the door leading to the stairs, not saying another word or looking back to see me watching him walk away.

Cal clears his throat before stepping us out of the elevator. "So, I'm assuming a drink is in order after that?"

Cal and I head to dinner, not addressing the elephant in the room. The restaurant is just past my school, so I show him the middle school which prompts questions he has avoided until now.

As we drive past, he turns to me from the passenger seat and asks, "How's being back after the shooting?"

I keep my eyes on the road in front of me. "It's different," I reply. "It was hard welcoming the kids back with a smile because it felt fake—like it was painted on. The first day, I think I cried three or four times because it felt so surreal that we were back together in a room where we all shared those moments.

"The kids are resilient though. They are just so strong at such a young age. I would say even stronger than me. They don't talk around it, and they feel safe in our space to ask questions and discuss what happened. A lot of them even shared how they coped and what helped them, and a few of them even shared their feelings about the need for gun control and reform."

"Wow, how old are they again?"

"Sixth grade, so eleven or twelve."

"They can have those kinds of conversations?"

"We had a pretty solid classroom community before the shooting. Taking the time to make sure all students feel comfortable and loved is important to me, so I spend a lot of time throughout the year ensuring students have solid relationships with me and each other.

"Co-creating a space that is safe, both literally and figuratively, allows us to have those deep conversations. It may not feel *literally* safe like it once did, but it is still a space where all voices matter, and students feel safe expressing their thoughts, opinions, or feelings."

"What about the shooter's brother? Did he come back?"

I shake my head, feeling my emotions getting the better of me as I think of Cole. "His grandparents thought it would be better for him to get a fresh start somewhere else. It was a hard pill to swallow for me, but I had to accept they were doing what was best for him."

I think of Cole every day, both when I'm inside the classroom and outside of it. It was another loss to mourn, but he deserves the world. I'm hoping to reach out to his grandparents to see how he is doing, maybe trying to stay in touch. A kid like that could use all the support to lean on, even if he is more than capable of standing on his own two feet.

"What about the other sixth grade teacher?"

"All of us teachers have been covering for her class until they find someone to fill the position more long-term."

Along with Cole, I think of Rita often, longing for her support and guidance, and I miss being able to see her every day by looking across the hall. I make sure to do my job for the both of us, knowing that she would do the same for me and my students.

The rest of the ride is quiet, just the music faintly playing. We're about to park at the restaurant when Cal asks, "What are you going to do about Emmett? He looked pretty surprised to see you."

"You're just full of questions tonight, huh?" I park the car, leave it to idle before unclipping my seatbelt. I lean back in my seat and sign. "But in all honesty, I have no idea."

Cal unclips his seatbelt, a hint of a smile on his face when he turns to look at me. "I think he still has feelings for you." Cal has light brown hair that gets darker in the winter. He is constantly running his fingers through it to push to the side revealing his bushy eyebrows and green eyes that occasionally look blue in the right light. He has the same olive skin as me with similar facial features, but he got the height that I didn't.

Some say they can't see the resemblance between us while others say we look like twins.

"He thought I was your date."

Holy shit.

My stomach drops. "No! I didn't even think of that!" I grab the steering wheel and press my forehead against it. I let out a groan, making my brother laugh. "He's never going to talk to me now."

"Were you even going to talk to him?" I ignore him and lightly hit my head on the steering wheel a few times, punishing myself for not registering the obvious. "Also, I'm choosing to ignore that you never told him you had a brother," he teases.

I turn to face him, my head still against the wheel. "I was working up the nerve to unveil all that history that comes with our relationship," I pause before adding, "and it never came up."

"Well, work faster because now you have even more explaining to do."

Cal gets out of the car and heads into the restaurant.

I let out one more groan before turning off the car and opening the driver's door to follow him in.

"You're helping me type up a text to him," I yell to him. He's a few steps ahead of me.

"Yeah, yeah. I know," he says, turning around to smile at me.

CHAPTER 47

EMMETT

I AM COMPLETELY WINDED by the time I get back up to my apartment. Between the stairs and seeing Drew, I don't know if my breathing will ever go back to normal.

I pull my keys from my pocket to unlock my front door. Pushing it open, I kick off my Vans and slam the door behind me, trying to release even a little bit of the tension I feel in my shoulders at the thought of Drew's arm around another man.

I was silly to think that she was hooked on me like I was on her, but I didn't think she was in a place to go on a date. Here I am thinking she loved me, but something was standing in her way. Little did I know, it really was as simple as her not wanting me.

I'm not sure what hurts more, the thought of her with someone else or the thought of not being good enough for her. This feeling reminds me of how Riley made me feel, inferior. I never thought Drew would make me feel anything like Riley did.

I throw off my beanie and pull my hair back into a loose bun. I don't have much of an appetite, which doesn't matter anyway because there's nothing but beer in my fridge. I grab one before heading to the couch to turn something on, anything to get my mind off what Drew is doing right now.

Calvin?

I've never heard her talk about a Calvin.

And when did she have time to go out and meet someone?

School must be going okay, but even before the shooting she never went out on Friday nights.

Stop it.

I need to stop obsessing.

Drew is not my business anymore

Even though seeing her arms around that guy made me want to throw him across the parking garage.

I turn on *New Girl*—a show Drew and I watched together, but I ended up liking it more than I thought I would. I've kept watching where we left off, ignoring the thought that it makes me feel closer to Drew.

I lean back to try and relax, trying to subside the buzzing on my skin and the tightening in my chest.

A few episodes go by, along with another beer, when I feel my phone buzz in my pocket. Thinking it's probably a text from Eddie, I choose to ignore it and let one more episode play.

I glance over at my oven timer and see it's about 9:30 p.m.

I head to the bathroom to take a shower, peeling out of my jeans and hoodie, before hopping in. It's not until I'm drying off that I remember my phone in my jeans pocket and the text I never checked. I wrap the towel around my waist, my hair dropping water on the floor as I bend down to grab it.

When I tap the screen to check the notification, I feel a flutter in my stomach that I haven't felt in weeks but have now experienced twice in one night. I click on Drew's name and the incoming bubble in so long I need to scroll through it to read.

It came in two hours ago.

> Hi Emmett.
>
> First of all, I think it's stupid that I'm doing this over text, but I don't know if you even want to talk to me. Second of all, Cal is my brother. I want to clear that up before we get any further. I know I never told you I had a brother, and it's a long story I would be happy to tell you, if you care. Third of all, I miss you, and I really want to talk to you. It wasn't fair of me to keep you in the dark about why I said the things I did in the parking lot. I owe you an explanation and an apology. My brother is staying with me until Sunday, but he's going to see some friends from our hometown tonight and won't be back until tomorrow. If you want to talk, I'll be home in a couple hours.

I finish reading and notice she sent two more texts just a few minutes ago.

> P.S. I'm sure you'll know when I'm home. I do have lead feet after all ;)
>
> P.S.S. That was stupid. I was nervous you weren't responding and thought it would brighten the mood. Please disregard.

I laugh to myself, at myself, at Drew, at this mess we're in. And I laugh at the fact she thought I wouldn't miss her too.

As if on cue, I hear the door above me slam and the sound of shoes being tossed, knowing exactly the corner she piles her shoes in.

I don't think I can move fast enough.

Drew misses me and wants to talk, and I'm not going to make the mistake of not hearing what she wants to say to me. There is no way I am going to give up the chance to tell her how much I miss her too.

These weeks have sucked. They have felt like Hell—or what I think Hell would feel like if it existed. Waiting to feel better but knowing deep down I never would if I wasn't with her.

Jumping back in with her may seem crazy and impulsive, but I snuck glances and moments with her for six months and then finally had a taste of her for those amazing weeks. Now, knowing what it's like to be without her, I'm never letting her go.

If she wants me back.

I shake the thought away, not having time for doubts, and I quickly get dressed, grabbing a pair of sweats and a hoodie, not even putting on a pair of boxers, socks, or shoes before running up the flight of stairs separating her from me.

I take the stairs two at a time, reaching her door in record time. Not having the luxury of letting myself in anymore, I knock three times, hoping she doesn't regret the text she sent tonight.

The door opens, and I feel my heart begin to beat again.

"Hi Drew," I say, hoping to pull some pink into her cheeks. Knowing that if I still can, just by saying her name, I never lost her to begin with.

Like the answer to my prayers, a flush appears on her skin, and her teeth find her bottom lip as if she needs to stop herself from saying what's on the tip of her tongue.

A moment passes before I ask, "Can I come in?"

"As long as you promise to stay?" Her pleading eyes pull me in, the hope in her voice making the past weeks without her worth it.

"Sweetheart, I never want to leave."

My lips crash into hers, and I'm home.

CHAPTER 48

DREW

I HAD every intention of sitting Emmett down and explaining to him that I needed time to learn that it wasn't time alone I needed, but time to figure out why I thought I had no choice *but* to be alone. The past three and a half weeks have been endless conversations with my therapist, Lacey, and Cal about how to unlearn what my mind so desperately wants to convince me, what my experiences and past have taught me, and how they construed my reality.

I don't need to do it all on my own, and depending on others doesn't make me weak—I know that now.

But that's not the end of it.

I know it now, and I'm ready to put the work in to re-learn, with the help of those who love me supporting me through it, and I want Emmett with me too.

If he wants to be.

I was so nervous typing up that text, but Cal helped me overcome the doubts, and the nerves, to send a text I've been wanting to send but haven't been ready to.

I can't help but have doubts with a mind constantly trying to show me the worst-case scenarios. When Emmett didn't respond for hours, I figured the ship had sailed. I had ruined my chances and read into our earlier exchange too much. I concluded that he didn't want to salvage this, had moved on, or just didn't want to hear what I had to say.

And I'm so glad I was wrong.

I can feel the heat and passion in Emmett's kiss as his lips reacquaint themselves with mine. He backs me up into my entryway and shuts the door behind him with his bare foot. I smile into his lips thinking about the view when I opened the door. Seeing his wet hair framing his face, in just sweatpants, and a hoodie, and bare feet, I knew he saw my text just a few minutes before he was at my door.

"What are you smiling at?" he says against my lips.

"You don't have shoes on." I nibble at his bottom lip, pulling a subtle growl to his throat. "In a hurry?" I ask.

"I was," he whispers as his lips begin to move down my neck. "The girl I love is finally letting me love her, so I dropped everything to come see her." Goosebumps cover my skin.

I'm the girl he loves.

"She just needed some time." My palms find his cheeks, and I turn his head to meet my eyes. "I love you too." I give him a light kiss to his lips before continuing, "Thank you for being patient with me. I'm sorry I wasn't ready before, but I am now, if you still want me."

"I want nothing more."

He kisses me hard before adding, "And I may have been in a rush getting up here, but now"—he trails his kisses back down my neck, finding the sensitive spot that drives me crazy —"I'm taking my time." I shudder, feeling his breath on my neck in between his kisses. "If that's what you want?"

He poses it as a question, although I think he knows my answer. Still, it's reassuring to know he still wants to make sure, but I don't want there to be any more doubts. "Yes," I breathe, and his lips are on mine again, reminding me that I never want to know what it's like not kissing Emmett.

My jacket is still on, as I had only just gotten home, and Emmett makes quick work of it, pushing it off my shoulders.

Before it can even fall to the floor, his arms are under my thighs, picking me right off my feet. I wrap my legs around his waist, never breaking from his lips. He walks us through my living room to my bedroom, and there is a familiar edge and eagerness to him as he carefully sets me down on the bed before bringing his knees to cage me in and press against me. His choice of sweatpants does not leave much up to the imagination, the pressure being exactly what pushes us past the point of no return.

I need to feel his skin on mine, or I will go crazy.

I reach to pull up his hoodie, finding that there's nothing underneath. He sits up on his knees to take it off, and I can faintly see the outlines of ink on his skin in the darkness of my room, making the budding pressure in my lower belly strengthen.

He gives me a knowing smirk because I've told him before how much I enjoy this view, and he returns the favor by reaching down to find the bottom of my sweater and pushing it up slowly, stopping when my sweater reaches my breasts, seeing there's no bra underneath.

I low groan escapes his throat as I finish the job he got too distracted to complete. As I pull the sweater over my head, left in just my jeans, I feel hands on my breasts, massaging one with each hand before taking my nipples between his fingers. I glance down to watch the erotic scene and notice the ink on his forearms now reaches the tops of his hands, two matching black and gray roses.

"Those are new," I moan, putting each one of my hands on top of his as he continues to massage. "I like them."

He gives me a knowing smile that, mixed with what his hands are doing, elicits a sensation that goes straight to my core. "I know what else you like," he teases before he slowly leans down to take one of my breasts in his mouth while continuing to massage the other. I close my eyes as the pressure builds, my back arching more into his mouth. He groans in response, always loving the reaction he pulls from me.

No surprise there.

"I missed the noises you make for me," he says against my skin, sending tingles down my spine. He moves his mouth to my other breast, swirling his tongue around my nipples, grazing his teeth against the sensitive skin. "But remember, not too loud." I can hear the smile in his voice because my eyes are closed trying to focus on not completely falling apart already.

He releases my breast from his mouth, giving me light, little kisses and drags of his tongue before his lips find mine again. "I think it's time to get you out of these," he whispers before undoing the button of my jeans and sliding down the zipper painfully slow. He wasn't kidding before when he said he wasn't in a rush.

He begins to slide them down to my knees and then stands up to give me more room to slide them all the way off. With him standing in front of me, I take the opportunity to sit up and slide my fingertips in the waistband of his sweats pulling a hiss from him. Emmett is just as sensitive as me, the time apart forcing us to forget what *this* was like.

Once again, I find there's nothing underneath, so I pull his sweatpants down, his erection at my eye-level. He brings his hand to stroke himself, and I lick my lips before taking him into my mouth, wanting nothing more than to make him feel good.

"Fuck, Drew." His voice, husky and strained as I take him in my hand and trace the underside of his shaft with my tongue before wrapping my lips around him again. One of his hands finds the back of my head and lightly grips me by my hair.

I rest my hands on his muscular thighs to keep myself balanced, and I feel him slowly begin to move his hips, thrusting into my mouth, fighting to stay in control of his movements. Just before he loses it, he pulls out of my mouth letting out an exhale.

"When I come, it's going to be inside my girlfriend's tight pussy tonight, not in her mouth." My heart bursts at the same time my body warms with anticipation. "Lay down, sweetheart. I've been dreaming of being between your legs for weeks." He kneels at the foot of the bed, and I feel like my skin is burning because it's so sensitive.

I need his touch.

I need his tongue.

I need him.

"I need to get you ready for me. It's been so long. You're probably so tight and wet for me, aren't you?" His breath is so hot against my sensitive flesh, and my hips slightly buck wanting to somehow release this pressure building. His hands find my thighs pushing them down, not letting me reach to meet his lips. "Did you miss this as much as I did? I bet you can't wait for me to taste you." More moisture pools between my legs.

I can't form a single word—my mind is so clouded. All I can do is moan in agreement with anything he says. If his fingertips grip the skin of my inner thighs any tighter, he'll leave bruises. He may like teasing me, but he's losing control right along with me.

Painfully slow, he traces one finger slowly to my center, finding the sensitive skin wet and begging for him. I let out a gasp as he moves his finger to part me, able to move easily. He finds my most sensitive spot and applies a light pressure as he slowly circles his finger. I moan, needing a release before I go insane. Rewarding me with a little more pressure and moving a little faster before I feel his finger slowly push through my entrance, his thumb moving back to my clit. I whimper at the perfect combination, and he slips in another finger easily because I don't think I've ever been this wet. I arch into him, feeling his hand grip my thigh tighter before his tongue replaces his thumb, and I unravel instantly. All the tension that has been growing since he walked in through the door releases, and euphoria takes hold as pleasure rips through me. But Emmett does let up, his tongue continues lapping me up, his fingers riding out my orgasm until it fades.

As I come down, I open my eyes and watch as he slowly retreats his finger and brings them to his mouth, licking them clean. Wetness instantly pools in my center at the view, and I can't believe this man is mine.

"Damn, I've missed this," is all he says before his lips are on mine, and I can taste myself on his tongue.

"Me too," I moan as my lower belly swirls. "Let's make up for lost time tonight, okay?" My heart tugs at the thought that I ever let him go.

His hands find my hip, lightly pushing me to roll over. His mouth now by my ear. "I was planning on it."

I can hear that the patience and control has completely melted away, and his edge is back. He grabs me by the hips, pulling them up so I'm on my knees but keeping my chest to the bed, exposing my most intimate self to him. Before I have time to breathe, he's pushing himself inside, the delicious stretching sensation I missed so much making us both moan in unison as he slides in, bottoming out with one slow thrust.

"Always so tight," Emmett says through his teeth. One hand gripping my hip, the other twisting in my hair, making me arch even more into him. I feel myself getting closer and closer to the edge again, even more so as I feel his pace quicken and his movements become harder. "Fuck, baby. I'm not going to last long tonight."

"Emmett." His words send me over the edge, pleasure taking me over once again.

His thrusts get faster and less controlled as his body takes over, falling apart a moment later, his chest falling on my back as his pace slows enough to gently pull out, my body feeling instantly empty as he does.

"Lay down on your back," he says before running to the bathroom. He comes back with a warm wet cloth, lying next to me, so he can gently wipe at the sensitive skin between my legs. He helps me clean up before throwing the cloth towards our pile of clothes and pulling me into his chest, his body molding into the backside of mine.

"I've been waiting for this since the morning you left."

I turn to face him, still staying wrapped in his arms, our naked bodies keeping each other warm. "I'm sorry I didn't give you a better explanation. I didn't know how to tell you what I know now."

One of his arms is around my waist, and the other finds my flushed cheeks. "What is it that you know now?" His eyes are soft, as he lightly moves his fingertips down my face. I bury my head in his chest, both of his arms tightly wrapping around me.

I speak into his chest. "I felt like I was depending too heavily on you, the same way I did with Reed. That night, the voice in my head told me that I wasn't strong enough to stand on my own two feet, and I refused to be that girl again.

"I grew up learning that love needed to be earned, and my first relationship used that to further alter my reality. It made me believe that I was nothing without the person who loved me. I realized this after the night Reed came over, and you heard us screaming." Emmett's body slightly tenses at the memory, and I know his possessiveness takes over when I talk about Reed. I melt into him a little more, reminding him that I'm his and continue, "It was that night that I concluded that I would never be that scared girl clinging to the sleeve of someone else just so she could stand.

"So when I started having thoughts about going back to work and thinking I wouldn't be able to do it without you, it scared me. It scared me and reminded me that I had to be strong on my own, not with the help of anyone else. But I know now that strength and support are two different things, and I can be strong but still need support."

I look up from his chest to meet his eyes, seeing him hang on my every word, taking it all in. I reach up to touch his cheek. "I'm just so sorry I hurt you in the process." My eyes fill with tears as he grabs my hand and kisses my knuckles, tears escaping at the gesture.

"And I'm sorry I never helped you see how truly strong you are. Drew, you are the strongest person I have ever met, and I wish you could see yourself through my eyes." I see his beautiful brown eyes cloud, tears threatening to fall from his eyes too. "I will always be here to support you, or let you borrow any strength you need, but please know that it's because I love you, not because I think you need it."

He gives me the gentlest kiss, our faces both damp with the emotions we are laying out for one another.

I feel so incredibly grateful to have him, and Lacey and Calvin in my corner, and it's hard to fathom I ever believed otherwise. I never should have believed I was better off alone, or that distracting myself with work was healthy, or that settling for someone who didn't see my worth was okay.

I have people who recognize and remind me of my strength, and these are people who never tell me I'm nothing without them. Those feelings of loneliness and emptiness I knew all too well have faded away, and my heart has never felt so full.

EPILOGUE: ONE YEAR AND FOUR MONTHS LATER

DREW

"EMMETT?" I say from the bathroom, putting on my earrings. "We're going to be late!" I check the time on my phone seeing that we have only ten minutes until we're supposed to be on our way to our double-date with Lacey and Tyler. We've been seeing them every other Friday since the end of last February.

"I'm ready!" Emmett calls from the kitchen, putting his Vans on.

This past week, I finished up my third year of teaching sixth grade at Northshore Middle School, and we are using the weekend to celebrate my year, starting tonight with drinks at our favorite place: Lenny's.

Over a year ago, Emmett and I had just gotten back together after a month of finding myself and realizing I didn't have to choose between Emmett's support and my own strength—I can have both.

After a long while of making up for lost time, we woke up the next morning sore in all the right places. We got ourselves ready for the day, barely able to peel ourselves away from each other before my brother, Cal, came home. He and Emmett had a re-introduction, and my heart exploded seeing two people, who are so important to me, meet.

It made me even more excited for Emmett to meet Lacey.

Cal and I spent the day together, and we met Emmett at Lenny's for a drink before dinner. Eddie gave Emmett a hard time for coming in on his weekend off, but he quickly forgave him when he heard the two of us made up.

"Move in with me."

After three vodka clubs, my inhibitions escaped me. I was staring at my off-duty bartender who refused to let Eddie or Annie make my drink, and I realized I wanted to experience everything life had to offer with him by my side but knowing that we should start small.

"Yes," he said, leaning over the bar to kiss me.

A few days later, he ended his lease early and moved his stuff upstairs to the eighth floor, and I have loved every second of it. Some may think it was rushed, but Emmett and I both have learned that life is short, and there's no need to waste time that could be spent with the person you love.

When I first met Emmett, I never thought we would end up where we are now. Just two years since we met for the very first time, I now feel like every day is part of a highlight reel.

"You're the one who is making us late." He teases as I join him to slip on my shoes. "Um," he says, "you need to change."

I look down at my usual attire, black jeans, black tank top, and Vans, and I notice the Vans on his feet opposite me, just like mine but twice the size.

"You don't want to match with me?"

He rolls his eyes, grinning with his teeth. "Fine, but come on." He hands me my purse. "We have to go."

Before he can turn to open the door, I wrap my arms around his neck, pulling his lips down to meet me. I love seeing him in his summer attire of a black and white checkered button-up, and black shorts, showing off some of the new tattoos on his calves. His shirt is short-sleeved, so his tattoos on his arms and hands are on display too. The few top buttons of his shirt are undone, revealing just a peak of his new chest piece.

My cheeks warm at the thought of that day. It takes everything in me not to rip open the rest of the buttons and bring him back to our bed, but I know that will make us even more late.

I can't help the flush in my cheeks at the thought.

His chest piece is a Cloudless Sulphur butterfly in the middle with symmetrical branches of leaves on either side. The meaning behind the yellow butterfly being a positive sign of hope and happiness for your life while also embodying the symbolic and spiritual meanings associated with all butterflies such as change, transformation, and hope. But this one has the special additional symbolization of true happiness and a bright light for the future.

Because the piece was going to take a few hours, I wanted to see if another artist was available to do a piece for me. I choose the same butterfly, as well as a snake to symbolize healing, and chrysanthemums to symbolize the loss and grief that doesn't dictate my life but is a part of it. The tattoo artist took my three ideas and molded them into a beautiful piece that wraps around my forearm.

In our past year together, we also finished watching all the Marvel movies in chronological order, which prompted our favorite date-night tradition of seeing any new Marvel movie that comes out in theaters. I find it much easier to stay awake in the movie theater now, mostly because of the handsome man seated next to me who turns into a horny teenager anytime the lights in the theater dim.

Emmett's hands find the back pocket of my jeans, initiating more than just the butterflies in my stomach as his lips meet mine. He gives me the whole damn rainforest.

Our kiss deepens before he slightly pulls away, apparently not wanting to be late for what I assume is to see his new best friend.

Lacey and I were so happy that Emmett and Tyler hit it off, bonding over their tattoos and shared experiences of being the partners of two best friends that are constantly either talking to each other or about one another. Their newfound friendship was just one more reason to stay so connected with my best friend who was there for me when I needed her most.

"You ready?" he says against my lips. He smiles, showing his teeth, my favorite Emmett smile.

I reciprocate with a smile of my own. "With you, always."

We walk hand in hand to the elevator that played a part in our meeting two years ago, knowing it will always be a special detail of our story. Emmett pushes the button and sneaks a glance my way as we wait. He quickly looks away and smiles, as if I caught him in the act.

"What?" I ask. He's giving me a weird vibe as he shifts from his heels to his toes as we wait. "You're that worried about being late?" But before he can respond, the elevator bell rings and the doors open, revealing a sight I never thought I'd see.

The back wall of the elevator is filled with pictures we've taken over our time together, selfies in bed, posed pictures at concerts, self-timer photos with Lacey and Tyler, Cal and Emma, and Annie and Luke who are still "just friends" . . . or so they say. Even Eddie and his new friend, Mia, are in a few. Eddie started bringing Mia around the bar and out with us over the last few weeks. He calls her his bandmate's little sister, but he isn't fooling Emmett and me.

My eyes instantly begin to water as they roam the photo collage that documents our entire relationship that bloomed from trauma so unspeakable, it's amazing to see how we flourished.

Emmett leads me into the elevator, and I see the floor of it is covered in rose petals, reminding me of the roses on his hands.

"Drew," he says, grabbing my other hand, so I'm facing him. "The first time I saw you, I thought you were too good to be true. I thought you were the universe showing me everything I wanted but couldn't have. But, when you looked at me with those eyes, I was done for.

"You have shown me what true love, passion, kindness, and strength are, and you are living proof of them every single day. Whether it's at your job, or at home, in my arms, or in our bed, you are the person I want to spend my life with. I want to spend forever supporting each other, no matter what comes our way." He drops down to one knee, pulling out a black velvet box I didn't even notice was in his back pocket. He lets go of my hands to open the ring box, and my hands go to my mouth at the sight of a black onyx stone surrounded with tiny diamonds on a rose gold band. "Drew" —he pulls the ring from the box, and I give him my left hand —"will you marry me?"

A sob escapes me, and I nod my head. Tears are rolling down my face, and I feel so thankful that this year has been one filled with happy tears instead of sad ones.

As Emmett slips the ring on my ring finger, I ask myself *how did I get here?*

I have never felt like I could take on the world, but I know I can with Emmett by my side.

Emmett wraps his arms around my waist picking my feet off the floor and kisses me into tomorrow.

Into our future.

He sets me down, and I can't believe this is happening. I take a second to look at the pictures and wonder how he pulled such a surprise off.

"I never expected this." I wipe the stray tears in my eyes

and feel my heart beat grow unsteady but in the best way possible. "Did you think of this yourself?"

"Of course," he says as he wraps his arms around me, his chest flushing against my back as we look at all the photos he collected. He lets out a chuckle. "I had help though. Lacey is waiting downstairs. She is making sure no one uses the elevator until we come down."

I laugh along with him, not surprised at all.

"And I hope you don't mind, a few more will be joining us tonight." I turn to face him, wrapping my arms around his neck, and I smile so big it hurts. "Tyler, Cal, Emma, Eddie, Mia, Annie, and Luke are all waiting for us at Lenny's. Everyone is so excited to not have to keep this a secret anymore.

I feel overwhelmed with love at the thought that all the most important people in my life, and the people most important to them, are going to share this night with me, but I find myself feeling selfish to make this moment between just Emmett and I last.

I kiss him deep, hoping he catches on that I want my *fiancé* all to myself for just a little bit longer.

"You're going to make us even more late," he says against my lips.

"They'll understand. Please?" I take his bottom lip between my teeth. He lets out a groan, one I know means trouble, and he takes my hand. We run like teenagers on the verge of getting caught back to our apartment.

When we get to the door, he pushes me against it, kissing me hard. He slowly moves from my lips to my cheek and down my neck, finding the spot only he knows how to find. I feel his breath in my ear as he grabs my left hand and brings it between us. I watch as he gives each of my knuckles a kiss, giving my ring finger an extra. Then, he meets my gaze, and I melt into those chocolate eyes I get to spend the rest of my life melting into.

"How could I ever say no to my future wife?"

ACKNOWLEDGMENTS

THANK YOU. That is all I can say. Thank you for choosing to read Drew and Emmett's story. Thank you for taking a chance on my debut. Thank you for supporting me on this crazy journey.

This book wouldn't have been possible without the help of New Book Authors Publishing. Thank you to Em and Alyssa who helped me get this book to all of you.

A huge thank you to Caitlin who helped me make this book even better for all of you. I can't wait for our work together on book two.

Thank you to Bookstagram and BookTok community where I found like-minded people who understand me in ways no one else does. Thank you for all the likes, comments, shares and for helping me share GMB with the world. Thank you to the bookish and indie author friends I have made. You all have taught me so much, and you make me feel so seen. Special thanks to Linna (@linnareads), one of the first people (outside my family) to read and review this book.

Thank you to my real-life found family who served as my inspiration for the characters in this book and the rest of the Lenny's Bartenders series. Thank you for pushing me out of my comfort zone and being my own personal fan club. Sydney, Stacy, Vanessa, Julia, Haley, Chloe, and Jonathan, if it wasn't for all of you, I wouldn't have the confidence to put myself out there. Knowing you are all there, cheering me on, makes this journey all the more exciting.

Thank you to the friends from different times in my life

who came out and supported me. I was so nervous to publish a book, scared of what people would think, but it turns out that I had nothing to be afraid of.

Thank you to my mom for being an alpha reader before I even knew what an alpha reader was.

Finally, thank you to my rock, my home, my better half, my biggest supporter. Max, I couldn't have done this without you. Literally. You push me to be the best version of myself each and every day, and you are my real-life book boyfriend. The one who sets the bar. The one who made it so easy to write about love because of how lucky I am to be loved by you. Also, huge shout out to you for being my own personal graphic designer. My covers and website and social media posts wouldn't be what they are without you.

I can't wait to show you all more of Drew and Emmett along with the rest of the Lenny's Bartenders crew.

So happy you're here.

ABOUT THE AUTHOR

Katy is the indie author based in Milwaukee. Her favorite trope is forced proximity, and she is a firm believer that found families are the best families.

Lover of all things romance, pop punk, tattoos, anime, rainy days, matcha, her husband, and her daughter, Katy's purpose for writing is to remind readers that you are deserving of the love you read about.

When she's not writing, you can find her reading, or adding to her never-ending TBR.

instagram.com/authorkatymichele
tiktok.com/@authorkatymichele
threads.com/@authorkatymichele
goodreads.com/katymichele
amazon.com/author/katymichele

ALSO BY KATY MICHELE

Lenny's Bartenders

Giving Me Butterflies (Drew & Emmett)

Crash & Burn (Mia & Eddie)

Back to You (Annie & Luke)

Hey Honey's Baristas

From the Ashes (Rumi & Jack)

Call You Mine (Ava & Anderson)

www.ingramcontent.com/pod-product-compliance
Lightning Source LLC
Chambersburg PA
CBHW070614300726
48975CB00006B/1811

9 798989 589517